Britain on the Brink

Book One: First World Adventures in Time and Space

by

K.M. Breakey

Copyright © 2025 by K.M. Breakey
All rights reserved.
v1.0

This book is a work of fiction. Names, characters, places, and incidents are either the product of the author's imagination or are used fictionally. Where public figures and businesses are referenced, they are done so purely for the sake of verisimilitude. Their interactions with characters invented by the author are fictional and are not intended to be interpreted as actual events, or reflect in any way on the character of these public figures or businesses.

No part of this book may be reproduced, scanned or distributed in any printed or electronic form without permission. Please do not participate in or encourage piracy of copyrighted materials in violation of author's rights. Purchase only authorized editions.

ALSO BY K.M. BREAKEY

Shout the Battle Cry of Freedom
Fearless Men, But Few
All Thy Sons
Never, Never and Never Again
Johnny and Jamaal
Creator Class
The World Clicks

"Remember that you are an Englishman, and have consequently won first prize in the lottery of life."

~Cecil Rhodes

Contents

1. White Male "Privilege" 1
2. Another Lap Around the Sun 4
3. The Time Tunnel 9
4. 1966 World Cup 12
5. Victory 17
6. Rule, Britannia 22
7. Back in the Time Tunnel 29
8. Home Again 31
9. Family Time 34
10. The Rose and Thorne 38
11. Breaking News 42
12. Horror 45
13. Newfordshire 49
14. Another Vision 52
15. Planning 57
16. Rivers Of Blood 60
17. Networking 64
18. Dinner with the Elites 69
19. Charles Winthrop 74
20. Disclosure 78
21. New York City 85
22. Back in the Present 94
23. Oswald (Ozzie) Fletcher 97
24. Debating at the Pub 101
25. Time to Fight! 107
26. Strategizing 109
27. The Ruse 111
28. Enoch Powell 117
29. The Funeral 129
30. The Martyr 138

31. Chaos in Newfordshire 145
32. Punishing Dissent 149
33. Update From the Lawyer 152
34. Sad Times 156
35. This Thing is Real! 158
36. How Does It Work? 161
37. The Fish Plant 165
38. Prisoner of War 168
39. The Stowaway 174
40. Vigilante Justice 180
41. On The Lash 186
42. The Paradox 191
43. What Now? 197
44. Things Aren't What They Used to Be 200
45. Logistics 206
46. A New Reality 209
47. Filling Time 214
48. Making Plans 218
49. Rhodesia 222
A Note to the Reader 226
About the Author 230
Also by K.M. Breakey 231

1. White Male "Privilege"
London, England
May 22, 2025

Jack Campbell took a seat in the posh penthouse boardroom. On the docket: *Corporate Excellence Through Diversity, Equity, and Inclusion.* Good Lord. Jack despised the nonsense and would tell you as much in private.

But he didn't say so publicly. No one did. Not in UniBank's hallowed halls. Because DEI demanded respect and wielded power. Some UK institutions were pushing back, following the Trump/Musk juggernaut in America. Not UniBank. They remained all in. *Diversity is at the heart of everything we do.*

Jack played along, even put pronouns in his signature. He learned early in his career – corporate life involves indignities, even occasional soul-selling. This was merely another hoop to jump through.

He was a Senior Executive at UniBank, one of the UK's largest financial institutions, a behemoth with tentacles in over a hundred countries. He joined in 2003 and worked his way up the ladder. He had a sharp mind, a steady hand, and his baritone carried a natural authority. He was the archetype white male executive – tall, handsome, charming. Ruthlessly efficient.

His workday was a steady stream of strategy sessions, high-stakes calls, and complex (sometimes shady) M&A deals in far-flung locations with regulatory grey areas. This had been Jack's world for twenty-plus years. It was rough and tumble – full of ego, conflict, and testosterone.

He mostly stayed above the fray, navigating the politics with finesse and building alliances to consolidate power and influence. Despite layers of bureaucracy, Jack was known as a man who got things done, no fuss.

He knew how to play the game, but the game was changing. Correction: the game had changed. This insidious *Wokeism Beast* had slithered and squirmed into the bank's corporate corridors – as if red tape and regulation wasn't bad enough.

It seemed harmless at first, but like an infection, it morphed and mutated and grew to the point that it seemed it may eventually destroy its host. Jack had seen it destroy a few careers and put a glass ceiling on others. Inevitably, its victims were that once alpha species known as *the white male*. They deserved it, so said the doctrine.

Jack studied the instructor. Chantelle Williams was a black female. No surprise, they almost always were. The fake eyelashes, fake nails, and blonde weave combined to give her a clownish countenance. Ghoulish even. She was also morbidly obese, but for her it was not a bother. Her self-esteem was off the charts.

The bank was paying her great gobs of money to shit on everything in sight, especially white people. *We're lucky to have her*, said the Director of HR, another black female. Chantelle had the jargon down pat – allyship, microaggressions, intersectionality. Words that didn't exist a few years prior.

When the Orwellian torture session mercifully ended, Jack said a prayer of thanks and bolted for the door. Not only was it 5:00 p.m. it was Friday. *And* it was his birthday. Fun times awaited.

On the tube home, he observed the same sign he saw every day: *Hey Straight White Man, Pass the Power*. He shook his head. The insolence. *The audacity*. All taxpayer-funded, of course.

He shook it off. Nothing was going to dampen his spirits.

2. Another Lap Around the Sun

Lily and the kids greeted Jack at the door. "Happy Birthday, Daddy!" Finn and Lucy screamed in unison.

"Thanks, kiddos," he swooped down for a hug and a kiss before turning attention to his wife. "Hello, beautiful. I survived another week."

"You survived another year," said Lily. "Happy forty-third, darling."

"Bloody heck Nora, I'm forty-three, am I?"

Lily nodded with a grin. "Fifty's right around the corner."

"I need a drink on the double."

"Go on, Ozzie's already here."

Jack strolled with purpose into the living room.

"Welcome home, sir." Ozzie bowed solemnly.

"Stand up straight you silly man."

"Sorry, me Dad taught me to respect me elders."

"I'm younger than you, mate."

"Will you get the old folks' discount at the pub now?"

Jack mixed a generous gin and tonic. "Where is everyone? I'm not stuck with you all night, am I?"

"Hey, it's your party."

Jack grinned at his best pal. "You were right about the struggle session."

"Oh yeah, not letting up an inch?"

Jack shook his head. "Pedal to the metal."

"Told ya."

"That kiss-ass Morgan lapped it up. What a broken man he is."

"Sorta like Steady Eddie?"

"*It's an issue of class, not race*," Jack mimicked their liberal friend Edward. "Tell ya what, I may be VP, but I'm low man on the totem pole at these bloody events."

"You're not allowed to say totem pole."

Jack feigned shock and horror. "This bloody wokeness thing, *whatever it is*, it's taken over at the bank."

"Be honest, mate. It's taken over the bloody country. The commies are in charge now."

"I should've explained that to the instructor," said Jack.

Ozzie scoffed. "She wouldn't appreciate the nuance. Too stupid, I guarantee it."

Just then, young Finn dashed through the room – a blur of youthful energy. "Slow down, champ," Jack scolded with a grin. *My God, what will England be like when Finn comes of age?* A scary thought, and not the first time it crossed Jack's mind.

Edward Squire and his wife entered, pulling Jack from the rueful reverie. "Steady Eddie," he and Ozzie called out in unison. The nickname, coined years ago, had stuck like glue. Eddie was calm, cool, collected. Nothing fazed him. Not even the rape and pillage of his native land. He was a raging lefty, and a target of ridicule for Ozzie.

Another couple followed, then another. The room swelled with hearty greetings and banter among familiar chums. Cocktails were proffered and before long conversation turned to football, as it often does at English gatherings.

"Don't start. Our side always comes round." Ozzie was a United supporter, and his Red Devils were off to a terrible start. "We've more trophies than your lot could dream of."

"You're living in the past, Ozzie."

"Ha, I would if I could."

"Don't get him started," said Eddie.

"We'll be on top again soon, don't you worry."

"You've been saying that for years. Christ, how many managers you had since Fergie?"

"We've got history, mate. What've you got with bloody Arsenal? Sweet sod all." Ozzie and Jack bellowed laughter.

"Keep laughing, lads," said Eddie. "We're playing beautiful football. Odegaard's class. And Saka's better than half your team combined."

"Enjoy it while it lasts," Jack chimed in. "You're good 'til Christmas, then you lot fold like a cheap tent."

"We're runner-up the last two years."

"Christ sakes, he's proud o' second place."

Jack lapped up the banter. Friendly fire now but with Cup Matches it could come to blows. *Literally.* Jack was a Liverpool man, like his Daddy, and his Daddy's Daddy.

"And for what it's worth," Ozzie added, "I lost interest years ago. Bunch of feckin' foreigners wearing English kits and a bunch of cucks watching 'em, more concerned with their team winning than saving their dying country."

"You always say that when your team's in the dumpster."

Both statements were true – Ozzie was as politically right as they come, and one of very few ethnic British males unafraid to speak his mind. To get a sense of Ozzie, picture Conor McGregor, but bigger, bolder, and English. For Ozzie, the Prem was another tool to distract Brits from their dispossession.

"Stop watching, lads. Stop supporting the bullshit."

"Ah, come World Cup time, you'll be there with the lot of us."

Scoff. "I see we hired a German to manage our squad of Africans."

"We'll have black players *and* white players," said Eddie. "As it should be."

Bigger scoff.

"Don't forget," said Eddie, "it was Kane who missed the penalty against France."

That stung. When England crashed out of the last World Cup, Oswald (Ozzie) Fletcher was devastated, despite what he might otherwise say. He was inconsolable. All the lads were.

"Wouldn't it be something if we won," said Jack wistfully. "What a day that would be."

"It could happen," said Eddie.

"It *should* happen," said Jack. "We invented the bloody game."

"Back in '66, my Dad got finals tickets for ten bloody shillings," Jack added. "What's that now, eight quid?"

"Yeah, and back then the competition actually meant something," said Ozzie. "The Dutch team was Dutch. The French French. Believe it or not, we fielded a roster full o' English lads."

"Imagine," said Jack grinning.

"We even had the remnants of our Empire. But the bleedin' traitors were selling us out fast."

"To this day," Jack continued, "my Dad says it was the greatest day of his life. Better than his wedding, he says. Even Mum knows it." Jack had heard the story so many times, it was like he'd been there himself, back in 1966, a full thirteen years before he was born.

The night went according to script. Plenty of good-natured banter with a dose of sarcasm and vitriol, for good measure. Always was with Ozzie in the room. Unfortunately, Jack's parents didn't make the two-hour trek down from Newfordshire. They weren't getting any younger and, truth be told, England's streets weren't getting any safer. There was also London traffic. Always a bitch.

The kids took centre stage frequently. "For my birthday, I want a football cake," Finn declared. "And pizza."

"Better than Paul's lad," Ozzie whispered discreetly. "That kid probably wants a frilly skirt." The twelve-year-old in question had recently announced he wanted to be a girl. The mother was delighted. The father, not so much. "If the alphabet people get their hooks in your kid," Ozzie proclaimed, "not much you can do."

The birthday cake made its appearance, and the obligatory *Happy Birthday* was sung, followed smartly by a rousing rendition of *For He's a Jolly Good Fellow*.

"Blow out the candles, honey," Lily said. "Don't forget to make a wish."

Jack didn't hesitate. *I wish I could go to the World Cup Final in 1966.* Then, remembering the godawful DEI Seminar, he went a step further. *I wish I could go back to the England of old. The real England.*

Zing.

A surge of energy ran through him like a jolt of electricity. For a few precious moments, a vision appeared. A crystal-clear image of Wembley Stadium. *Old Wembley.* The very stadium that hosted the 1966 World Cup Final.

"What'd you wish for?" Ozzie demanded. "You didn't waste it on those Liverpool foreigners, I hope."

Jack came back to reality and made a *zip-the-lips* gesture.

Cake was served and the sugar blast sent the kids into overdrive. They were bouncing off the walls, and with alcohol on board so were some of the adults. By the time it was over, Jack was done and dusted. He couldn't wait to lay his head down. He'd probably be asleep before it hit the pillow.

"That was some proper good fun," said Lily.

"It certainly was," Jack agreed. "I'm rightly knackered now though. Didn't even have that much to drink."

"You're getting old, dear."

"*Hey.*"

She grinned. "You go in and rest, I'll do the washing up and check on the kids."

"Aw, thanks honey."

Her grin morphed into a leer. "Don't fall asleep, though, loverboy. I'll be in later with a special present." She was a vixen, Lily was.

Jack grinned back in anticipation.

3. The Time Tunnel

In the bedroom, Jack was overcome with a sense of wellbeing and gratitude. He was a blessed man, his troubles trivial. But this particular spirit of goodwill was above and beyond the norm.

Birthday-related, perhaps? Or something to do with that vision of Wembley? *What was that* by the way? Some weird premonition?

Zing.

It happened again.

Another flash of Old Wembley. More than a flash. *A vision.* Distinct and real, no detail spared. This one was more powerful. More prolonged. More persistent. He gazed into Lily's vanity mirror and a surreal outline of his visage stared back, the likeness blurred, an aura of light surrounding it.

Jesus.

Quite suddenly, a strange sensation engulfed him – mind, body, and spirit. He felt weightless as the image in the mirror blurred further, yet he still perceived it with absolute clarity. In fact, he perceived everything with perfect clarity.

Clarity of thought.

Heightened consciousness.

A deep and fearless curiosity to see what this was all about.

It was no medical event. Not a heart attack. Jack felt threatened not in the least. On the contrary, he felt an overwhelming urge to succumb entirely to...*whatever was happening.*

Bright light filled his field of vision. His body relaxed, his breathing and heartbeat slowed. He surrendered...and was soon floating through...was it space? Time? Yes, and yes. There could be no doubt. He was travelling through the cosmos, backward in time, observing a parade of visions pass by.

Life events. Momentous events. The COVID pandemic. The Manchester bombing. Brexit. The Fall of the Berlin Wall, a stalwart Ronald Reagan demanding, *Mr. Gorbachev, tear down this wall!* Chernobyl. The John Lennon assassination. The election of Margaret Thatcher. Jack witnessed and perceived them all and many more.

At the same time, his personal life was laid bare: his wedding day, the birth of his children, the death of his beloved Grandad. It was as if he was on a three-dimensional – scratch that, *multi*-dimensional – moving walkway. Actually, more like a tunnel. *A Time Tunnel.*

He was perceptive to the events around him. He could see, hear, even smell everything as he observed time pass in elaborate waves of sensory profusion. He felt the wind in his hair, the smells of childhood, the emotion of each moment. But Jack wasn't overwhelmed. On the contrary, he comprehended with effortless clarity.

Otherworldly clarity.

Then he saw his destination. How did he know? Was it instinct? Or did it just happen? He wasn't sure. But it made sense, notwithstanding. July 30, 1966. Saturday. Wembley Stadium.

He panned the swarming crowds and gradually zoomed until he was transported inside. He saw the pitch, the players, the fancy electronic scoreboard. The infamous thirty-nine steps leading to the Royal Box where players collected trophies.

This was old Wembley.

The *Time Tunnel* slowly faded as visions crystallized into reality and Jack's consciousness settled into this time and place.

Boom.

He was there. In the flesh.

4. 1966 World Cup

Jack had arrived. In 1966. In his seat. Section 38. Wembley Stadium. The place Pelé once called the Cathedral of Football.

He glanced about, wide-eyed, as the crowd buzzed. He spotted West German flags, but Union Jacks were dominant. The skies were grey and bore the threat of rain. But rain would not come. Jack knew this well because his Dad had told him.

His Dad had told him everything and cor blimey, Jack was living it now. As if he'd been transported onto a movie set. But it wasn't a movie set. It was real. Every detail.

How is this happening?

Jack pinched himself. Nothing happened. He pinched himself again. Still nothing. *What the? If it's not a dream and it's not reality – what is it?*

He surveyed himself. Same green shirt and plaid pants he'd had on at the birthday party. Thank God he'd been wearing sandals. For that matter, thank God he hadn't changed into pyjamas. Is that how this thing worked? He checked his pockets. No wallet, but his trusty mobile had come along for the journey.

He took several deep breaths and got his bearings. He was a few rows up from the action and could clearly see the lush turf – perhaps a wee bit slick from earlier rain. And the players themselves, from both sides, warmed up on the pitch. He could see them clearly, right down to the expressions on their faces. His eyesight, *sans glasses*, was perfect. He had the eyesight of his younger self.

There was England's most beloved footballer, Bobby Charlton. A legendary figure, ambassador extraordinaire for the sport. That's how Jack knew him. On this day, Sir Bobby was twenty-eight years of age, but his mythical status was already fully formed. Eight years prior, he'd survived the Munich Air Disaster which claimed many of his teammates. He scarcely skipped a beat, going on to win the FA Cup, League Titles, the European Cup, and (spoiler alert) soon to be World Cup. Off the field, Mr. Charlton was humble, as the British are. But on the field, he was renowned for stamina, grit, and a ferocious strike, no matter left or right foot.

There was the twenty-eight-year-old version of Norbert "Nobby" Stiles, the hardnosed five-six defensive midfielder. *The Iron Tackler*, they called him 'cause he always went in hard. Some say too hard. And of course, the great Geoff Hurst – substitute for the injured Jimmy Greaves. Not a single fan knew it – *save Jack Campbell* – but Mr. Hurst was about to produce a performance for the ages.

Jack scanned the fans in his vicinity. Mostly commonfolk it appeared, living their best lives – buoyant, joyful, full of expectation. To say the English squad had the country behind them was understatement. Nay, this team carried the dreams of fifty million Britons. Today, team and nation were one and the same.

As Ozzie said, *England was still a real country in 1966*. Still ninety-nine percent ethnically English. Yes, this means ninety-nine percent white. Based on what Jack could see, Ozzie was bang on. Jack had yet to see a non-white face – in the crowd or on the pitch. That included the West Germans, so it did.

At that moment, the chap two seats over held out his hand. "Good day, sir. I'm Sheldon Cook."

"Hello, sir." They shook hands. "Jack Campbell."

"I heard you were coming," the man stated. "Peter cancelled last minute, and his brother made some calls.

Seems you were the lucky recipient. How do you know Peter?"

Jack hadn't considered who was *supposed* to be in this seat. But by some divine providence, it had become available to him.

"We go way back," said Jack. "Haven't seem him in a while, mind."

Sheldon nodded smilingly. He was a family man, with two bright-eyed youngsters either side of him. Introductions were made and Jack was taken by the joy on their faces. Pristine, untainted happiness.

Sheldon was roundabout Jack's age – the 2025 version of Jack, that is. *Am I forty-three here?* He wasn't sure what the hell he was.

"Think we can take 'em today?" Sheldon asked.

"I've a good feeling," said Jack.

"Me too, but me nerves are shot."

"My Dad told me they'd win. He guaranteed it, and he's usually right about these things."

"I wish I had his confidence. Is he here?"

The question threw Jack for a loop. Good Lord, his Dad *was* here. Jack opted to lie. "Unfortunately, not. But he'll be watching on the telly." Jack was starting to relax. He made a grand show of asking the young lads about their own sporting exploits. They were near in age to young Finn.

"My own boy and girl play, too."

"Your girl plays football?" The boys laughed in unison.

Jack shrugged toward the boy's father. "She's a tomboy." *Note to self. It's a different era. Girls don't play the Beautiful Game in 1966.*

A vendor wandered into the vicinity and barked out his offerings. *Meat pies, crisps, fizzy drinks, tea.* Sheldon got the man's attention and ordered the works for his kids, including a glossy Match Programme. He turned to Jack. "What do ya need, mate? My treat."

Jack smiled sheepishly. He had no money. "Very kind of you, I'll take a Coke. Thank you, Sheldon." As the transaction unfolded, Jack came clean. "Appreciate it, mate. Truth is, I lost my wallet earlier." He gestured vaguely: "Been a hectic day."

"Sorry to hear, old sport." In modern-day England, there'd be high suspicion toward a move like that. But here, trust and goodwill were in abundance. "Tell you what, I'll get you a programme, too. You need one to enjoy the match."

Sheldon waved off Jack's protests. "We're on the same team today, laddie. We're all family."

Jack skimmed the publication with interest. There were articles about key players, their respective sides, their respective countries. By modern standards, it was an amateurish production, but this only added to its charm. For the first time, it sank in – England's opponent was *West Germany*. My God, this truly was a different world. A world where the Iron Curtain still divided Europe.

Jack studied the rosters and player bios – nothing but white faces on both sides. And just look at those English lads. *Proper* English lads, they were. Jack felt a surge of National Pride such as he'd never felt. Englishmen weren't supposed to feel such a thing. *We're supposed to feel guilt and shame.*

Sorry, not today.

Jack had seen a copy of the programme once before at a festival. It was a sought-after collectible, worth a fortune. This copy was obviously mint condition. Hot off the presses. Without thinking, Jack whipped out his iPhone to snap a few photos.

A split second later, it dawned – the space-age gadget wouldn't jive with the time. Heck, these people barely had colour TV. For them, an iPhone was outright sorcery. In some parts of time and space, they'd burn him alive for witchcraft.

Too late. One of the bright-eyed youngsters, the older of the two sitting to Jack's left, got an eyeful. "*What is that?* Wow, look Daddy."

Jack quickly shut the phone off, but not before Sheldon got a glimpse. "Don't know, me boy. What have you there, mate?"

Jack sheepishly attempted to cover the phone with his hands. "It's just a, uh, a special kind of camera."

"Looked like a miniature television to me," said the kid.

Sheldon nodded. "Who are you, James Bond? You get that from Q, did you?" Both youngsters giggled.

Jack regrouped. "I...uh...I work for the government." He said it with a serious tone, then grinned and pocketed the phone. "Not for Q. I'm not allowed to talk about this device. It's a prototype."

Sheldon looked at him quizzically. He wanted more, and the awkward moment lingered. However, blessedly it was three o'clock and the game was starting.

Another note to self: No photos! And no Googling players. He grinned. *There's no internet here, you silly goose. Probably no Wi-Fi either*, he chuckled at the absurdity of explaining Wi-Fi to Sheldon.

5. Victory

The wait was finally over for the packed stadium. Jack knew from memory, 96,000 in attendance, ten percent of them German. Pre-game festivities were brief – national anthems and not much else – and the referee's piercing opening whistle was bang on 3:00 p.m. local time.

Both teams looked smart in the classic 4-4-2 formation. England in their iconic kit – red jersey, white shorts, red socks. Nothing flashy. No gauche sponsor logos, just the classic embroidered Three Lions crest. The West Germans sported white jerseys, black shorts, white socks. Elegant simplicity.

London bookies made England the 1-2 favourite, but not a single English fan took anything for granted. The game found rhythm quickly. Less than a minute in, free kick Germany fifteen yards outside the England penalty. Moments later, Bobby Charlton with a wonderful touch. Then, a twenty-year-old Beckenbauer – *Der Kaiser in the flesh* – making superlative plays on the ball. He was a midfielder on the day, not yet the magnificent sweeper he'd become. But he was already special.

For the umpteenth time, Jack marvelled at what he was witnessing. This was straight from a science fiction movie. Going back in time?

How is this happening?

Yet it was happening. It was as real as the stars in the midnight sky, and Jack embraced it. Why not? This was a game for the ages and he might as well savour the moment.

The crowd didn't have to wait long for a goal, but not from the side they wanted. At the twelve-minute mark, poor clearance by the English defender allowed Helmut Haller to put the ball past keeper Gordon Banks.

Yikes. Germany up 1-nil.

It momentarily took wind out of sails, but six minutes on Geoff Hurst tied the match with a powerful header, and English fans were redeemed. By halftime, the game remained all square at one.

The crowd was in fine spirits and Jack and Sheldon relived the tying goal, and a few other close calls. But the youngster to his left soon interrupted. "May I see your camera again, sir?"

Jack smiled at the young man, who was about a year older than Jack's own lad. Showing off the iPhone was tempting. Oh, the fun he could have playing wizard to these folks. He resisted the urge. It felt…*dangerous*. Already, Jack was sensing the burden and responsibility of *time travel*.

"I wish I could, son. But I'm under NDA." Neither the boys nor Sheldon knew what that meant but Jack didn't dwell. "Whereabouts you live Sheldon?"

"Notting Hill. Born and raised."

Jack frowned. "How's the neighbourhood?"

"We love it. So vibrant. Full o' culture, y'know?"

Jack's frown deepened. He was aware of Notting Hill's embrace – *that wasn't exactly the correct word* – of Caribbean immigrants starting as far back as 1948 with the fated Windrush arrivals. In 1966, few Londoners felt threatened by the influx. After all, this was England. *Their England.*

Jack knew different. In fact, the inaugural *Notting Hill Carnival* was set to occur just a month hence. By 2025, the event would be known for violence, with bookies posting an over-under on the number of stabbings. Vast swaths of Notting Hill would eventually become inhospitable to white Britons – Jack knew well – like so many other areas.

The *Great Replacement* – ethnic cleansing Ozzie called it – would be rapid in Sheldon's neck of the woods. Already it was in full force, and poor naive Sheldon was putting positive spin to it, God love him.

Jack was tempted to warn the man – *get out now* – but Sheldon was still talking. "...close to everything, Stamford Bridge for one. We're Chelsea fans, you know. Blimey, it took us just fifteen minutes to get here today."

"You drove?"

"Course we did, mate."

Jack raised his eyebrows in appreciation. In modern-day London, traffic and parking made driving near impossible. On the day of a World Cup Final? Crikey, forget about it.

"Wha'bout yourself, Jack? Where do you live?"

"I'm in Twickenham." Jack decided to be honest.

"Ah, you're a rugby fan, then?" It was the home of English rugby.

"Ah sure, but it's a distant second to this great game."

"Beautiful spot. Pricey." Sheldon rubbed thumb and forefingers together. "Government's paying well these days, yeah?"

Jack shrugged noncommittally.

"I suppose if you're coming up with space-age gadgets like the one in your pocket, it's money well spent."

Another shrug.

"Soon, we'll have flying cars and men on the moon," said one of the youngsters.

Jack smiled at the shiny optimism.

"And smart robots," added the other. "My science teacher told me people in the future won't even have to work. Not if they don't want to."

"I'm not so sure about that," Jack offered. It was obvious he was being cagey, but he didn't know what else to do. He didn't know the rules in this strange...*circumstance*. Erring on the side of caution seemed advisable.

Again, mercifully, the match started and all eyes turned to the pitch. "Here we go again," Sheldon announced.

For thirty minutes, the two sides battled fiercely, trading chances including a glorious one by Bobby Charlton himself. To Jack's mind, the English lads had the edge in play, perhaps buoyed by the crowd's rousing rendition of *The Saints Go Marching In*, which had become England's theme song this World Cup. They also belted out a menacingly loud and powerful *Rule, Britannia*, and it touched Jack's soul like nothing before ever had.

My God, he felt the full force of English blood and soil. And then, heightening the moment to a state of pristine ecstasy, a magical moment unfolded. In the 78th minute, following sustained pressure, Martin Peters took a nifty pass from Alan Ball, and struck a clean winner past keeper Hans Tilkowski. The Wembley faithful went into a rabid frenzy.

With just twelve minutes left in regulation, it had to be the clincher. The Cup was England's. It must be. And as the minutes ticked by, it became more and more obvious. England had this. The trophy was finally coming home.

However, tragedy struck in the 89th minute. After a goalmouth scramble, Wolfgang Weber put home the tying goal with a minute in regulation. West Germany had pulled off a miracle. The shock equalizer forced thirty minutes of extra time. The singing stopped and the smiles vanished. A hush came over the stadium, save ten thousand Germans who were predictably ecstatic.

The anguish in the faces of Sheldon and his boys was enough to break Jack's heart. He wanted to console them, tell them it was all gonna work out fine. Again, he resisted the urge.

Why, he wondered. Fear? Caution? Uncertainty? Yes, that was it. *Uncertainty.* For all he knew in this strange parallel universe, West Germany wins. Was there a guarantee the game would play out according to the historical reality?

It had so far. Thus, chances are, it would continue to. "Chin up, lads. Extra time it is. We've got this."

"We were *this close*, Jack."

"Don't worry, I've a good feeling."

"Blimey, me heart can't take much more o' this."

"We'll be fine." Jack offered a confident smile, and it seemed to cheer them. Their mood was lifted further by

England's play out of the gate, with Alan Ball, Bobby Charlton, and Geoff Hurst all leading aggressive attacks.

Sensation came in the 101st minute when Hurst took Allan Ball's cross deep in the penalty and blasted a shot from close range. It slammed the underside of the bar and bounced straight down, appearing to hit the goal line, before being cleared by the German defender.

Confusion ensued. The Swiss referee signaled for a corner, but England protested. Shockingly, the Russian linesman took England's side in adamant fashion. *It was a good goal*, he proclaimed. Despite passionate protests from the West Germans, the decision stood.

"It was in," screamed Sheldon, and his boys echoed the sentiment. Like any proper Englishman, Jack had seen the replay a million times. He'd be first to admit, it was questionable. A portion of the ball certainly crossed the line, maybe most of it. But the whole ball? He wasn't about to bring that up now, though.

No sir.

Because again, he was lost in the elation. The singing was back with greater fervour and the minutes ticked away. At the 120-minute mark, more theatrics. Close to the final whistle, the referee checking his watch, and Germany pressing for an equalizer, Hurst caught the German defence napping. He found space down the left flank and bore down on the German keeper. He struck a left-footed laser from inside the box and it found the back of the net.

My God.

It had to be the clincher, *and* it completed Hurst's hat-trick, cementing him in football lore for eternity. But again, controversy as English supporters had stormed the pitch early. No one cared. Nor did history. Asterisk or otherwise, a win was a win. As with Maradona's *Hand of God*, it only added to the lore.

And it was a win. A 4-2 final. English fans were intoxicated with joy and pride, Jack included. England was on top again, right where she belonged. Jack forgot he was in a different era.

He forgot about everything except the precise moment he was living.

6. Rule, Britannia

West German grumbling did nothing to dampen spirits of the rabid English fans. They were in a state of mass delirium, as was Jack.

England were World Champions. *Finally.* Glory restored where it belonged, to the country that gave football to the world. Forget Germany. Forget Latin America. Forget talk of the Southern Hemisphere growing dominant, producing not only the best teams, but the best players. Forget all of that.

England was king of the hill. Top of the heap. Like a phoenix from the ashes, National pride rose up in an unstoppable tsunami of ecstasy. When Bobby Moore collected the great trophy from Queen Elizabeth II, Prince Philip at her side, the Duke and Duchess of Kent looking on, Jack knew in his heart – this was bigger than football. It was spiritual. A religious experience.

No country could match England's pomp and circumstance, and now, no country could match England on the pitch. He wasn't the only one who felt that way. As fans poured out of Wembley, he picked up random snippets of conversation: "I can't believe we've bloody done it."..."I never doubted our lads, not for a second."..."This is surely the first of many."

Pride and happiness swelled in Jack's chest, so powerful he felt he may explode. It wasn't only the win, it was the atmosphere. The people. *The English people.* Smartly dressed all. No ballcaps, no trainers, no hoodies. Not a drug addict nor aggressive panhandler in sight.

And let it be said, not a burka to be seen, either. Not a hint of violence in the air, even as West Germans mingled among English. The *Progressive* beast hadn't spoiled England. Not yet. Even here in the heart of London.

"I'm meeting me mates at the Lion's Pub," said Sheldon. "We've a table waiting. Fancy joining us?"

"I think I shall," said Jack. The thought of a few pints was irresistible.

"We witnessed it together, mate. Brothers for life now." The two embraced, and the young lads looked on approvingly.

The crowds in the street were thick and energetic, and Jack marvelled at the orderliness. The people were well-behaved and courteous. Even mild-mannered in this, their moment of great glory. And the city itself – English to the core. For once, the people matched the architecture.

Jack had heard of these days, when you could safely walk London's streets day or night. When everyone spoke English, and practically everyone was White. The rumours were true. He suddenly realized, he hadn't seen a *person of colour* the entire day. If he spoke the term – *person of colour* – odds are no one would know what he meant.

He was witnessing British people in their natural habitat. British people as they were meant to be in nature. The unabashed joy in Sheldon and his lads was a thing to behold. Unlike Jack, Sheldon didn't fret for his children's future.

"Are you quite alright, Jack?"

Jack exited his reverie with a grin. "Never better."

"You were lost in space for a second there."

"Just enjoying the moment." Jack gestured toward three gorgeous lasses strutting past in miniskirts. "Can you blame me?"

"Not at all, mate."

It was the start of the Swinging '60s, and risqué garments were all the rage. A symbol of cultural change, perhaps not in the right direction, Jack reckoned. Despite the showy display, the women were decidedly more chaste than their 2025 counterparts. The skirts were certainly revealing, but the girls came across not as slutty, but as graceful and elegant.

"I'm taking it all in, Shel. I haven't walked these streets in a good while." He glanced around happily. "Almost feels like I've never walked them."

It was true, the environment was familiar, yet vaguely foreign. Take the vehicles. A shiny TR4 here, a sleek Jaguar E-Type there, no doubt with the plush leather interior. Vauxhalls galore. Black Cabs galore. Even the odd Rolls Royce. Shocking how many of the cars were British-made back in the day.

Also, no bike lanes. No dreaded ULEZ cameras. No kebab shops or curry houses. Crikey, around here *Curry* was a surname. And again, it had to be acknowledged – no non-whites. Scratch that, *almost* none. By now, Jack had seen a few.

Nevertheless, this was London to the core. Pure. Untouched. Unspoiled. Jack was practically shaking with ancestral recognition. Like an electric charge through his nervous system. However, there was a parallel current of sadness. A mourning for what had been taken, almost as surely as if London had been razed to the ground.

Sheldon shot him another puzzled look. "You're due for a pint, laddie."

"Couldn't agree more."

"This way, follow me."

Upon entry, Jack was hit with another dose of ancestral nostalgia. The pub was classic English, probably centuries old. Pubs were one aspect of British life that had resisted change, which is probably why the Brits loved them so much.

Yet here in 1966, Jack witnessed authenticity that didn't exist in 2025. No TVs, no mobile phones, no craft beer, no loud music to dampen banter. Because that's what pubs were for, right? Fellowship and pints. Nothing more, nothing less.

On this, perhaps the most glorious day in recent English history, the place was jammed. A modern-day Fire Marshal would've had a meltdown. *And the smoke.* It was thick in the air. Everyone smoked, it seemed, and ashtrays overflowed.

There was a masculine energy in the room. A working-class vibe. It was male-dominated to be sure, but women weren't banned, not at all. Discouraged maybe but not banned. The banter was hale and hearty.

> *"The lads were class today. Absolute legends, each of 'em."*
>
> *"No one can take this away from us."*
>
> *"The whole country's celebrating tonight."*

The men were present, in the moment, and Jack met a fine sampling of Londoners. Bus drivers, longshoremen, postal workers. Professional Class, too. He even swapped shoptalk with a banker.

"Who you with?" The man asked.

Telling the truth was out of the question – UniBank wasn't formed until the 1990s. "Barclays." Jack went with a safe bet – the largest bank in England.

"Brilliant, mate. I'm in currency trading, myself. You know the drill – exchange rates, letters of credit, that sorta thing." He smiled. "Me hand's still sore from updatin' ledgers." He mimicked the motion. "Month end, y'know."

That's right, Jack realized. *Forget computers, calculators weren't even on the scene. It was an analog world and these poor saps did everything by hand.*

"You know Jamie Cuthbert?" The man was asking. "He's a good lad. Cheeky bastard, once ya know 'im."

"The name rings a bell."

"What sort of work you do there, Jack?"

What to tell this chap? The banking Jack undertook bore no resemblance to this man's world. "Let's not talk shop, mate." He raised his glass. "Not today."

"Right. Fair play." The man raised his own glass.

Just then, the barmaid strolled past and some of the men flirted. "Angie, if I ever leave me wife, I'll be comin' for ya, luv."

She was no shrinking violet: "Thanks for the warning, Paul."

"Aye, she's a cheeky lass, *in't she.*" He pinched her bottom.

To another man, a younger and better-looking specimen, Angie flirted back with full vigour. But the spirit of the moment was never far. Glasses were repeatedly raised, and pints aplenty consumed. From time to time, the singing kicked in:

> *Rule, Britannia! Britannia, rule the waves!*
> *Britons never, never, never will be slaves.*

And again:

> *Rule, Britannia! Britannia, rule the waves!*
> *Britons never, never, never will be slaves.*

Sheldon's young lads took it all in and made friends for life with others their age. Jack briefly pondered the fact that his own Dad could be at this very pub, but a quick swill washed away those brain-twisting concerns.

By now, people were ordering food, and Jack realized he was ravenous. The menu was as British as they come – fish and chips, bangers and mash, cottage pie. The Asian food blight, as Ozzie called it, had yet to take hold. Jack settled on steak and kidney pie, a bargain at 26p. Sheldon was still footing the bill, and happy to do it.

The sustenance served the men well. It fortified them for another set of rounds. For the family men, however, 9:00 p.m. was nearing. Time to call it a night. Sheldon, for one, had had enough, and his young lads had turned a wee bit mopey.

"Been a great pleasure, Jack." Sheldon extended his hand.

"Pleasure's all mine," said Jack, pulling Sheldon in for a manly hug. "Can't thank you enough for the uh, hospitality, shall I say. Next time, it's on me. That's a promise." Hugging among men was not common in 1960s England, but with alcohol on board, Sheldon accepted the overture.

"Happy to do it, sir." Sheldon said, then turned serious. "What're you gonna do now? How you getting home? Shall I give you cab fare?"

It was a jarring question, and it jarred Jack from the spell of alcohol, World Cup glory, and the love of fellow countrymen. He had no place to go, and the look on his face betrayed that.

"You could stay at mine. We've a spare room, nothing fancy. The wife wouldn't mind." Sheldon grinned. "She's an agreeable sort for the most part."

"I'll be fine," said Jack unconvincingly.

"Or I could book you a room, it's no trouble."

Jack smiled. "Something posh and grand if you don't mind. Perhaps the Dorchester?"

Sheldon smiled at the small joke, but he was ready to leave. His young lads, moments earlier full of mischief, were drooping badly. "I must get these tykes home to bed." He tousled his eldest's hair.

Jack stared into space awkwardly.

"You're a good man, Jack, that I can tell. But, if you don't mind me saying, you seem a little lost at times. Like maybe, you're not in the right place."

Jack rallied his senses. "Look, I'm right, mate. I'll be fine. Gimme a minute now, would you? I'll 'ave me a quick Jimmy Riddle and walk out with ya."

Jack would obviously have to figure something out. He waltzed into the loo, passing a few of his new mates along the way. For a second, uncertainty was replaced by the previous jubilation. *What a day, what a day!*

With business done, Jack studied his reflection in the mirror, and any sense of normalcy was abruptly punctured.

What is this place? How am I here? How will I return? Will I return?

Emotions overcame him. *If I live out my days in this idyllic England-of-old replica – is that what it was? – would I be happier? Perhaps I would. This version of England is clean and pure. Friendly faces all. It is home.*

Yet, it wasn't home. Jack had a home in England to be sure, but not here. Not this era.

He thought of Lily and the kids and his heart ached. Not only for them, but for all the native English living in modern-day dystopian England. A hellhole by comparison, no one could argue otherwise.

Jack could not *and would not* desert his family. Nor his friends. He had to go back. People needed him. His fears for the future rose to the surface. Fears for his children's future.

He had to go back. But how?

Would it happen spontaneously? Was there some trigger?

Or would it never happen?

7. Back in the Time Tunnel

Alone in the bathroom – *miraculously, still alone* – he looked deeper into his reflection. *What if I'm here forever? Stuck here? What of Lily and the kids? Is there another version of me still there?*

He found himself praying to God.

Thank you for this blessed experience. I don't know what it means. I don't understand how it happened. It's been wonderful but I'm ready to go home. To my own time and place. I need to go home.

An image of Jack's bedroom flashed, so vivid and real it startled him. He closed his eyes and tried to channel it. At first nothing happened, then more faint visions appeared.

Was it the Time Tunnel?

Changes were happening. His vitals were slowing, that same peculiar sensation was engulfing him – mind, body, soul. He opened his eyes and saw his reflection was blurred and strangely lit.

Simultaneously his thoughts clarified. Everything suddenly made sense. The meaning of the experience was in his consciousness, and he was at one with it. Bright light filled his vision. His vitals slowed further and he surrendered. Before long, he was in the *Time Tunnel*, travelling through the cosmos, this time moving forward through a parade of temporal landmarks, viewing them with the same heightened perception. Princess Di's wedding, the Falklands War, the Queen's death.

The events played out in infinite detail, and he comprehended them with infinite clarity. He could probe deeper at will, extract any level of detail, yet paradoxically, he kept moving, as if time spent exploring didn't count.

Finally, his destination – the master bedroom of his Twickenham home. Present-day London. Did he choose to get off? Or did it just happen? He wasn't sure.

The *Time Tunnel* faded as his bedroom crystallized into reality and Jack's consciousness settled into present-day.

He was back, gazing at his reflection.

Vital signs, calm as you please.

8. Home Again

Jack was exactly where he'd been when the vision of Old Wembley hit. His reflection was no longer blurry. It was clear and most definitely real. He heard Lily puttering in the kitchen.

He'd been whisked back to the present. His bedside clock reported 1:47 a.m., precisely the time the vision had hit. The wee hours of Saturday morning.

What the...?

Had time stood still while he was gone?

Consciously and deliberately, Jack steadied himself. *What happened? Was it all a dream?*

Yes, that's it. A dream. Must've been. An amazing dream to be sure, more realistic than any dream I've ever had! But a dream, nonetheless.

I must be getting old, Jack reasoned. *Perhaps I've been working too hard. Or drinking too much. Or developing an overactive imagination?*

Ah, flippin' heck. It was just a dream. Leave it at that.

A vague sense of relief washed over Jack, but it was short-lived. Doubt crept back in. Because it sure as hell didn't feel like a dream. Dreams are murky and strange, full of illogical sequences and non-sequiturs.

That's if you remember them. And even if you do, the memories are fleeting. They slip away quickly and vanish forever. The events of a dream never actually happened and thus never find purchase in long-term memory.

This was different. Jack remembered *everything*. Every last detail. Every interaction with Sheldon and so many others. The World Cup match, the city streets, the pub. Even the loo from which he was transported back.

These things happened. They were incredibly vivid. And they made sense. So unlike a dream. And how was it a dream when he wasn't even sleeping. He hadn't gone to bed. Some sort of hallucination perhaps?

Christ.

For good measure, he checked his phone. *Damn.* No pictures. He was about to take one, but the phone – it was too modern. Too space-age for 1966. He had to keep it hidden.

But if he had taken a photo, would it be there?

Of course not. Give your head a shake, man. Snap out of it. Get some sleep. You obviously need it.

He began to undress. He stripped off the green shirt and the plaid trousers.

Wait, what's this?

Oh my God!

There it was. Folded and jammed in his pocket. The glossy Match Programme. Mint condition, save a crease down the centre so it'd fit in his pocket. He flipped through it, as if doubting its presence. As if to prove it was really there.

Gordon bloody Bennett!

It was no dream after all. Jack knew all along.

Oh my God! Oh my God! Oh my God!

He paced the room frantically trying to process this revelation. He'd read novels about time travel – the paradoxes, the parallel universes. He'd seen movies. Who hadn't?

Was I actually there? Was Sheldon a real person? What was his last name again? Jack couldn't recall. *He'd be long dead now, wouldn't he? Or well into his 90s. But his kids would be alive. Maybe in their 70s.*

Crikey, if I was really there – forget if, I was there – did my interactions affect the future? Did I affect Sheldon's life?

What about the banker? Or the bus driver? Or Sheldon's kids? How did I get there? How did I get back?

Questions flooded his brain. He remembered praying. Was that what happened? Or had he willed himself back to the present?

It was too much to process at this late hour, and Jack was suddenly overcome with exhaustion. The urge to sleep came on quickly. He stripped off the rest of his clothing and hopped under the covers.

Later, he vaguely sensed Lily's arrival, her attempts to initiate a bit of naughtiness. No dice. Jack was out for the count.

A heavy sleep had descended.

A well-earned sleep.

9. Family Time

Jack rose early the following day. Rested. Refreshed. Invigorated. Inspired.

The memory of his *adventure* washed over him pleasantly. He didn't panic. The shock that this incredible thing happened was over. And it *did* happen. He had proof.

But what did it mean? He had no answer there.

He followed his weekend routine. He made coffee, flipped on the telly. BBC Sport was previewing the day's matches. Was a full slate, including the featured match, Man United vs Liverpool. The usual suspects were to meet at the Rose and Thorne to take in the action. At stake, bragging rights for either himself or Ozzie, though if United lost Ozzie would pretend not to give a toss.

The female broadcaster worked through respective lineups, covering recent hot streaks, injuries, other assorted minutiae. Jack couldn't concentrate.

How could he?

The reality of England in 1966 – of London – had penetrated his soul with a mighty blast of ancestral recognition. Jack struggled to put language to his feelings. Finally, a suitable phrase dawned. It was as if he'd been home. A profound sense of being home. Of being whole. Of relaxing – truly relaxing – for what may have been the first time in his life.

Everyone was British. *Ethnic British.* Everywhere he looked, he saw his countrymen. He was safe and protected. Among family. It wasn't just safety, it was the utter absence of violence, or even the threat of it. He implicitly trusted the people he interacted with. And they trusted him.

Look at Sheldon, helping financially with not an ounce of hesitation. It was an act borne of high trust. Something you did for kith and kin and never thought twice about. What a beautiful way to live.

This world of purity and honour existed in England's recent past. Jack had heard tell, but now he'd seen it firsthand. Most of today's British had little awareness of what had been taken from them.

Jack did. He had experienced the wonder and magic of the recent past, and it stirred something in his soul. Quite suddenly, a new thought emerged. An intriguing and tantalizing thought.

Can I go back again?

Will it happen again? Can I make it happen again? If so, how? And will I go to the same time and place? Or somewhere else in history?

Random thoughts ran roughshod, one curious notion leading to the next, then twisting around on itself. Time travel was full of mind-bending paradoxes.

Where would I like to go? What would I like to see? England had only the one World Cup victory, but Liverpool had a heap of Champions League wins. Maybe the AC Milan beatdown of 2005? Or Andy Murray's Wimbledon victory? Would there be a seat waiting for me? The universe made room for me at the World Cup. Would it always be like that?

Some deep intuition told him, perhaps not.

What other moments would I like to see? Concerts! Early Beatles. Led Zeppelin. Pink Floyd. I could spend time in the '70s. Witness the emergence of Punk, or Ska, or New Wave.

Wait.

I must think bigger. Beyond sports and entertainment. Perhaps the Victorian era, when Dickens and Hardy chronicled British life. Or the Industrial Revolution. Or the great battle of 1066 – the Norman Conquest. What would I do whilst there? Would it be dangerous? What if I was killed? Would I also die here in 2025?

A provocative thought. And slightly terrifying.

How would I get by in these environments? Would there always be a friendly chap to hold my hand? How would I blend in, wear the right clothes, say the right things? What would I do for money?

Abruptly, Jack's musings were terminated, as was his peace and quiet. The kids were up and that was a fact that could not be ignored. They joined him on the couch, which is to say, they climbed all over him. From here on out, the usual events of a Saturday took over.

"Are you coming to my match, Daddy?" Finn asked.

"Of course I am, sport."

"What about mine?" Lucy asked.

"Your mother's got you covered." When schedules conflicted, this was standard operating procedure.

"I'm playing forward today, Daddy," Finn announced. "I'm gonna score a goal."

He tousled his son's hair. "The first of many it'll be."

Finn switched gears quickly. "Can I play Lego?"

He meant the video game, not the old-fashioned physical blocks. "You know the rules, not 'til after breakfast. You hungry?"

Finn nodded.

"And you Missy?"

"Starving." Lucy was such a sweet little lass, far easier to manage than her boisterous brother.

"I am too," said Lily, strolling in wearing pajamas, just as sexy as the day Jack met her. "You were a tired chicken last night, honey."

A complex set of ethical questions rose to the fore. *Am I to tell her what happened? She'll think I'm a nutter. Hell, maybe I am a nutter.*

"Ozzie wore me out," he answered.

"He always does." Lily's posture took on a determined air. "Right then, who's up for eggs on toast?" All hands went up, Jack's included.

He sure lucked out with Lily. For starters, she was gorgeous – no two ways about it. A true English rose. An Anglo-Saxon Goddess but also bestowed with the great gift of happiness and joy. She brought it to every interaction. Saw the bright side of everything. Her aura was like a drug.

Jack fell in love immediately, but alas Lily had many suitors, and she didn't flock to Jack like he was the Messiah. This took him aback. He was always the fair-haired boy and rather used to getting what he wanted.

It upped her worth considerably and when the connection was finally made, Jack didn't squander it. After six months of *going out*, it was obvious they'd spend their lives together. Lily had one condition.

"I want kids." It was non-negotiable.

Jack wasn't opposed. "Sure. A son for me. A daughter for you." Alas, Finn and Lucy appeared as if they'd always been there. Jack could scarcely recall life without them.

They were blessed and happy, though life was hectic. Like this morning, Lucy's match at ten, Finn's at half-ten. Different grounds, naturally. Not a bother. They made it work.

That day, Finn was a beast on the pitch and did indeed pot his first goal. Lucy played more cautiously but enjoyed the team spirit and bonding. By half-one, the production was over, and Jack had the green light to pursue male bonding at the pub.

10. The Rose and Thorne

By the time Jack arrived – *surprise, surprise* – most of the lads were several pints deep. Jack cast a critical eye over the premises. Sure, there were TVs. And yeah, conversation competed with music. But for the most part, the place was untouched by the progressive zeitgeist. Right?

Ha, not so fast.

He spotted a Rainbow Flag by the fireplace. *Christ, do they have to be everywhere?* Imagine trying to explain that to his 1966 chum Sheldon. On the plus side, the clientele was almost entirely ethnic British. That was something.

The much-anticipated match was set for three o'clock, plenty of time to revel in the pre-match guff. Not the same as being at Old Trafford, mind. Jack had occasional access to corporate seats, and he used them to bring the kids. But for this lot, the pub did the trick just fine. Ozzie stopped shelling out years back. *I refuse to hand over me hard-earned wages to the globalist ghouls.*

It was a near-full-house and Jack jostled for position at the bar. He spotted an unattended Match Day Programme and flipped through the pages with interest. It was slicker and glossier than its 1966 counterpart. But it had a *soullessness* to it. A mass-manufactured sterility. The 1966 edition, on the other hand, was dyed-in-the-wool British.

The musing brought Jack back to his recent excursion and set him in a wonderful mood. A genuine bonhomie that shone brightly. Ozzie didn't miss much, and he knew Jack as well as anyone.

"You're rather chipper this afternoon. What's up, Campbell?"

Jack shrugged.

"Something's up. You win the Lotto? Got a bird on the side, do you?"

"Just happy to be out with the lads. Even you, Ozzie."

"It's drugs, innit? If you 'ave some, I'll join ya."

"This is my drug." He held his pint high, and they clinked glasses. "You lot are my drug." He gestured wildly, and Ozzie regarded him skeptically. Ozzie could smell bullshit a mile away, which is precisely why he despised the Wokeness Brigade.

He and Jack met through top-level rugby and despite differences became fast friends. Ozzie was broad-shouldered and manly, had been since the age of fifteen. By his early twenties, he was already balding and it phased him not in the least. He was a roll-with-the-punches sorta geezer.

Ozzie enjoyed a good scrap when it was called for, even a brawl if that's what it took. He was a tough lad. He delivered a few sound beatings in his day and took a few himself. Had the scars to prove it. Jack was the taller and heavier of the two, but if it ever came to blows, Jack didn't like his chances.

At twenty-three, Ozzie met and married his ex-wife and quick as a wink, they had two nippers at their ankles. The younger, Bryan, was already nineteen and Ozzie's spitting image in appearance and temperament. He was the favourite by a longshot. The older lad, Jonathon, was a snowflake – Ozzie's word. They were not currently on speaking terms.

It wasn't a smooth ride for Ozzie and the wife, either. Ozzie was a handful and they had several separations before splitting up for good. *Me ex-wife's a right cunt*, Ozzie was known to say. But he was nice to her, truth be told. It's just that dysfunction was in his nature.

He was a heavy equipment mechanic by trade, and that suited him. He was never a top student, definitely not cut out for corporate. He was, however, damn good at his job and it showed up in his pocketbook. Despite years of child support and a healthy booze budget, Ozzie was doing fine financially.

Then there was Edward Squire. *Steady Eddie.* He was Ozzie's polar opposite. Buttoned-down, reserved, pompous. In other words, steadfastly English. Practically an archetype.

He hated being called Eddie. He preferred Edward, and absolutely no one at the pub indulged the preference. He wore a beard and still appeared unmanly, according to Ozzie. Eddie came from family money – nobility he was known to say – and was head boy at grammar school, and proud of it.

He and Jack met during their university years, and what do you know Eddie never left academia. He became a tenured Professor of Literature at King's College of London, which suited perfectly since a blind spot for politics was a prerequisite.

Politically, Eddie was as left leaning as they come. He embraced the government's ridiculous posturings with unnatural vigour. No policy was too outlandish for Steady Eddie, and this put him in Ozzie's crosshairs. *You're a flamin' cuck,* Ozzie would say. Eddie offered the occasional retort – *and you're an ignoramus* – but usually it was a sarcastic "charming" or "oh dear God."

The first half wound down with Liverpool up one-nil – a beauty by the Egyptian Mo Salah – and the banter dialed up full tilt.

"Your side can't compete, Ozzie. Not when we've got maybe the best player in the world."

"He's overpaid, mate. You know it. He'll be soon forgotten."

"Better than your high-priced talent, flopping all over the pitch."

"Oi, spare me, coming from a Liverpool supporter. We've scored more proper goals than your squad ever will."

"Brilliant, from a guy who never played footie."

It was true. Ozzie eschewed the Beautiful Game in favour of his beloved rugby. Some of the aforementioned scars came courtesy of many a ruck and maul.

"I played football."

Jack laughed. "U10 doesn't count, son."

"I count it."

"I'm sure you do." More laughter. "And I'm sure your lad's 've been practising their penalties again, no doubt."

"You back on that?"

"It's their bread and butter, mate. It's all they got."

"I'll give you a penalty," Ozzie held up a fist. "Be a shame to mess up that pretty face."

"Woooo, I'm scared."

"You should be. Your *face* should be."

"At least I support a real club," Jack continued. "Not a nursing home for gold-diggers. United's spent enough money to buy frickin' Portugal. And they're still terrible."

"Let's see what happens in the second half, ya numpty."

All in good fun. Cheeky jabs were part of the experience, and even Steady Eddie was known to participate, but he had no dog in the fight today. Admittedly, Jack was more rambunctious than usual, and Ozzie commented on it a second time.

As for Ozzie, high spirits were the norm. When the teams took the pitch for the second half, he cautioned Jack: "Match ain't over Twinkle Toes. We'll show ya what—"

The comment was never finished because the broadcast abruptly switched to the BBC:

> *"We're interrupting this programme for a Special News Report."*

11. Breaking News

A hush fell over the pub as a sombre anchorperson delivered the grim news:

> *"We're interrupting this programme for a special News Report. Earlier today, emergency services were called to Newfordshire-By-The-Sea following a major incident earlier today."*

Jack's ears perked. That was his hometown, the beautiful and quaint village in which he was raised. Concern for his parents welled up.

> *"At approximately ten past three, police were called to one of the town's two local primary schools on Abbott Crescent after receiving reports of a stabbing. These live pictures..."*

The screen flashed to images of the street in question, where a significant police presence was gathered. An area was cordoned off with yellow crime scene tape. The BBC person droned on:

> *"Police detained two males and seized several weapons. The men were taken into custody for questioning. Police believe others may have been*

involved. We can confirm reports that there were multiple stabbings, multiple casualties, and possible fatalities.

"Police continue to assess the situation and work with emergency partners to tend to the injured parties. While Police acknowledge this was a critical incident, they are stressing that the situation has been contained and there is no imminent threat to the public. We will provide further updates as they become available."

They switched back to the football, where talking heads described action on the pitch as if this horrible, unspeakable event never happened. But it had happened, and the patrons were shaken. Few were paying much mind to the match's second half.

"Oh, fucking Christ," Ozzie was the first to speak. "*Another Southport.*"

The shock and pain of another attack on their young. The slaughter of beautiful English children. It was too much to bear. Some of the men were checking their phones for news. They knew from experience, the public broadcaster would leach out information slowly – they'd bring in "experts" who would speak in solemn tones, and wear looks of grave concern. But they'd dance around the issue on everyone's mind.

Who did it?

"Look at this," Ozzie was reading from his mobile. "Courtesy of the BBC...no names have been released, but witnesses describe the perpetrators as British men who had recently moved to the area. *British men.*"

"And there you have it," said Eddie, knowing full well Ozzie's suspicions.

"Did you hear me? *No names released.* You know what that means. We all know what that means."

"Probably that they want to get it right before going public."

Ozzie scoffed in disgust. "And if *Abdullah Ooga Booga* was a suspect, they'd claim he was British."

"Well, if *Abdullah Ooga Booga* was born in Britain, they'd be right. He'd be just as British as you and me," said Eddie calmly.

"Ah, you bloody cuck. Are you for real?"

"I find your tone objectionable."

Ozzie lowered his voice while upping his intensity: "I'm talkin' *indigenous* British, Eddie. Come on, mate. Shared history. Shared blood. *Shared DNA.* I trace me name and me family to the Middle Ages. I'm Anglo-Saxon to the core. We all are. *Even bloody you.* We've our ancestors' blood flowing through our veins."

"That may be all well and true, but we've been an immigrant nation for a very long time. Don't forget, not so long ago, Britain invaded many parts of the world. Maybe the world has a right to come here."

"So mass migration's revenge then, innit? That's what you're saying, yeah?"

"Not at all. It's what Britain committed to when she established her Empire. An Empire for *all* her subjects."

"Bollocks. We sailed the Seven Seas and brought civilization to the savages. We taught 'em to stop massacring each other, stop marrying their cousins. Gave 'em science and electricity, clean water, feckin' railways. We even abolished slavery for fuck sakes. We did all that. The British. Now, plonkers like you want to give our country away so you can feel good about yourself."

"Not give it away. Share it. Don't forget, immigration helps Britain economically," said Eddie.

"It's been against the wishes of our people since Day One. Since the bloody Windrush sham."

"They had every right to come. You reap what you sow, Oswald."

"We never asked for it, we never voted for it. And they're still coming in goddamn dinghies across the channel, bringing their savagery. We never used to have acid attacks and grooming. And we sure as hell never had bloody child stabbings. Did we?"

The telly flashed back to the BBC. "That's enough you two," said Jack.

"Yeah, shut the fuck up Eddie, would ya?"

12. Horror

The same female anchorperson, looking even more sombre:

> *"This is a special BBC News Update on the story we've been following. We can confirm multiple emergency services teams were called to Newfordshire-By-The-Sea following shocking scenes at the Lord Abbot Primary School. Two men were arrested in connection with the attack and the police have identified two other persons of interest. The perpetrators' names have not been released, and the police have not determined a motive. The wounded are being treated at multiple hospitals in the surrounding area. Let's go to John for a live report. John?"*

They cut to an on-scene reporter:

> *"Amy, horrific scenes in Newfordshire as children ran screaming into the street, some of them bloodied. A spokesman for the Newfordshire Police said he believed the attackers were targeting children and that the injured adults were bravely trying to protect the children. Amy?"*

Back in-studio:

> *"Prime Minister Bloodworth has made the following statement:*
>
> *'The victims of this horrendous tragedy are in our thoughts and prayers. This was a coldblooded and callous attack, and the nation is deeply shocked and saddened.'*
>
> *"The attack is the latest amid a recent rise in knife crime in the U.K. that has stoked anxieties and led to calls for the government to do more to clamp down on bladed weapons."*

The TV screen returned to the match, the score still one-nil.

"What about the attackers, ya cunts?" Ozzie screamed.

Another man pointed to his phone. "I'm hearing they were *Muzzies out looking for revenge.*"

X – formerly Twitter – was rife with conjecture, opinion, and speculation, particularly in far-right circles.

"Of course it was bloody Muslims." said Ozzie. "It won't take Scotland Yard to solve this crime."

"You don't know that," said Eddie. "And you better be careful. Don't forget we have hate speech laws."

"Ah, ya bloody imbecile. I'll tell ya, whoever it was, they hate the English enough to kill our children. And Muzzies fit the bill, don't they?"

Eddie shrugged. "Not all of them."

"It's a stabbing. That's what they do."

"They don't have a monopoly on—"

"Shut the fuck up, Eddie. Wait and see, they'll be foreigners. Like always. Then, give these pricks time," he pointed at the TV, "they'll be talking 'bout racism and struggles with mental illness. Enoch Powell was right about everything, but I doubt even he thought it'd get this bad. Children butchered in broad daylight, blown to bits at concerts. Rivers of blood, ain't that the truth?"

Eddie started a response but Ozzie was having none of it. "I don't wanna hear it, ya bloody cuck. London's gone from a hundred percent white to thirty-three in fifty years. You think that's normal?"

"It was never a hundred percent."

"Shut it." Ozzie pounded a fist on the table with enough force to make the glasses shake. "It's replacement, that's what it is. And now London's a shite-hole, not safe after dark. Not safe anytime. I hate it."

"It's always been overcrowded, Ozzie."

"And London's not enough for 'em now, is it? They want our countryside, too." Ozzie scoffed. "They spread like a bloody cancer. Nowhere's safe from the disease. And what do you and your lot say? *Oh, look at the spicy food.* I got news for ya, mate. We could've skipped over the barbarity and got the bloomin' recipes, yeah?"

Eddie was taken aback by the intensity of the attack and wisely stayed quiet. There was anger in the room, not just from Ozzie. Silence descended for a spell, and was broken when the television flashed to another update:

> *"We're getting confirmed reports that twelve children and four teachers have been killed. The children range in age from six to eleven. The youngest victim was six-year-old Grace Price of Newfordshire."*

A photo of the cutest blonde child imaginable appeared on screen.

> *"Two adults were also injured and remain in critical condition. It's believed they are teachers at the school and were attempting to protect the children, Newfordshire Police said."*

> *"Multiple witnesses described hearing blood-curdling screams and seeing children covered in blood emerge from the school. One witness said 'It was like a scene from a slasher movie.'"*

Jack recoiled from the horror. The magnitude was setting in. It was Southport times ten. He suddenly had a desperate need to make sure his loved ones were accounted for. His own precious children.

He stepped away to call Lily and she picked up first ring. "I'm watching," she said. "Mum called ten minutes ago. It's so horrible."

"Where are the kids?"

"Finn's playing downstairs. Lucy's at Molly's house, I talked to the mum. They're safe and sound. Can you pick her up on the way home?"

"Of course."

"Will you come soon?"

"I'm leaving now. I've lost interest in the match. It's horrific, darling. How are you doing?"

"I'm, uh," she hesitated, "I'm feeling lost. What has happened to my precious England?"

Jack sighed. "Love you and see you soon." He returned to the lads. The room's energy was gone, except Ozzie who was still pontificating.

"Lads, I'm done," Jack announced. "I need to go home and hug my kids."

"We all do," said one of the men.

With that, the crowd began to disperse, the men shocked and confused. Such chilling scenes are difficult for the Western mind to process.

Sadly, the Brits were getting plenty of practice.

13. Newfordshire

Back home, Jack hunkered down with family. He hugged his kids a little tighter than normal. Lily, too, for that matter.

What if it had been Finn and Lucy?

It was an unbearable thought. They were so young and innocent, so untouched by life's ugliness. But it could have been them, no two ways about it. They'd been to Newfordshire countless times to visit Jack's parents. They revelled in the lush back garden, with its stone walls, its nooks and crannies.

Newfordshire was a picturesque seaside village. For Jack, it was like reliving his childhood. Like going back in time – funny to think of it that way.

But it was.

Notwithstanding this new infamy, Newfordshire had fared better than most seaside towns. Jack's Mom was known to whisper, *we're one of the few they haven't infiltrated*. She'd say it with a nervous grin. Yes, the town was still largely British, but rumours of a mega-mosque were persistent.

Of course, the town had changed enormously, but for other reasons. Its rich maritime history was mostly gone. Jack's Grandad and the men before him were fishermen. Jack's Dad had a go at it, but by then the industry was decimated. Overfishing, environmental concerns, and enough red tape to cover a football pitch.

Jack's father got out early and found a lucrative office job, balancing books for the town's cannery. Like Jack, Mr. Campbell had a head for numbers, and he ran the outfit meticulously. He did alright for himself over the years. Coupled with his inheritance, Jack's father was a wealthy man.

There'd been talk of Jack taking on the position, but long-term prospects were dicey. The trend for the area was tourism, which held no interest for Jack. Alas, it was the end of the line for the Campbells of Newfordshire. And it wasn't easy for Jack or his parents. Newfordshire was his home and the sea his childhood playground.

In the end, Jack made his own path, which involved moving to London. He left in 2001 and never looked back – at least not career-wise. At the time, London was clamouring for bright lads like him, even white ones, and banking was the industry of choice.

Early on, Jack worked in sales and posted impressive numbers. As he transitioned to management, he proved a natural. From his corner office overlooking the banks of the Thames, Jack inspired up-and-comers as easily as he appeased massive egos that were part and parcel of the rich and powerful.

The fiscal horrors of 2008 left a mark, but Jack came out alright. So did UniBank, with the help of bailouts. But on a day like today, financial success meant little. Not with the country going to hell in a handbag. That was Jack's sense.

Later that evening, Prime Minister Bloodworth said little to change his opinion:

> *"The entire country is deeply shocked by today's tragic events. Our thoughts and condolences are with the victims and their families. I want to stress, we believe this is an isolated incident and it is not being treated as terror-related. We urge people not to speculate on details of the incident while the investigation is ongoing."*

If he was trying to pacify, the effect was the opposite. Even Lily was upset by the tone. However, Bloodworth was right about one thing – the country *was* in shock, and not for the first time. Every ethnic Brit was starting to realize the special hell they were living in.

Even the liberals. Perhaps even Steady Eddie.

14. Another Vision

The *Newfordshire Massacre* was a global story through several news cycles. Editorials were written and there was much soul searching. The perpetrator, as Ozzie predicted, was a recent arrival from Africa. A Muslim with hatred in his heart for indigenous Brits. There was no other way to phrase it.

Amid rank-and-file Brits, there was anger. Jack felt it, and not only when he talked to Ozzie. Precious young ones had been viciously slaughtered. It was utterly beyond the pale, and it would happen again. Sure it would. This wasn't the first time, and it wouldn't be the last.

How far we have fallen.

Memories of Jack's recent *travels* flooded back. From World Cup glory to horror. Ten years ago, he scoffed at Ozzie. Jack refused to acknowledge the signs. Ozzie was right all along. People called him racist, white supremacist, *Nazi*. But he was right about everything. By now, every native Brit knew it to be true.

A wave of guilt washed over Jack. He was partly at fault, smugly scoffing at Ozzie, telling himself everything was normal when he knew in his heart it was not. Was it a collective complacency? Certainly, but it was more than that. The root cause was a hostile and traitorous government. Why else would their leaders – Labour and

Tory alike – allow the constant in-flow? Not only allow it, encourage it. Enable it. Defend it.

The government was supposed to protect its citizens. That should be top priority. England's had been doing precisely the opposite for a very long time. If anything, they made special efforts to keep the borders open and flood the tiny island with dissimilar people and cultures. They portrayed this as good and normal, while promoting a parallel message that new *citizens* were victims of racism and must be afforded special privileges.

Every day more piled in, and every day Brits noticed with increasing alarm. Was it too late to fix? Probably. It was even too late to complain. The loudest complainers got fired. Debanked. Imprisoned. Ozzie escaped consequences thus far, but he mostly worked for himself. And his forays on social media were anonymous. He was no dummy.

Jack had listened to Ozzie enough over the years – not always voluntarily – to understand what had happened. He would've eventually figured it out on his own. The betrayal was so obvious. It was no conspiracy theory.

Did it have to be like this? Was this always England's fate?

Zing.

A surge of energy ran through him like a freight train. Another vision. *The Palace of Westminster.* Home to the Houses of Parliament – the House of Commons and the House of Lords. In these stately chambers decisions were made – *or not made* – which allowed and encouraged England's decline.

The image morphed to infamous British MP Enoch Powell, and Jack observed snippets of a much-renowned 1968 speech:

> *"...on present trends, there will be in this country three and a half million Commonwealth immigrants and their descendants."*

> *"In this country in fifteen or twenty years' time, the black man will have the whip hand over the white man."*

> *"...total transformation to which there is no parallel in a thousand years of English history."*
>
> *"I am filled with foreboding; like the Roman, I seem to see "the River Tiber foaming with much blood."*

The vision vanished quickly, but its memory lived on. Westminster's glorious gothic architecture. And the speech – *Rivers of Blood* as it was known – was a masterpiece of Britishness. A forceful argument expressed politely, elegantly, convincingly. The message: importing hostile cultures ultimately creates violence, chaos, and the breakdown of civil society.

The vision was strikingly clear, as it had been with Old Wembley and the World Cup.

Is this another premonition about where I must go? And for what purpose? To warn the British people, perhaps? To change Britain's historical trajectory?

It seemed a daunting task. Near impossible. Enoch Powell tried, and it didn't work. Two days after his address – which wasn't even delivered at Westminster – Conservative Party Leader Edward Heath dismissed Mr. Powell from the Shadow Cabinet, and the press commenced a series of vicious editorials / smear campaigns attacking Powell's appeals to racial hatred.

Never mind that ordinary Brits everywhere felt Mr. Powell said precisely what needed to be said. Never mind that overnight he became the most popular politician in England. Never mind he was not only a great and brilliant man, but a courageous patriot. The most courageous of his time by a wide margin.

Nay, none of that mattered. He said the unsayable, and he had to go. Soon after the address, Powell was driven from respectable society by Establishment Machinery. Britain is a democracy they say? Makes one wonder.

Jack pondered. Altering the past to affect the present. It seemed an impossibility. The greatest minds of all time had yet to figure out the paradoxes of time travel. Could Jack visit his ten-year-old self? Or go back further and prevent his Mum and Dad from meeting? Ergo, Jack is never born. Ergo, Jack doesn't exist.

Brain-twisters aside, Jack wondered. What if it never happened – the migration of millions into his once green and pleasant land. His once safe land. What would England be like now? He could scarcely begin to fathom.

And why 1968? The start of England's racial replacement was twenty years prior with the arrival of the HMT Empire Windrush. According to official lore, hundreds of British Caribbeans, whatever that meant, were here to fill post-war labour shortages.

He'd heard Ozzie skewer the fantasy more than once. The Windrush wasn't even the first to bring so-called British subjects from former far-flung colonies. But certainly, the most famous.

By '68, foreigners were no longer a rarity in some parts of England, such as Powell's Wolverhampton constituency.

Jack scolded himself. *What's wrong with foreigners?* A deluge of counterarguments flared, as did the ubiquitous guilt. Decades of conditioning had warped his thinking.

What's wrong with them coming to our fair land? Did we not go to theirs? Seems reasonable. Tit for tat, yeah? They're human beings, just like us.

The arguments sounded fine on the surface. Convincing even. And they installed themselves like a virus in the hearts and minds of modern-day English.

Some people, however, had immunity. Like Jack's best mate, Oswald Fletcher. He was subjected to the same propaganda, but he never bent the knee. Not even a bit. *They don't belong here, and I don't want 'em,* Ozzie proclaimed. His immunity was so strong, it triggered immunity in others. Like Jack.

For good measure, Jack recited what he knew to be truth: *The British are not a hateful people, and we never were. Certainly, we were curious and certainly we made mistakes. We even overstepped on occasion. Hey, nobody's perfect. But we were adventurers. We brought civilization to the four corners of the world. Roads, electricity, potable water. When we chanced upon beastly savages – in some* cases, there's no other way to phrase it – *our first thought was to help them. We didn't come to slaughter (as most tribes of history have). Nay, we came to explore, learn, and share. Because we are Englishmen.*

He could hear Eddie's snide retort – *only racists believe that hogwash* – and it angered Jack.

15. Planning

That evening, putting Finn and Lucy to bed was a chore. The children sensed anxiety in their parents and pushed the limits.

"I'm not tired," Finn bellowed. "May I *please please please* watch one more episode of Supertato?"

Jack tapped his watch. "Bedtime's an hour ago, champ. Off you go before you fall asleep standing up."

Lucy giggled and turned to Lily. "*Please*, Mumsy."

"You heard your father." It took all her might to stay firm. After the day's events, she hated letting them out of her sight. "I'll be up to kiss you good night."

By nine, they heard the last peep. "You think they're actually asleep?" Asked Lily.

"I'm not gonna jinx it by checking."

Lily sighed deeply. "Quite a day."

Jack nodded. "That's one way of putting it."

"It's too horrible to even process."

"I just hope justice is served."

Both knew it wouldn't be. "Shall I put on the kettle, love? Cup o' tea makes everything right."

"You go ahead, darling. I've had enough tea for the night. I've had enough of everything."

"Me too, but I promised Mum a call."

Jack nodded. "Take your time. I'm gonna hop off, read my book, maybe take my mind off things."

"Good for you. I'll be in soon."

Jack leaned in for a kiss. "Night night, love."

But Jack wasn't going to bed, nor was he about to read a book. They were little white lies. If things went according to plan, Jack was going on an adventure. And this time, he'd be prepared.

He slipped on casual trousers, a white shirt, and one of his classic blazers. A blue trench coat and basic black shoes completed the ensemble. Call it dressy-casual. *Imagine turning up in space-age trainers*, he reasoned. *That'd surely raise an eyebrow.*

Now, what to bring? And make it snappy. If Lily walks in, I'm not sure how I'd explain this little game of dress-up. Obviously, my phone, but be bloody careful with it. Money? I can't count on another benevolent chap like Sheldon. Can I? I won't take the chance.

As luck would have it, he owned a small collection of vintage notes given him by his father. When the UK's money system was decimalized in the '70s, people hoarded them. Jack had over a hundred quid across various denominations. He fished out a ten and three fivers. That oughta do.

Is it time to go?

Jack nodded decisively and gazed with purpose into the bedroom mirror. His likeness gazed back, clear as a bell, nothing out of the ordinary. He searched for a suitable strategy.

Am I to concentrate? Or is it better to relax?

The process was unclear. After a few minutes, Jack proactively visualized Westminster, trying to forcibly recreate the vision, and summon a *time travel* event.

It wasn't working, and his mind wandered. *What if I end up at Wembley again. Or somewhere else?* Another thought dawned. *What if nothing happens? What if I never go back again?*

Suddenly, that seemed a likely outcome. It was probably a one-off. A miraculous one-off to be sure, but probably there was no gift of *time travel*. Then, an even more disturbing thought – *perhaps I never went back at all. Maybe it was a hallucination? Maybe I am going insane.*

Crikey, if Lily walks in at this moment, she'd surely reach that conclusion.

After ten futile minutes, weariness came over Jack. He felt ready to give up. He took a final glance in the mirror…and…*wait! What's this?*

Is it happening?

The quality of his reflection blurred.

Oh dear God, it's happening.

The strange sensation engulfed him, the weightlessness, the clarity of thought. Then the bright light washing over him, ushering him into an altered state of consciousness.

He surrendered fearlessly and was back in the *tunnel*, traversing backward in time, floating through the cosmos, observing historical events, perceiving them in all their infinite detail. Seeing, hearing, smelling.

And there it was – *The Palace of Westminster*. He focused attention on it and began descending into that time and place. Parliament Street. April 20, 1968. A Saturday.

He saw passersby. He saw motorcars of the era. The *time tunnel* was fading, the visions crystalizing into reality, as Jack settled into this new time and place.

16. Rivers Of Blood

    Jack arrived – *landed you might say* – on Parliament Street outside the Palace of Westminster. No one seemed perturbed by his entrance. No one seemed to notice. Passersby went about their business.
    For several moments, Jack was overwhelmed. He looked at the friendly faces, the uncluttered roads, the ample parking. Emotions flooded his nervous system. Joy. Nostalgia. Melancholy. It was as if he'd shed a skin. He was home again. He felt a kinship with the people in his midst. They were his people.
    There was no trace of weary defeat in their eyes, and certainly no homeless. There were, however, a few non-whites scattered about. Scarcely enough to raise alarms, mind. Foot traffic was lighter than normal, it being Saturday. Otherwise, everything was as it should be – immaculate. Nothing out of place. Utopia in comparison to modern London. Everything clean and bright and shiny.
    He turned toward the palace and took in its grandeur. His eyes swept across the structure, from the Victoria Tower to the Central Tower's famous spire, to the most famous of all, the Elizabeth Tower, known as *Big Ben* after its main bell, and iconic four-faced clock. He'd seen Westminster countless times, but it was as if he was seeing its glorious splendour for the first time.

Britain was known for dreary weather, but this fine Saturday in April of 1968, spring had sprung and the sun shone, even at 5:00 p.m. The city glowed with optimism, with dignity, and Jack's heart filled with pride. He marvelled at the order and grace and beauty.

As his shock and awe subsided, a new thought formed:
Now what?
Earlier in the day, Enoch Powell delivered his infamous address. Am I to meet the man? If so, how? And even if I can meet him, what do I say? Do I tell him the situation is more dire than he ever imagined? That the Rivers of Blood he predicts will be the blood of children? Not even the great Mr. Powell could envision that.

Wait a moment. It's Saturday. Parliament wasn't even in session today. Not only that, the address wasn't even delivered here – it was a hundred mile north in Birmingham, at a meeting of the West Midlands Conservatives.

Jack was crestfallen. Now what?
Do I wait 'til Monday? Then somehow sneak into Westminster and secure an audience with Enoch Powell. No bloody chance. They didn't even have tours in '68 – Jack looked it up. Evidently the halls of Parliament were less accessible back then. Something to do with the Cold War.

What to do? What to do?

Jack wandered up Parliament Street, his shine now tinged with uncertainty. Suddenly, all became clear. When all else fails, what does any proper Englishman do? He goes to the pub, of course.

As if by magic, a public house appeared across the street – *The Red Lion* – its letters boldly proclaimed in ornate gold and black.

Upon entry, the first thing he noticed was the smoke – it was thick in the air. The place was busy, but to Jack's delight he found an empty stool. Luck or some grand design, he wasn't sure.

He ordered a pint from the portly bartender and absorbed the ambience under the soft glow of antique chandeliers. The walls were lined with black and white photos, each surely telling a tale of intrigue and adventure.

The pint appeared and Jack placed a five-quid note on the counter.

"Aye mate, have you anything smaller?"

"Sorry barkeep. You hold the change, I might fancy a few tonight."

The bartender nodded appreciatively.

"Any word on Enoch Powell's speech?"

A puzzled look from the bartender. "Come again?"

"He gave one today."

"Did he now? I hadn't heard. And I'm usually the first to hear."

A young man two places over piped up. "I'm only just back from Birmingham. What a speech it was."

"Rivers of blood?" Jack asked.

"Something to that effect, yeah." Curious stare. "Were you there?"

Jack shook his head. "A friend called me. But he didn't say much. How'd it go?"

Others in the vicinity took notice and the man smiled conspiratorially. He was clearly ecstatic about Enoch's address. "All I can say is *finally* someone's drawing attention to this. Giving a voice to the threat."

"You're talking immigration?" Someone asked.

"I'm talking *invasion*. Have you seen Wolverhampton?"

With that, the men were off to the races. "Aye, it's getting a bit much now, innit? The foreigners, I mean."

"Tell you what, lads. The streets don't feel safe, not even in London. Not like when we were nippers."

The young man sipped his bitter. "Not like before the war. 'Twas before my time, but me Dad's told me, so he has."

"Forget before the war, mate. I'm talking five years ago. The world's changing fast."

"Too bloody fast, if you ask me."

"Sure, it'll take some getting used to," someone added. A moderate. "Ah, but there's no end to it. Not sayin' it's bad necessarily, but the government oughta cap it at least, yeah?"

"Come off it, Jimmy. *It's bad.* They come here, take our jobs, live ten to a house, and expect us to foot the bill. Certain parts o' town, you won't hear English spoken."

The moderate nodded. "Fair points, but I s'pose they're trying to make a living, same as you an' me."

"Why here? That's the question."

"Government says we need 'em."

"I've been hearin' that for ten years. I call bollocks. What about our own lads, huh?"

The moderate muttered a response.

"That's what Enoch Powell's been banging on about," the young man bellowed, keen to put himself back in the spotlight. "Wait 'til you hear what he said today. I'm tellin' ya, there was an explosion of relief. *Finally,* we're gonna talk about this."

"Rivers of blood?" The moderate asked. "He said that?"

"Look, he may have engaged in some hyperbole. Blood in the river, whatever he said." Dismissive gesture. "Listen to the speech. It's a warning to all of us."

Jack marvelled at the dialogue. It was remarkably like what you might hear in 2025, though less bitter, less angry, less fearful. *My God, if they only knew what was coming.*

An elderly gentleman sidled up to Jack. A kindly looking fellow with intelligent eyes. "See what you started."

"Wasn't my intention." Jack grinned sheepishly.

"I've not seen you here before."

"I'm Jack Campbell."

"Sheldon." The men shook hands. "Sheldon Cook."

"*Sheldon Cook?*"

"Yes sir."

Another Sheldon Cook?

Coincidence? *Couldn't be.* It had to be a sign. There were divine forces at play, and this gave Jack a mighty boost of confidence, as if confirming he was in the right place, doing the right thing.

17. Networking

"Well, Mr. Campbell. Welcome to The Red Lion."

"Thank you, sir. May I buy you a pint?"

"Ah, splendid." His eyes twinkled. "You won't need to ask twice."

Fresh ales in hand: "Shall we have a chat then, Mr. Cook?"

"Certainly. And please, call me Sheldon and I shall call you Jack."

Jack nodded.

"Right this way. I see a table has freed up."

The man had a posh accent and exquisite elocution. He wore a tweed jacket and possessed aristocratic Anglo-Saxon features. *The markers of upper class*, thought Jack.

Through conversation, Jack discovered this particular Sheldon Cook was a former MP in Churchill's Conservative government, the post-war Second Edition. He was born in British India – Darjeeling to be specific – in 1890. *Incredible.*

"And you still follow the political game?"

He chuckled. "It's in my blood."

"And Enoch Powell. You're aware of his uh, *leanings*."

"I certainly am. His latest tirade has not hit the news cycle, but when it does..." he made an elaborate gesture.

"Which side do you take?"

Shrug. "Why the British side of course. I've no patience for bleeding hearts. You hear our people," he gestured toward the men still debating the *New British* in their midst. "It's the working class that always bears the brunt."

"Everyone will feel it eventually," said Jack, with the benefit of hindsight.

Another shrug. "I'm not so sure about that."

"I am."

Sheldon raised his eyebrows. "Well, if so, thankfully that's a long way off."

"Perhaps not as far as you think."

"You don't exude a spirit of optimism, Jack."

"I'm a banker by trade, Sheldon. A numbers man. And if you do some basic arithmetic, you'll see how quickly the tide can turn."

"So, you're saying we're doomed?"

Jack pondered how much of his hand to show. "You tell me, Sheldon. I'm an outsider. You've been in the game a long time. Do you think Mr. Powell can make a difference?"

Sheldon's turn to ponder. "He's just fifty-six years of age, certainly young enough. Extraordinary chap, to be frank. I'll have you know I've heard his name as a possible successor to Heath." Sheldon paused to frown.

"But?"

"I'm not sure he's the stomach for this fight, over the long haul if you know what I mean. He's a reserved and gentle chap. A scholar at heart, you understand."

Jack nodded. "Speaks six languages, I'm told."

"I've a feeling he'll be shut down," said Sheldon.

"Really?" Jack played dumb. He knew well Enoch's fate.

"He's gone too far this time. I can only imagine the fallout. The press will have a field day."

"Let's try another question. Is Mr. Powell an outlier? Or representative of his Conservative fellows? Are others ready to step forward?"

"He's not alone in his beliefs, I assure you. But, how to put this – the issue is political dynamite. His contemporaries prefer to stay silent – it's the easier path. The maddening thing is that some choose not only silence, but they attack. Even from our side of the aisle."

Jack sneered. "It's cowardice, plain and simple. Now's the time to speak up. The longer they wait the harder it gets." Jack wanted to add: *The politicians can say these nice things, but in 2025 our children will be slaughtered in the streets.*

"I'd say you're spot on there. Shocking to see how our cities have changed. I mean, the Africans are one thing. Now the sheer number of coolies." He paused to shake his head. "And no one says a word about it."

Jack recoiled from the slur – an involuntary reaction. They'd arrest Sheldon for less in modern-day England. Here in 1968, Sheldon had no such restraints. No doubt the N-word got frequent use as well.

"It's taboo," said Jack. "The race issue."

"This race issue could very well be the death of us. Are you following the developments in Rhodesia, Jack?"

Jack nodded in fascination. He was familiar with the fate of his British cousins in that once glorious country.

"I fear for the Rhodies," Sheldon continued. "Thank goodness South Africa's holding firm."

If he only knew, thought Jack.

"One thing's certain on the race angle – we'll never have it as bad as our friends across the pond."

"The Yanks?"

Sheldon nodded happily.

Jack hid his smirk. "That might not always be the case."

"Indeed," Sheldon nodded. "Terribly upsetting really. I expect as much from the chattering classes. But I always felt British Conservatives had a firmer backbone."

Jack hid another smirk. "What does *The Iron Lady* say on the matter?"

"Who?"

Whoops. The famous nickname had yet to be coined. "Sorry, Margaret Thatcher. My Dad nicknamed her."

Sheldon grinned. "Mrs. Thatcher's given lukewarm support to Mr. Powell, and I expect that will continue. She's a woman of her word."

"She'll be Prime Minister one day, mark my words."

Sheldon bellowed laughter. "A female Prime Minister. That'll be the frosty Friday."

"You heard it here," said Jack with a grin.

Sheldon rubbed his chin. "We'll see. It's not enough to have friends in your corner," he spoke in a sombre tone, "when traitors are lurking. Snakes in the grass. Vile specimens, indeed."

Jack felt a hot flash of anger. Truer words were never spoken. "This influx of foreigners, Sheldon. It should not be happening. The public doesn't want it. Yet politicians, by and large, say nothing. Newspapers won't print the truth."

"Oh, heavens no. For Mr. Powell's latest foray, I reckon tomorrow's press will skewer him."

That's right, thought Jack. *No internet. No social media. News travels slowly, and word of mouth is still a powerful thing.*

What can I say to this man – to this generation – to trigger change? At this moment, immigration is literally the only thing that matters – all other problems are manageable. Immigration, however, is permanent. Perhaps if I shock him? Issue a dire warning?

"You know Sheldon, it won't be long before we Brits aren't welcome in parts of London. We'll be jeered, intimidated, even attacked."

Sheldon shook his head. "Oh, I can't imagine it ever getting that bad. At some point, reason will prevail. Surely it must."

"Don't bet on it. You think suddenly the people in power will find courage? You think the traitors, whoever they are, will suddenly decide Britain's had enough?"

"Come now, sir."

Jack persisted. "They want it all, Sheldon. It'll be far worse than anything Mr. Powell imagined."

Sheldon shot Jack a curious look. "You sound as if you know these things to be true."

Jack maintained eye contact: "Perhaps I do, Sheldon. Perhaps I do."

"Remarkable." In that moment, something in Sheldon's eyes changed. As if he became aware that perhaps Jack *did* know things.

Jack recognized the shift. "Could you arrange a meeting with Mr. Powell?"

"Oh, that would take time. Enoch will be a busy man in the coming days. I've heard tell he's off to Canada soon."

Jack winced.

"Don't fret, mate." Sheldon glanced outside. "Look, the rain's started and by Jove, look at the time. The trouble and strife will be waiting." Alcohol had loosened him up. "Are you hungry, Jack? Would you come to the house for tea?"

"I wouldn't want to impose."

"Nonsense, we've plenty of space and plenty of food. I should warn you, though, I've a few friends coming. I daresay they may like to make the acquaintance of a chap like you."

"Very well then, I accept."

"Ah, jolly good."

"I'm not convinced Enoch's your man to fight the war you wish to wage."

"Who then?"

"We'll discuss that tonight. The young writer Charles Winthrop will be there. Have you heard of him?"

"Indeed, I have. I've read some of his work."

"*Some* of his work? He's only written the one book."

Jack was caught out again. Winthrop would publish several novels in the 70s and 80s, but his '68 debut made a splash. A political thriller.

"He has more coming, I assure you." Jack said. "He's a visionary."

"Splendid. I've a feeling you two will get along like a house on fire."

18. Dinner with the Elites

Sheldon's driver was waiting outside in a shiny Rolls, and he whisked Sheldon and Jack through London's uncluttered streets to a prestigious Marlborough Place address. Wrought-iron gates opened to reveal a stately manor with manicured lawns, hedges, all the trimmings so to speak.

The foyer was ostentatious, a grand chandelier cast its glow over paintings, family portraits, and a sweeping circular staircase. Further inside, the parlour's high ceilings inspired awe as Sheldon's guests mingled.

Introductions were made. Drinks and hors d'oeuvres were served. In due course, the gathering migrated to the dining room, and they were seated at an enormous mahogany table. The group numbered ten, Sheldon plus three men of his vintage, and their wives. John, Stephen, and Adam were all prominent political figures, Sheldon assured Jack. Also present, the famed author, Charles Winthrop. The men drank and smoked and conversation roamed across many topics.

"You might consider a more modest tone, Adam," John was saying. "Lest we forget, you kept your seat by the skin of your teeth."

"I've a knack for navigating storms," Adam replied confidently.

"And creating them."

Adam shrugged. "I survived. That's all that matters. I'm a survivor, like the pound sterling." He leaned back and puffed his cigar.

"Speaking of storms," said Stephen, the oldest of the bunch, "I'm reminded of the great Commons debate of '63."

"The snowstorm?"

Stephen smiled broadly. "Half the benches were empty. It was a wonderful opportunity to get things done."

"Did you consider using it to strike down the Commonwealth Immigrants Act?" Jack decided to inject himself into the dialogue.

Stephen recoiled as if to say *who is this newcomer?* "You've brought an Enoch Powell disciple into our midst, Sheldon."

"You dislike Mr. Powell?" asked Jack.

"Not at all. He's a lovely man. I only question his…how shall I phrase this…his *political judgement*."

The men around the table laughed.

Jack was disgusted by the indifference. The complacency. What could he say to convince these men they *must* support Mr. Powell at all costs. "I see most of the immigration officers at Heathrow signed a *We Back Powell* petition."

"I've not heard that," said Adam, exchanging glances with Sheldon. "And I'm with the Home Office."

It was true – Jack had done the research. "You must know the people of Britain don't want more immigration."

"Ah, the commoners," said Adam with amusement. "They don't know what they want half the time."

Jack scoffed. *This is hopeless. These men are so separated from the British people, so smug in their wealth and superiority. But they must know. They must! Is it malpractice or treason? Or simple cowardice?*

As if reading Jack's mind, Sheldon jumped in: "We understand what you're saying, Jack, but politics is a process. Decisions made through consensus don't always appear to make sense. That's democracy, and I've come to believe it's a good thing."

"It's *not* a good thing. Not in this case. Decisions shape nations and if you and your ilk don't face hard truths, you'll destroy Britain."

More laughter. "Next, he'll be lecturing us on the Empire," said Adam. "You must be fun on the cricket field, old sport. All doom and gloom."

Jack scoffed again. If these men were not the enemies of Britain, they might as well be. Especially this Adam fellow. The only sympathetic face at the table was the other non-politician, the writer Winthrop. *After dinner, he and I must chat*, thought Jack.

Meantime, conversation switched to football. "Any thoughts on England's chances in Mexico?" The 1970 World Cup was fast approaching. "Qualifying's begun I see."

Jack chimed in. "Britain will never win another World Cup."

Looks of disbelief around the table. "Nonsense, Jack." Sheldon said it in a scolding tone. "After our recent victory, the way it united the country. The lads will be keener than ever to perform at top level. I believe we'll win a great many in the future." Hearty agreement from all.

Jack continued unabated: "What's more, in a few decades, there'll be nothing but foreigners on England's national team." Jack hated being rude, but if ever there was a time – these men needed to be shaken from their slumber.

"Now you're being silly," said Sheldon, standing as if to pre-empt further outburst. "I'm going to wash away that comment with a toast. To England, gentlemen – *and ladies*. A land of wit and weather, and fine gentlemen who always find a way to muddle through any crisis."

"Here, here. To England." They repeated.

The conversation turned again, this time toward nostalgic tales of bygone days when Churchill loomed large.

"Winston had a gift, he did," Adam said. "He could stir the soul of an Englishman like no other."

"Even the commoners."

"Especially the commoners," said Adam. "They fight our wars, you know."

"He could stir a drink as well," Stephen chimed in.

"He was utterly magnificent on stage," Adam continued. "Truly an orator for the ages."

Sheldon nodded. "During the war, he made us believe we could endure anything."

"We proved we could. We British are made of stern stuff."

"And his wit was legendary," said Sheldon, and regaled the table with the infamous tale of a woman approaching Churchill: *If you were my husband, I'd poison your tea.* To which he replied: *Madam, if you were my wife, I'd drink it.*

A roar of laughter.

"To Stephen's point, the man loved a good drink, no question. Many a late-night session was brandy-fueled, I dare say."

Jack decided to ruffle feathers again: "Say what you will, gentlemen. Churchill's legacy is rubbish. He may have said some interesting things, but he was an obese drunk and his tenure was the start of Britain's decline."

This provoked intense dismay. *Egads. Preposterous. Blasphemy.*

"As I understand it, he pushed Britain into the war to save himself from bankruptcy."

"Where did you find this man, Sheldon?" Adam's tone was light, but there was a degree of malice now.

"Why at the pub of course." Sheldon regarded Jack. "I knew immediately he would add colour to our table."

"That's one way of putting it."

"Again gentlemen, join me in a toast." Sheldon had a flair for the dramatic. "Here's to Winston Churchill. A force of nature. The greatest Briton of them all, who saved us from the Nazis..."

But not the communists, Jack thought, but didn't say.

"...and to all of us – there's not many left – who had the privilege of knowing and loving the great man."

"May history judge him kindly," Adam added, searing Jack with a glare.

Sheldon wasn't finished. "Though our empire may fade, the great *British Lion* shall never cease to roar. The world shall never forget what we've achieved."

Jack let it be. He'd done enough stirring of the pot. It would have felt wrong criticizing Sheldon and his lofty words. He was such a decent man. So likeable and warm.

They all were (save Adam) and maybe the good will in their nature – *the near-pathological altruism* – maybe that was part of the problem. They imagined, naively, that everyone was like that. That every culture was capable of English fair-mindedness and high principle, which was not the case.

Nor was it the case with Adam. Jack took an instant dislike to the man. He was clearly a champion for *the new British* and seemed utterly unconcerned with protecting the native people and culture.

After dinner, the men retired to the parlour for more drinks, cigars, and conversation. Jack's earlier belligerence surprised even himself. It wasn't in his nature, but he felt it necessary. Unfortunately, it seemed to have little effect. Overall, not an ounce of progress. History would not be altered one iota. The men were more interested in themselves and their stories. And the stories were indeed entertaining.

But I've not been placed here to be entertained. There must be a higher purpose. Right? However, fulfilling that purpose might be harder than I thought.

At that moment, Jack noticed Charles Winthrop at his side.

19. Charles Winthrop

"You're a brave soul, Jack." Charles remarked. "Those are powerful men. Not used to being challenged in such a manner."

"Perhaps that's the problem." Jack grinned. "Congratulations on your novel, sir. I see it's been wonderfully received."

"Thank you, though one tepid review in *The Times* hardly counts as wonderfully received. Unless you know something I don't."

Jack smiled conspiratorially. "I've a feeling more positive attention's coming."

"I'm glad you think so. Have you read the book?"

Yes, but it was so long ago I forgot most of it. Can't say that. "Not yet, I'm afraid. I shall get to it soon, I assure you."

"That's what they all say," Charles smirked.

"I mean it, and I must say, if you're spending time with this lot, you're the perfect man to write political thrillers."

Jack surveyed the young Charles Winthrop, a man destined for literary greatness. Jack had indeed read his debut, *Reckonings*, and several more since. Winthrop wrote page-turners with depth. He had the knack of capturing low and high-brow readers.

"I find contrarians like yourself far more interesting," Charles said.

"*Ha*, I'd say they think I'm a crackpot. All doom and gloom, the sky is falling."

"Do you truly believe England's in peril?"

"I know it to be true."

Raised eyebrows. "Such certainty."

"You're a writer, Charles. Can you not envision a dark future?"

"Oh, I don't know. This London town hasn't changed much in a hundred years. I don't expect it'll change much in the next hundred. *Ha*, I sound like my father. I just feel it'll take more than a few wogs to put down the British people. Am I so wrong?"

"Have you seen Birmingham recently? Or Wolverhampton?" Both towns were already severely afflicted by demographic change.

"Indeed, I have." He nodded sagely.

"More towns will follow. London, too. Mr. Powell's speech was the tip of the iceberg."

"You sound like a man who's seen the future."

"If I told you I have, would you believe me?"

Charles chuckled. "I *might*, actually. But I might also ask for proof."

Jack maintained a rather severe eye contact. He and Charles were at the room's periphery, isolated from the others, who were engrossed in their own antics. *Go on. Show him your phone.* Jack wasn't sure the voice in his head was his own.

Show him! What have you got to lose? An iPhone from 2025 is surely evidence you're from the future. Either that or outright sorcery. Remember the look from Sheldon Cook #1 at the World Cup? To hell with it, I shall throw caution to the wind.

Jack withdrew his phone and presented it to Mr. Charles Winthrop. The device came alive, unlocking itself in response to Jack's face. Jack had wondered if it might fail to respond in 1968 for some unknown reason. Violation of some obscure law of quantum physics or some such thing. Thankfully, that was not the case.

"*What is that?*" Charles demanded. Unreserved astonishment.

"It's a mobile phone from the future." Jack calmly scrolled through icons.

"A phone you say?" Amazement. Disbelief. Curiosity. Phones of Charles' era were mechanical devices with clunky dials. Charles was awestruck by the elegance. The sleekness. "Doesn't look like a phone. Where's the dial? Where are the wires?"

Jack chuckled haughtily. "Where do I begin? First of all, it's more than a phone. Far more. It's a...a...it's an *everything-device*. The future's digital, Charles. And wireless."

Jack demoed several apps – the timer, the calendar, the calculator. He flipped on the flashlight. He opened the Supertato game recently downloaded for young Finn, and it ran smoothly in disconnected mode.

Charles was riveted, and that was an understatement. "*It responds to your touch?*"

"Sure. Or my voice. Of course, its functions are limited at the moment. There's no Wi-Fi, no internet."

"Internet?"

"Long story. Think of it like a global communication network. If we had internet, as we will in the future, I would essentially possess – right here in my hand – the equivalent of all the libraries of the world."

"Impossible." Charles shook his head vigorously. "Impossible. Even the top science fiction writers of our time, none of them would have the gall to concoct such a device."

"It's also a camera." Jack took a selfie and showed Charles. Then he took a photo of Charles himself.

"You take my photograph and immediately it appears. *In colour*. Where's the film? I am...*very confused*." He studied the image intensely. "I'm astounded and bewildered by what you're showing me."

"I could go on. This thing can do so much more. It's a phone, a camera," he paused to scroll photos. "Here's my car, my wife and kids. Here's me on my birthday last weekend."

Charles shifted nervously.

"It's a music player, a television, a map. There's practically nothing it can't do."

"How can something so small possess such power? It doesn't even plug into the wall. This is surely a magic trick. Some witchcraft."

"It's science, Charles. It's essentially a computer. You have computers in 1968."

"Sure, I saw the Atlas a few years ago at Oxford. I also saw the UNIVAC on a trip to America. Computers are enormous. They fill entire rooms."

"Well, they get smaller in the future. Trust me."

"Impossible."

"I understand it's beyond your expectations."

"How far in the future are you from?" It was a preposterous question, and the look on Charles' face betrayed its preposterousness.

Jack didn't answer. Instead, he opened the music player and spotted *Abbey Road* –cached and ready to go. "Are you a Beatles fan, Charles?" Jack clicked on *Here Comes the Sun* and the classic opening notes kicked in as the iconic photo of John, Paul, George, and Ringo appeared.

Adding to the *miraculousness*, the song and album hadn't even been released yet. So palpable was Charles' awe that others began to notice. As Sheldon approached, Jack pocketed the phone.

"What was that?"

"Oh, just a card trick." He winked at Charles. "I'm an amateur magician."

"Ah right, I love a bit of magic. Show me, please."

"Nah, the show's over."

Jack stood firm until Sheldon lost interest and returned to the others.

"I suggest you keep this," Jack patted the mobile in his pocket, "to yourself, Charles. Lest others think you're crazy."

"Too late for that I'm afraid." Charles had recovered his composure. "We must talk more."

"Absolutely." Jack nodded and smiled.

20. Disclosure

The pair found refuge in a quiet alcove overlooking the estate's back garden. An astute servant, noting their retreat followed and offered tea. Jack couldn't help but notice the luxury and splendour surrounding them at every turn.

With tea served, Charles launched right in: "So you're from the future?" He smirked. "It's an absurd question, but it seems I already know the answer."

"It is absurd," Jack agreed. "I don't understand how it happened myself. But I believe I've been put here to warn the people of England."

"Warn them of?"

"A vast influx of foreigners. *An invasion.*"

"Precisely what Enoch's on about."

"Precisely."

"How bad does it get? I mean, once the government realizes it's not in our best interests, surely they'll put a stop to it."

"You'd think good sense would prevail, but no." Jack shook his head. "Look, we don't have long to talk. Sheldon will surely seek us out. But let me say this – the government – with due respect to Sheldon and his cronies – the government will become the enemy of the British people."

"That's not possible. Not in a democracy. We'll simply vote them out."

Britain on the Brink

"No matter who you vote in, they'll follow orders. Liberal Democracy." Scoff. "It's the worst form of tyranny." It was a classic Ozzie line.

"Follow orders from whom?"

"That's a deeper question." Jack drew a breath. "Look, it pains me to say this – but within fifty years, Britain will be a shell of her former self. A laughingstock. Large parts of Britain, particularly London and other large cities, will be majority non-English."

Charles gasped.

"It's not only Britain, mind you. All of Western Europe."

Jack withdrew his mobile again. He was limited without the internet, but the device cached an astonishing amount of content. Ozzie's messages were available, and there were many. Images and memes that captured the modern-day dystopian nightmare.

"Brace yourself, Charles."

Jack started with a banger, a widely circulated prep school photo, the children smartly dressed in classic English uniforms. The catch? Only one white kid in a sea of black and brown. Expressions were jolly and jovial, save the lone Caucasian who appeared lost, alone, and frightened.

"That's not Britain."

"Oh, it is." Next, a football team – every player black, save one Middle Eastern chap. "This is the French National squad. Like I said, the problem affects all Western Europe. The English squad's not much better."

Charles frowned. "Who in their right mind would believe that's a French side?"

"You'd be surprised. A weird collective mental illness takes hold. Like the country and everyone in it has gone insane. Nothing makes sense."

Next, a video of police brutalizing a young and peaceful English lad. "This is what they do when you protest."

"What's that man's crime?"

"Oh, he was probably carrying a Union Jack."

Charles expressed a look of utter shock.

"Or maybe complaining about Muslim grooming gangs."

"Grooming gangs?"

Jack shook his head. "Tell you later, if there's time." He fired up more content. A DEI meme which he skipped over – *too hard to explain.* A meme stating *the UK was conquered without a single shot fired.* Video of an overloaded dinghy setting ashore on a Devon beach, a contingent of Africans stealing off into the nearby town.

"How is that possible? Where are the police? Where is the bloody army?"

"The government turns a blind eye. In fact, they put these migrants in hotels while ethnic British are homeless, freezing in the streets."

"Did we lose a war?" Charles' brow furrowed. "It looks like we've been conquered."

Jack chuckled. "If you believe my friend Ozzie, we lost World War II. But that's a different kettle of fish. We actually lost a *new* type of war. A narrative war. A war to capture people's hearts and minds."

"Not sure I understand."

"Let's just say we're run by our enemies and the media's complicit."

"I don't understand how any of this can happen. We won World War II. My father was at VE Day. He listened to Churchill speak. He's told the story many times over."

Jack shrugged. "All I know is, in my era barely a third of London is ethnic British."

"When you say ethnic British…"

"I mean *actually* British. You know, white. The others, *ha*, they call themselves British. But once they sense dominance, they glory in their true ethnicity. They flaunt it. They gloat."

"Look at this headline."

Indians Own More Property in London Than Native White Britons

"It's real, I promise you. And look at the comments."

Who's colonized now BITCH!

"Such vulgarity."

Jack scoffed. "In the future, everything is defiled and degraded. Especially the British people."

Charles loosened his necktie.

"We're being wiped out, Charles. Erased from the land. They call it *The Great Replacement.* And they bring nothing. When Britain colonized foreign lands, we brought roads, technology. Sanitization, medicine. These people bring only problems. They're locusts on a field of corn."

"I've no idea what to say."

"That's not even the worst of it. In the future I come from, we have bombings, stabbings, butcherings, beheadings. Riots and carnage. Rape of children by the thousands."

"Rape of children?"

Jack nodded.

"And our people don't fight back?" Utter disgust. "Why such cowardice?"

"By the time enough people got angry, it was too late. The enemy had the whip hand, as Enoch said, and they weren't afraid to use it."

Charles snorted.

"This early trickle of quote unquote *coloured people* into our fair land. Make no mistake, it's an act of war. A *new* type of war, one that's difficult to fight against. If England doesn't stop it now..." Jack trailed off.

"How?" Asked Charles.

"Good question." Jack leaned back in his chair. "Already, it's taboo to criticize. Very soon, Edward Heath will sack Mr. Powell and send a message – the immigration topic's off limits. Toxic. Political suicide. The London Times – a supposedly conservative paper – will provide cover. They'll call Mr. Powell's speech evil and shameful. A deliberate appeal to racial hatred. Listen to me Charles, every day the British people don't fight, the battle will get harder. You're condemning your descendants to hell on earth." Jack sighed. "Unimaginable horrors."

They sat in silence for a spell. Jack had a lot more to say, but he was suddenly feeling off. Nauseous and weak. *Something I ate?* He pressed on, nonetheless.

"I realize it's a lot to take in." Jack grinned to lighten the mood.

"Again, I've no idea what to say." Charles paused and stroked his chin. "If I may quote Dickens: Are these shadows of things that *will be,* or shadows of things that *may be*?" Spoken in his best *Alastair Sim.*

"Who am I to say? And by the way, that movie's still popular where I come from."

Charles chuckled mirthlessly.

"The Beatles are still popular, too," Jack added. "Even though they split up two years from now."

"Noooooo."

"However," Jack raised an index finger, "the Rolling Stones are still together and still making music."

Another chuckle. "Interesting. Sorry, I'm still struck by those Africans piling out of that watercraft."

"The dinghy, yes. They keep coming. An endless supply." A powerful thought crystallized in Jack's head. "You know, this whole thing was described long ago – *from my perspective that is* – by a French author named Jean Raspail. He wrote a novel called *The Camp of the Saints.*"

"Never heard of him."

"The book hasn't been written yet. I believe it comes out in 1973."

Charles made a face. "This is all so very strange."

"It's a dystopian novel. It describes an apocalyptic invasion of third-worlders to France's southern shore. It turned out to be remarkably prophetic. It describes precisely what we've witnessed – the destruction of Western countries by mass immigration."

"Was it a bestseller?"

"Not sure, but eventually it becomes famous. Dissidents of my era worship it. And of course, governments and media demonize it. They call it racist and xenophobic."

"And you're telling me about this book because…"

"Because you, sir, are a writer." Jack laughed. "Look, I got nowhere with that lot in there. But with you, I see a perfect action item. You must write the British version of *Camp of the Saints.*"

"So, this French fellow wrote his book, yes?"

"Yes."

"And history was not changed?"

"True. But you're not just any writer, Charles. You are a magnificent writer. You must write a better book. And you must promote it with urgency. If you do it right, Raspail may not even write his book. I'm giving you a five-year head-start. I'm giving you a chance at immortality."

By now, Jack's nausea had worsened considerably, and he was doing his best to ignore it. He sipped his tea and took several deep breaths. Clearly, that last line struck Charles deep. Immortality is precisely what every writer desires. Jack watched the wheels turn. This was 1968. Charles may get bad press, but he wouldn't get cancelled. Not in '68. If the book had potential to sell, he'd find a willing publisher and bookstores willing to carry it.

"I have so many questions," Charles finally said.

Jack sensed his time was short. "I've given you the gist. And I suggest you keep the sensitive bits to yourself."

Charles chuckled. "You've asked me to write a book about it, sir."

Jack laughed. "I mean about me. *Your source.* Where I come from. All that."

"You mean *when* you come from."

"That too."

"Who else knows of your…*travels?*"

"Nobody. And I want to keep it that way."

Both men noticed Sheldon approaching. The timing was excellent – progress had been made. A semblance of a plan. Whether Charles Winthrop would write a prophetic world-changing novel or not, only time would tell.

But I'm a Time Traveller, Jack realized with delight. *Very soon, I will know*. This struck Jack as extremely funny and he burst out laughing. The sickness he'd been feeling had also lifted, and somehow this added to the mirth. His laughter was so authentic, it was contagious and Charles joined in.

"My, my, you two are getting along famously."

Both men nodded as the laughter subsided. "A most interesting fellow you've brought into our midst," Charles responded.

"The others would agree, perhaps for different reasons." Sheldon was a smooth operator.

Jack turned to Charles. "Very nice chatting with you old chap. But I suppose we must be sociable and join the others."

"It would be appreciated," said Sheldon. "And perhaps no more disparaging remarks about our former Prime Minister, hmm?"

"Certainly not," said Jack.

"I must say, the men took great offence," said Sheldon sincerely. "As did I."

"My apologies."

"And as for Enoch Powell…"

"I've nothing else to say. I promise."

Sheldon grinned. "Come back in a fortnight. There'll be fireworks by then, I'm certain."

"I agree with you there." Jack stood, and as he did, he noticed nature calling. "May I ask where the lavatory is?"

"Right this way, sir," said the hovering servant.

Jack walked off feeling pleased. What an extraordinary conversation. If not for his mobile, the young writer would have surely thought him insane. But with the evidence presented, Jack's arguments – and his grim predictions – were difficult to refute.

In the bathroom, he reflected further. *Charles believed me. He believed every word. But will he write the book? And if he does, will it trigger changes in Britain's arc of history? It could. With enough urgency, perhaps the tide of time can be altered.*

Without warning, a vision seized control of Jack's frontal lobe.

21. New York City

The vision was vivid, *and it wasn't Britain.* Nor was it 2025. The World Trade Center, first an aerial view, then street-level images shifted to a nearby television studio. Inside the studio, an older version of Winthrop sitting calmly under bright lights.

Jack tried to seize on the image, to embed himself in that space and time, but it became elusive and vanished.

Damn. I lost it.

It was surely a sign he must go there. His desire to be in that moment was overwhelming. Charles Winthrop on American television. *Oh my God, he'd written the book. And he wasn't cancelled. Oh my God!*

Jack had to see it. Nothing else mattered. And here he was, in a bathroom gazing at his reflection. The precise setting where *time travel* seemed to initiate.

Do I need a mirror to make it happen? He stared at his reflection and allowed his mind to relax. He made no attempt to corral stray thoughts, nor consciously shoo them away.

It worked. The images returned with a vengeance – 1990s New York when the Twin Towers stood tall and proud. Charles Winthrop, now in his fifties, sat calmly in the talk show studio.

The image blurred as Jack detected the familiar sensations – the slowed breathing, the hyper-awareness. He surrendered to the moment and was back in the Time Tunnel, travelling, transitioning, traversing time and space with heightened near-infinite perception.

World events played out in infinite detail. As he neared the moment of the vision, he was overcome with curiosity – he had to see the Charles Winthrop interview. Evidently, he could. It was happening. Jack's consciousness was altering and returning as he settled peacefully into this new time and place. Autumn of 1997.

He was seated alone at the back of the studio audience. A shadowy figure it seemed. He could not be certain he was even physically present and could thus interact with others in this near-past alternate-reality world. Fine. Jack was happy to observe.

The show was in progress and a massive screen behind the set displayed Charles' book:

> *The Great Replacement*
> by Charles. W. Winthrop

He *had* written it, and look what he called it. Incredible. *I've altered history.* Jack's mind was blown and it took several moments to focus his concentration on the interview.

"... a controversial novel..." The interviewer was saying. "Prescient, certainly. People call it the most important dystopian novel of the 20th century."

Charles smiled sheepishly. "I've heard this."

"More prophetic than Orwell's 1984."

Charles nodded.

"Powerful words, yet you've distanced yourself from the discussion. And from the book itself."

"Well Laura, I've been busy with other projects. Don't forget, I wrote *The Great Replacement* in 1969. I barely remember the plot." The audience chuckled. They suspected a fib.

"You've not spoken of *The Great Replacement* in years. Decades even. Why now? Why here in America?"

Charles' turn to chuckle. "I'm still recovering from the attacks I suffered when the book came out. I still have the scars."

"Yet you stood your ground."

"It wasn't easy. They tried to ruin my life, and they almost did. It took a great toll on me." Charles paused. "Don't forget – the book is still banned in Britain."

"Perhaps symbolically, but I'm told many thousands of copies are in circulation. Even libraries are carrying it these days. Many a Brit considers your second novel to be England's saviour, almost a holy text. Let's face it, Charles. Your book altered the course of British History."

"You're putting that on me again?"

"It's a compliment. Your book changed the UK in a good way." Jack had discerned that Laura was a Fox News personality, based on the set branding and her positive demeanour toward Charles. "So many Western countries are suffering under the weight of immigration, legal and illegal. Yet Britain resisted. Uniquely."

Charles acknowledged with a shrug.

"I'll remind the audience, when *The Great Replacement* was released, it became a bestseller overnight. Everyone in Britain had a copy."

"And then?" Charles added with a grin, and the audience chuckled.

"The government stepped in. They stopped the presses, didn't they? No more copies were ever printed in Britain and the book was never published in America. Or anywhere else for that matter. Until recently, that is."

"Correct."

"The mainstream media cooperated by squashing the story."

"And me in the process."

Laura nodded sympathetically. "Back then, there was no internet, no social media. The book essentially died."

"I like to say it was murdered."

"Touché. But the lessons of the book lived on in the hearts and minds of Brits, *and only Brits*. And now, just as Britain once showed the world how to be an Imperial power, they now show the world how to wield sovereignty."

Charles nodded.

"Did I get that all straight?"

"Well done, Laura. *Well done.* You've covered it all." Charles seemed reluctant to wade in further. "Let's see if Britain's resolve lasts, though. If Labour gets in for another term…"

Laura nodded. "Sadly, it appears the globalist forces are taking hold in Britain."

Charles nodded. "In ten years, you might say my book *delayed* history rather than altered it."

"I don't know, Charles. Never count the British out. They've a strong backbone. They've shown it. In your book, fictional British people across all classes rose up and challenged authority."

"That's how I wrote it."

"And life imitated art. The real British people took the lesson to heart. And thus, England stood alone while other countries opened their borders. Like here in America."

"Yes."

"Meanwhile, our media painted Britain as the bad guy. Isolationist. Xenophobic. They harped on your colonial past."

"Dear God, I get so sick of hearing that."

The crowd laughed.

"People say your inspiration was Enoch Powell, and his famous speech. Yet your book goes so much deeper. They say your book provided a workable defence against the progressives."

"Again, that's how I wrote it. It was just fiction."

"It was more than fiction, Charles. It was prophecy. I must ask, besides Enoch Powell, who was your inspiration? How did you see the future so clearly?"

Charles paused for what seemed a very long time. He rubbed his temples. Jack watched every nuance of the performance.

"It's hard to describe," Charles began. "I saw visions. Political, scientific, cultural. I don't know where they came from. I can only say they must have come from God."

"Amazing. A divine inspiration of sorts. Would you change anything about the book?"

"I don't think so. Look, it caused me problems in my home country, in my personal life…yet it remains popular. No, I would change nothing."

"Yet in your subsequent works, you steered clear of politics."

Jack shrugged. "Certainly, British politics." He laughed. "I suppose if you look for it, you'll find politics in my books."

"You were initially billed as a writer of political thrillers. Yet after *The Great Replacement*, you found your niche, *your calling*, in science fiction. Was this a reaction to the backlash? Was this some…"

As Laura continued to probe, Jack was captivated. They moved on to exploring technological predictions in *The Great Replacement*. Bloody 'eck Nora, evidently Charles Winthrop used the term *iPhone* in his book. Had he no shame?

Jack chuckled. *Am I indignant? Do I want credit? Acknowledgement?* It was a humorous and odd situation. So, *The Great Replacement* had a Sci-Fi bent, with uncanny predictions of smartphones and the internet. Charles Winthrop was actually credited with inventing terminology (*the internet*) and hastening the arrival of the concepts themselves. He was hailed as a visionary.

Wait a second, it's 1997. And they already have smartphones? Perhaps he did accelerate the pace of innovation.

Another mindblower.

But his political impacts were more far-reaching. He dramatically altered British history, for the better. Fascinating that it changed Britain's path, but nowhere else.

Laura was speaking in a different tone now – a tone of closure. The interview was wrapping up. But not the event. An opportunity was presenting itself – an in-studio Q&A.

By now, Jack was fully and physically present in the studio, and he couldn't squander the opportunity. He waved to one of the assistants, circulating in the studio audience with microphones. He was chomping at the bit, but several others were ahead in the queue.

A black man asked a question about racism in modern-day Britain and proceeded to interrupt Charles' answer. Next, a white conservative fellow asked a convoluted question about the Middle East. Charles stage-whispered to the host: "Your audience mistakes me for a politician."

She smiled and nodded. "Do we have any questions about Mr. Winthrop's literary works?"

Jack was on deck and that was the perfect segue. He was far enough away that Charles probably wouldn't recognize him. Plus, it'd been thirty years since their encounter. Funny, Charles had aged, Jack had not. It was possible Charles had no conscious memory of the meeting. Who knew how these things worked?

Jack would consider that later, because the floor was his and he went straight for the jugular. "Mr. Winthrop, how do you feel your book compares with *The Camp of the Saints*?"

Charles was puzzled by the question, and after a beat became visibly rattled. He hemmed and hawed before Laura stepped in: "The Camp of the Saints?" She shrugged and turned to Charles. "Do you know what he's talking about?"

Charles looked like he'd seen a ghost. Perplexed, frightened, slightly horrified.

"No one knows what you're talking about, sir," said Laura. The assistant tried to take the mic, but Jack held on.

"Do you remember me, Charles?" The words came but for some reason Jack had to fight to get them out. More nausea. *Jesus!* He attempted a follow-up: *we spoke many years ago at Sheldon Cook's house.* The words were slightly unintelligible. As if a hidden force was holding him back. Jack was starting to come across, not so much as a crazed lunatic, but someone with a screw loose.

Meanwhile, Charles was having his own troubles. He mumbled a response, but his discomfort was evident. He was visibly shaking on the stage.

"We need to talk, Charles." Jack blurted, but a security guard appeared and snatched the mic. That was the end of Jack at the event, and the end of Charles, too, for that matter. Laura announced he'd taken ill. She thanked everyone, and pretended nothing weird had happened.

Jack's plan to speak with Charles after the event was a non-starter. The security guard, and another that turned up, escorted him from the premises. No rough stuff, but a firm hand.

On the street, Jack was feeling fine again. *What happened there? It was like some invisible force acting. A resistance? As if engaging Charles was forbidden. Or at least strongly discouraged. Like it might mess up the cosmos, cause a glitch in the matrix. Crikey, what if I tried something truly insane like finding the 1997 version of Lily? Or myself!*

Jack gave his noggin a good shake. What now, he wondered, and like magic an idea materialized. *I must buy Charles' book.*

Need a bookshop. From force of habit, he reached for his mobile, but of course it couldn't connect. Cellular of the day was weak, the 3G era still a few years off. Even so, there'd be no Google Maps. Then again, this was *alternate reality*. Who could say for sure?

Jack went old school and asked a passerby. "Certainly," the man responded. "There's a Borders down the street. World Trade Center, Building 5."

Passing the Twin Towers was emotional. Their scale was hard to fathom, and to think they'd be gone in a few short years.

Crazy!

5 World Trade Center, a low-rise in comparison, offered up a plethora of retail. Borders was easy to find and so was Charles' book. It was front and centre. Why wouldn't it be? The man was in town promoting it for the first time in years.

Jack retrieved a copy cautiously, almost reverentially. The cover was clearly inspired by images Jack had shared. A young English couple surrounded by a sea – *a swarm you might say* – of non-whites. British landmarks in the background were faded and dull, and a great mosque loomed large. On the back, a photo of young Charles precisely as Jack remembered him.

Jack skimmed a few pages, but his mind was racing too fast to concentrate. What about *The Camp of the Saints?* He found an in-store computer and searched. Nothing. He searched for *Jean Raspail* and a list of books appeared. Still, no *Camp of the Saints*.

Was it unpopular? Or was it never written? Likely, the latter. Or perhaps written in a different form, under a different title? Who could say? And who cared, Jack had the big prize – *The Great Replacement*. He made his way toward the checkout, but en route his heart sank. He had no cash – not for this era. Obviously, his credit cards wouldn't work.

What to do? What to do?

Shall I nick it? He glanced around. Not many shoppers. No security guards to be seen. *I'll do it,* he decided, and casually slipped the book under his coat like a seasoned pro.

Unfortunately – or fortunately – he lost his nerve at the exit when he spotted a gate sensor. *An alarm will go off. Isn't that how it works? They deactivate books at checkout.*

Jack wasn't thrilled with the idea of getting arrested in 1997 New York. God only knows how that would play out. Was this another form of resistance? Did some controlling force *not* want him to have the book? Or was it simply poor planning on his part?

Who knew, but Jack devised a compromise. He found a small alcove and flipped through the novel, snapping pictures galore. He didn't have the patience to photograph the entire book – *468 pages* – but he captured a healthy sample, including the cover and table of contents.

A new thought crystallized – *why am I doing this? If history has changed, I can pick up a copy when I return to 2025.* He chuckled nervously. *Makes sense, right?*

But did it? Did anything make sense in this strange world? What exactly was this time and place? Was it real? Or a simulation? More brain-twisters.

Whatever the case, Jack had had enough. He wanted to go home. To see his wife and kids. All of a sudden, he missed them tremendously. He tried to picture young Finn and Lucy, but their images were elusive. As if they weren't real, only shadows. His desire to return rose up with a near-violent urgency.

If the world had changed – *and clearly it had* – then good Christ, maybe his own life had, too. Maybe he'd taken a different path? It was a troubling thought process, and not one he wished to explore.

That single conversation with Charles Winthrop – a clever Englishman capable of creating change – was a catalyst triggering an entirely different chain of events, with England at the heart of the schism. Jack tried to remain calm, think it through, apply reason. But the more he thought about it, the more unlikely his place in the future seemed secure.

I must go home now. I must see my wife and kids. I must! The thought was all-consuming. *A mirror. I need a mirror to make the transition.*

The bookshop had a bathroom, but the queue was long. His maniacal demeanour startled some of the folks waiting. He tried to calm himself, control his panic, and though his mind continued to spin, he slowly wrested control of his vitals.

When they finally returned to normal, the vision appeared. His bedroom. Lily's mirror. He kept his breathing steady and passively accepted the vision. He didn't force it nor try to examine it. He simply acknowledged it. *Presto*, he was in the Time Tunnel hurtling through the space-time continuum, hyper-perceptive, hyper-aware, no trace of panic.

He witnessed familiar scenes and took a special interest in the events of September 11, 2001. Other events breezed by, from America, from Britain, from all over the planet.

It was the ride to end all rides.

22. Back in the Present

But all rides must end.

Jack was back in the familiar confines of his master bedroom, in his familiar Twickenham home. His cardiovascular system was calm. He gazed into the vanity mirror. He glanced about to get his bearings. He heard puttering in the kitchen.

He spotted a photo on the dresser – a family shot of Lily and the kids. Relief washed pleasantly over him. He collapsed onto the bed and thanked God and the heavens above for his safe return. The bedside clock reported 9:17 p.m. Amazing. Time had scarcely moved – or perhaps hadn't moved at all.

How can that be? I was in 1968 for several hours, then another couple in '97. Is that free time? Am I aging while I'm gone? Will I ever know the answers to these questions?

Curiosity ran rampant. If Jack's life hadn't changed, had *anything* changed? He snatched his mobile and Googled *The Great Replacement*. Plenty of *conspiracy theory* results. Evidently, the term was coined by French author Renaud Camus in the 90s, *Le Grand Remplacement*.

Jack searched *Charles Winthrop* and a long list of books appeared, with *Reckonings* singled out as his best. Jack furiously scanned the list but sure enough – *The Great Replacement* was not there. No sir.

Lily poked her head in, startling Jack: "You're still not in bed?"

He held his phone up. "Got caught up in this thing."

She shook her head. "I'll be soon in, love. Put that away."

He nodded with a grin, but he wasn't done yet. A few more searches. Evidently, *nothing* about the world had changed, including the brutal Newfordshire slaughter. A jolt of despair hit.

I'm back where I started. All that effort, the dinner table debate, revealing the iPhone. What purpose did it serve, other than a fascinating experience. A fascinating experiment. Nothing changed. Not in this version of reality – this real-life horror movie of modern Britain.

For a moment in space and time, Jack saw a glorious world where Britain stood up to the menace. Where Britain alone was the model – she fought back and won. At least partially.

What was that time and place? Jack asked for the hundredth time. *Was it real? Did it happen? Of course it happened. It was no dream. Just like the World Cup.*

Wait just one second.

Jack had proof. He snatched his mobile and scrolled photos. *Oh my God.* They were there. Pages and pages of *The Great Replacement*. The front cover. The back cover. That alternate reality happened. *Somewhere it happened.* Not here, not where he currently was. But somewhere in God's matrix, *The Great Replacement* was written, and it changed history.

The photos were another souvenir for his collection. Would've been nice to have the book, but what if Lily spotted it? She missed nothing and always asked tough questions. She'd already asked about the World Cup Programme. *Where'd you get it? It must be worth a fortune.* He gave her a song and dance, and thankfully she didn't press further.

A new thought flashed like a thunderbolt. There was a difference between the two keepsakes. A monumental difference. The Programme was part of his own timeline – the time and place he belonged. Charles' book, however, was not. It was from some other world. Some other dimension. *If I were to seek out Charles Winthrop tomorrow and show him this book he wrote – but didn't write – what then?*

Jack thought further. *So, my time travel adventures haven't changed present-day reality. But in a sense, they have. Me having this book – okay, images of the book – that's a difference. A huge difference. A discontinuity. A glitch in the matrix. At least a potential glitch.*

Again, mind-bending flip-flops thrashed in his head, and he suddenly felt exhausted. Lily would be in soon. He undressed and got into bed, but his mind kept racing. *How can I make changes that stick?*

He looked at his phone again. The pictures were there. They existed. The book was created by a conversation he had with a 1968 version of Charles Winthrop. But aside from the images, the book existed only in an alternate reality.

A new thought emerged.

I must plan bigger changes. If one conversation causes that much change, then what is possible? Then again, why? If the changes don't take in reality – my Anchor Reality, my anchor time and place – what's the point? The point is, he argued with himself, *maybe I can make them stick. Maybe I can force them.*

The door creaked open and Lily appeared in a lacy black negligee.

Hello, Nurse!

Jack did a double-take as she stepped into the room, blonde locks flowing, sultry white skin against silky lace. It took his mind off everything else.

"Put the phone down, sir." Her voice was husky. She struck a provocative pose. "Do you like my outfit?" Jack did very much. He'd not seen it before and it left little to the imagination. "Think you can handle me?"

"I'm willing to try," Jack said, and she crept onto the bed seductively. When she got within reach, he seized her and kissed her passionately. "I missed you so much, darling."

She giggled. "It's only been a few minutes, dear."

"Feels like longer," he said, and stopped talking after that.

23. Oswald (Ozzie) Fletcher

Jack slept soundly through the night. The cosmic adventures didn't penetrate his dreams, but their memory returned the moment he awoke. As before, he was refreshed and invigorated. The *thing* happened again, as he hoped it would.

He'd spent time in 1968 – then 1997, a strange new version of 1997 – and in both cases, he'd handled himself well. Not an expert but compared to his first trip – he maneuvered with relative aplomb.

This bolstered his good will. *Time Travel* was not only a gift but a skill to be nurtured. A jolt of excitement shot through his central nervous system, and he leapt from the bed leaving Lily to snooze.

It was early and the kids were sleeping. Jack savoured the quiet time. He made coffee and flipped on the telly, keeping it low. Sadly, his mood was burst by a BBC update on Newfordshire.

Despair rose up ferociously. Coming from 1960s England to this hellhole was a rude shock. A painful reminder that he'd changed nothing. Despite his *aplomb* in the different times and places – he accomplished nothing.

But flippin' heck, it was fun. If only I could tell someone. Keeping these new powers a secret will be a burden. Now I know how superheroes feel.

His ruminations were punctured by a phone call. Christ, 7:20 a.m. on a Saturday. *Ozzie*. Who else?

"Do you know what time it is?"

"Mornin' Goldilocks. You watchin' BBC?"

"No, too depressing."

"Bloody hell, mate. The cunts are whitewashing everything."

"As expected."

"But I have sources. The death toll's up to nineteen. The murderous bastards, they attacked in a swarm. Not like Southport with just one lunatic. This time, there was a gang o' four."

Jack shuddered. "What was the motive?"

Bigger snort. "Come on, Jack. The motive is they fucking hate Brits. It always is."

"Have they caught them all?"

"Course they did. They got 'em within an hour. Doesn't take Sherlock bloody Holmes to solve these crimes. They took off in a getaway car, plenty o' witnesses got the number plate."

"Daft plonkers. Well, let's see if justice is served."

"Don't hold your breath. This one's terrible, Jack. Ten times worse than Southport."

"You know for a fact they were Muslims? Has the BBC confirmed?"

Scoff. "They've said bugger-all, which confirms they weren't white. My mate Paul – he's got contacts on the scene – he says it's Muzzies." Ozzie cleared his throat. "Tell ya something, Jack. I've always had a racist streak in me. Never denied it, you know as well as anyone. But I never hated anyone." Snort. "That changes today. If they're on my island and they're not British, *I hate 'em*. Give me the chance, I'll deport 'em all. I'd kill 'em if I could, no word of a lie."

"Easy mate, watch what you say. You don't need another *knock on the door*."

"Fuck that. I've had my share of run-ins. They haven't made an example o' me yet and I'm sick o' playing by the rules. We'll never win playing by the bloody rules."

"But what can we do?"

"Deport the bastards, that's what. Ship 'em back to the hellhole they came from. Or deal with 'em here, right and proper. They used to stay in London and Manchester, places like that. Now they're spreading like an infection. *Newfordshire*, Jack. *This happened in Newfordshire.*"

Jack heard rumblings. Evidently, Finn and Lucy were up and would soon descend.

"I gotta go, Oz. Kids are at me."

Ozzie ignored the comment. "And you never say a word about it, do ya?"

"Ozzie, come on. We've been through this. What am I supposed to do? I step outta line, HR's coming for me. I got two young nippers to worry about. I lose my job, I'm no good to anyone."

"It's your nippers I'm worried about. Something's gotta change, mate."

"I'll see ya at the pub later. Who's playing?"

"Who the fuck cares?" Ozzie blurted. "They've taken football from us, too."

"Ah, they haven't Ozzie. Come on."

"We'll be chatting about more than football today, Jack. I've a few mates coming...see ya there."

Ozzie was a specimen. A commoner and proud of it. He spoke his mind. None of the uptight reservedness Brits were known for. But he was more than outspoken. He had courage. Not only the physical kind you need for a fight or a rugby match. He had moral courage. He didn't care a lick what people thought. He was gonna have his say. It was a rare trait in modern Britain. A dangerous one, too.

More rumblings. *Right, I've about thirty seconds of peace left.* Jack savoured a sip of coffee as tiny footfalls started down the hallway. They picked up steam and frequency, and before long:

"Daaaaaad!" Finn launched himself onto Jack's lap, his wild hair perfectly matching his energy.

"Oi, *Finn*. Easy lad, watch the coffee. Christ, you're a bloomin' tornado." Finn tried to live up to the billing by spinning in place.

"Where's your sister?"

"Here I am, Daddy." Lucy came in for a hug with considerably less vigour. Jack gave them both a good tickle and they squealed with delight. Meanwhile, Lily appeared in housecoat and slippers. "What's all the racket?"

"We had a tornado earlier," said Jack, setting Finn off on another flurry, this time Lucy joining him.

It was the stuff of life and Jack wouldn't have it any other way. Notwithstanding the unpleasantness with Ozzie, 'twas a perfect start to the day.

24. Debating at the Pub

Finn and Lucy's football matches were blessedly at the same park, greatly simplifying logistics. The weather was bright and sunny, one of those glorious mornings where English landscapes burst with colour.

Unfortunately, the Newfordshire incident was fresh in the minds of the parents. There were hushed whispers, and a close watch was kept on the children. There was even talk of Jack skipping the pub that afternoon, but it was Lily who insisted. Bless her.

Jack needed it. He loved the camaraderie. The tradition. The retreat from life's pressures. The familiar buzz greeted him on arrival, but today the pressures would enter the fray. Ozzie wasn't kidding about bringing mates – he had a small troop in tow, all with fire in the belly.

Ozzie was already on a roll – no surprise there – and he glanced up for a moment. "Ah, he's graced us with his presence."

Jack pointed at the screen. "I see the good guys are up." Liverpool had a one-nil lead over Aston Villa.

"We're paying no mind to that rubbish," barked Ozzie. "Now, where was I?"

"Colonizing the planet," someone yelled.

"Right, as I was saying…we colonized the bloody planet, then faded into the sunset. We've been resting on laurels for a century."

Eddie laughed at the characterization. Fair play, he was sticking to his liberal guns. However, poor Eddie was in for a rough ride this day.

"You're laughing, are ya?" Ozzie singled Eddie out. "Even after our young ones are cut to ribbons."

"That's not what I'm laughing at, Ozzie."

He glanced at one of his mates. "Told ya, he's aggressively beta." Snort. "He's an alpha at being beta." Ozzie was taking no prisoners. "We need remigration and we need it now. It's our only chance."

Eddie laughed again. "That'll never work. Every case will be in the courts for years, I promise you."

"We'll do it another way then. And while we're at it, we'll deport your likes."

"I told you many times, Ozzie. These people are fleeing war and persecution. It's only fair we Brits do our share."

"Do you hear this bollocks?"

"Germany takes in more than us."

"I don't give a flying fuck about Germany. Or any other country. I care only about Britain. They're destroying our thousand-year-old nation, and they expect us not to notice. Or pretend it's not happening. Fuck that."

"No one's destroying anything, Ozzie."

"This is the problem, lads," Ozzie nodded again toward Eddie. "It's his trademark kiss-ass move. He's tellin' the regime – *I'm one of the good ones*. Trottin' out the state-sanctioned response. Pretendin' all is well, even cheerin' it on. Give it to me harder, sir." Ozzie bent over in a sexually suggestive position.

It wasn't friendly teasing, and the gesture offended Eddie. "Vulgarity won't win arguments, Ozzie. Now, if you watch the news, even GB News is saying—"

"The *news* he says." One of Ozzie's mates piped up.

"*GB News*," Eddie repeated. "They're right up your alley." The channel was sometimes called UK's Fox News and was certainly right-leaning compared to echo-chambers like the BBC and Channel 4.

Ozzie jumped in: "They're as phony as a three-pound note. Just like our bloody *conservative* politicians. They fold like a cheap tent on anything that matters."

"Give 'em a day or two," said Ozzie's mate. "They'll be preaching the Islamophobia rubbish. Just like with Lee Rigby and the Manchester bombing. They're as bad as this bloody wanker, singing kumbaya." He pointed at Eddie.

"Worse actually," said Ozzie. "Cause they pretend to be on our side. Bloody hell, Eddie. We're being genocided and you claim it's a good thing."

"There's no genocide."

"Ethnically cleansed, if you wanna soften it."

Eddie smiled smugly. "It's pointless debating a fanatic."

Ozzie turned away in disgust. "He's a college professor, he's used to a room full o' sycophants. He can't handle any real debate."

Eddie scoffed.

"I'll tell ya, lads. Nothing changes 'til we fight these bastards, and we better be ready to die for it," said Ozzie.

"Who exactly are you fighting?" asked Eddie.

"The traitorous cunts running our country," said Ozzie's friend.

"*And the ones they're bringing in*," said another man. "They all hate us. They want us dead and gone. We gotta drive 'em out."

"The traitors in Westminster." Ozzie snarled. "You give me one chance..." He shook a fist menacingly.

"You better be careful, Oswald. The real world's not the same as posting anonymous memes."

"Look at this numpty. He expects me not to fight. To roll over."

"You'll lose your job. They'll probably throw you in jail. You'll lose everything."

"And if I don't fight, *we all* lose everything. Including you, ya daft prick."

"Democracy in action," said Eddie.

"Democracy he says." Snort. "It's tyranny, mate. And if it is democracy, then I say abolish bloody democracy."

"And hang the scoundrels in Westminster," said the mate. "Especially that fuckstick, Bloodworth."

"He's way down in the polls," said Eddie. "He'll be voted out in the next General."

"And they'll replace 'im with another fuckstick, I promise ya. These scoundrels, they're our mortal enemies, there to do one job – destroy Britain and the British people. Once Bloodworth's spent, the next in line takes over. Doesn't matter the party."

Eddie: "On that note, I think I'll watch the footie now."

"What about you then?" Ozzie turned his ire toward Jack, who'd been quiet during the melee, but taking it all in nonetheless. He sure as hell wasn't paying attention to the football.

"What *about* me?"

"You know what's going on, yet you do nothing. You *say* nothing."

"What am I to do?"

"Christ, you sit through those DEI sessions – how's that workin' for ya? How's your *mental health?*" Big air quotes.

"Perfectly fine, thanks."

"Aye, I don't see how. If I wasn't fighting the cunts, I'd go insane. Don't you get the urge to speak up?"

Jack was irked by the attack. Sure, he knew the truth. Ozzie *knew* he knew – they were best friends after all. Ozzie also knew Jack couldn't say much. But Ozzie was Ozzie.

It was also true Jack had a brand-new perspective. He'd gone back in time and would go again. For what purpose, he wasn't sure, but there had to be one. Whatever the case, keeping it secret wasn't easy. That's partly why he was quiet today. He was off balance, and Ozzie havin' a go at him didn't help.

Ah, God love Ozzie and his ilk, they were fighters. Ozzie was six pints deep, but he'd lose none of his courage the following day. The guy had nerves of steel, and credit where due – he was deceptively intelligent. But it always came back to courage. Ozzie's moral courage was a rare gift.

Heck, maybe he could inspire change. A course correction. Jack knew from recent experience, small changes trigger big impacts. He'd seen it. And by Jove, what then of big changes? Maybe they'd create worlds that were unrecognizable.

Was that rationale valid in present-day Britain? Jack wasn't so sure. Precedents from the past were interesting, but were they relevant?

Nowadays, you can't sneeze without the government knowing. It's an electronic prison. How do you fight back when you can't organize? Or even discuss the problem?

Ozzie and his ilk were doing it anyway. Risking everything. Again, Jack marvelled at the courage.

And what am I doing? Playing the regime's game. It keeps the pay packet coming. A pang of shame descended, not Jack's first trip down that rabbit hole. *If I throw in with this lot, though, I lose my job. Doesn't seem like a good plan.*

A new thought materialized: *I must fight back in my own way.*

Then the vision hit.

Out of the blue and with great fury.

Enoch Powell. A slightly older version. A new setting. Northern Ireland Parliament. Stormont. 1974. Mr. Powell, an Ulster MP for South Down, delivering comments in his trademark style – methodical, disciplined. Intellectually sound.

He was speaking against something called the *Sunningdale Agreement*. Jack perceived the setting and context with clarity – evidently Enoch wanted no part of concessions to Irish Republicanism. The IRA had other plans, but Enoch was unafraid to buck trends. He believed if Northern Ireland went, Scotland and Wales would follow. For Enoch, the only acceptable outcome was direct rule from Westminster.

This vision was short lived, and another soon took over, this one much closer to modern-day England. A familiar face materialized. Sir Roger Scruton. Philosopher. Public intellectual. He was speaking his famous quote:

> "The silencing of Enoch Powell has proved more costly than any other post-war domestic policy in Britain."

Just like that, Jack exited the reverie, or whatever it was, and became painfully aware Ozzie was staring at him strangely.

"What's with you? Looks like you've seen a ghost."

Jack put on a confident grin. "Just sad to see my squad down to bloody Aston Villa."

"*Christ*, you gotta get out more often."

The moment passed, and Jack tried to make sense of what he'd seen.

What are these visions? Premonitions? Suggestions? Where do they come from? Divinity? Some higher power? Whatever they are, whatever they mean, God willing, I'll be going back soon. This time, I shall take more chances. I may even be a tad reckless. Why not? Why not indeed?

To what end, Jack had no idea.

25. Time to Fight!

Meanwhile, Ozzie was getting a tad reckless in the present day and age. He was a tough and confident fellow, Ozzie. Never backed down from a fight, and on the rare occasion he came out worse the wear, never lost a smidgeon of fighting spirit. Never showed an ounce of fear.

Jack feared this battle may be different. He feared for his friend's safety, as Ozzie and his merry band of dissidents were planning a trek to Newfordshire.

"We leave tomorrow morning," he announced. "*The time to fight is now.*"

"Go easy, mate," Jack told him.

"Hey, we're Englishmen. We're civilized. We're not gonna riot. But we are gonna make our voices heard. We're gonna stand our ground – because it *is* our ground. It's our country damnit."

They had signs and placards: *Enough is Enough, Stop the Boats, We Want Our Country Back.*

"Say hello to me Mum and Dad, would ya?" Jack said. "Mum's known to fret, as you well know."

"Join us and you can tell her yourself."

Jack shook his head. He was accustomed to his posh life with Lily and the kids – nice house, fancy car, creature comforts. "I choose to remain a member of polite society. Associating with you is dangerous enough." It was a small joke, but there was truth to it.

"There won't *be* polite society in ten years." said Ozzie, as if reading Jack's mind.

"The media's already talking about—"

"*Fook* the media, the bastards. They're not reporters, they're propagandists. Regime whores. Call 'em what they are."

"They're saying far-right thugs will be dealt with."

"Ha, according to their definition, I am one." Snort. "These pricks lie like a broken clock. Orwell's Ministry of Truth didn't have a patch on them."

By ten the following morning, Ozzie and his pack of patriots were on the M5 driving northward through their green and pleasant land. A great troop of them, and Jack scarcely knew most of the lads, many of them youngsters. Full of beans, bringing that hooligan energy, but for country and nation, not some random corporate crest.

They included Ozzie's younger son, Bryan. A chip off the old block, named after the great midfielder Bryan Robson. The boy was nineteen years old and a brick of a lad – square-shouldered and square-jawed like his Daddy. Jack had known him since birth and could personally attest – he was top drawer. Britain was lucky to have him.

Yet, like all of them, he was vulnerable to the insanity. He could easily be crushed underfoot by the commies in charge and the media would play it up as a good thing.

Jack shuddered. Anything short of country-wide revolt and the chances of victory are slim. Too many Eddies. And, he must admit, too many Jacks. Another pang of shame hit. Got Jack thinking. If the news was fake – *and it most definitely was* – then what of the history books? They were probably far faker. In fact, probably all recorded history was questionable.

But, by the grace of God and his new special gift, Jack had the ability to check for himself.

That's exactly what he planned to do.

26. Strategizing

Jack contemplated the vision of Enoch Powell in Northern Ireland. Was that the place to go? He was getting a *been-there-done-that* sense. Sure, it was Belfast. Sure, it was 1974. But why not go further back?

Am I allowed to? And if so, how far? Windrush? Churchill? Queen Victoria? Cromwell? Perhaps I could caution early colonizers – look here my good man, I could tell them. This is a dangerous game. It will come back to haunt Britain.

Interesting, but perilous and full of unknowns. How would I blend in? How could I make a difference? Win over the military? The monarchy? Become a man of influence?

Christ, if they saw my phone in the Elizabethan era, they'd burn me at the stake. Again, the fear. *If I'm killed in my travels, am I killed in real life? Maybe I'm invincible in these alternate worlds. Immortal, even. So why not go in shooting? Take chances, assassinate evildoers, whatever it takes to trigger change, danger to myself be damned. Heck, if I'm in a spot of trouble, I'll just hop back in the Time Tunnel.*

He smiled to himself. His confidence wasn't that high – not even close. Also, doubts lingered. *Why go back at all if the changes don't take, except in strange parallel universes.*

He repeated the question. *Why am I doing this? For one, it's entertaining. It's also enlightening. And heck, maybe one day I'll figure out how to make changes stick. Meantime, I'll experiment. Learn a few things. Maybe apply lessons learned to today's world.* A flash of optimism hit. *Who knows, maybe we can win this war against all odds. Underdogs have been triumphant time and again throughout history.*

Besides, the urge to go back was irresistible. It was like a drug. An escape. Jack didn't know the answers. Perhaps he'd *never* know them. But he had to go back. He knew that in his heart. Still, probably best to follow the visions. Stick to the guiderails, at least for now. Come to think of it, he wasn't even sure how to exit the *Time Tunnel.* Maybe following visions was the only way.

A plan began to form. Thus far, he'd been winging it. Adapting on-the-fly to old worlds, new worlds, alternate worlds. Fine. That would continue. But better to prepare.

That meant bringing seed money to match the era and devising a means to acquire more. Like gambling on events for which he knew the outcome. It meant proper attire. It meant researching people, places, and things and devising strategies to connect with influencers, rather than simply charging about.

For this next trip, Jack reviewed news archives. He sought to understand Mr. Powell's travels since *Rivers of Blood*. What drove the man to leave for Belfast. Had he found a new calling? Or was it purely opportunity?

Evidently, the Loyalists figured a firebrand like Powell could help their cause. And Enoch entered the fray at the height of *The Troubles,* with car and pub bombings all over Ireland and England. Jack was stunned. He knew about the violence – every Englishman of his vintage did – but to read of them afresh was an eye-opener. Such a waste of Irish and English blood. So very sad.

Back to Enoch. Had the man given up protecting Britain? The persecution, was it simply too high, even then?

I will have the answers soon, Jack thought.

27. The Ruse

That evening, he and Lily were out with friends – Lily's friends to be specific. Her bestie from childhood, Helen, and the husband Oliver. A decent chap, though he and Jack never fully bonded. That evening was no different, not with all Jack had on his mind. He had a hard time shelving it to make polite social talk, but he managed. He was an executive after all. Compartmentalization skills were a strong suit.

Lily noticed, nonetheless. "You were distracted tonight, dear."

"Worried about Ozzie, that's all." It was certainly true.

"I understand."

"I'm gonna hop off early tonight, darling. Meet you in bed?"

"That's getting to be a habit with you."

"I am getting on in age."

"Ah, you've a few good years in you yet." She gave Jack the sweetest of smiles.

Another pang of guilt. He was keeping secrets from his beloved. That had to change. And it would, *but not tonight, Josephine.*

In the bedroom, Jack went to work. He changed clothes and gathered items. Didn't take long, he had it all planned. He stood in front of Lily's mirror and relaxed his mind and body. This time, no false starts – the sensations commenced straightaway. The weightlessness, the clarity, the bright light.

Soon, he was in the *Time Tunnel* hurtling through time and space, observing history and events, perceiving them. In due course, he saw Northern Ireland's capital circa 1974, and he understood perfectly it was his destination.

He'd been several times, IRL as they say, but took in the surroundings with fresh eyes. The tree-lined streets, the elegant neighbourhoods, the shops, the people – everything marked with an Irish aesthetic.

He saw the lush grounds of Stormont Estate, until recently home to Northern Ireland's Parliament, and began his descent. The tunnel faded, and with little fanfare Jack settled into this new time and place. Monday May 31, 1974. 4:00 p.m. A Friday. It was an off-day for Westminster Parliament and Jack happened to know Mr. Enoch Powell was in Belfast to meet local groups and hear their concerns. It was a time when politicians still cared about such matters.

Mr. Powell's presence on this day in 1974 was not written in public records. Jack, however, was privy to the knowledge courtesy of *the visions*. Or was it some deep intuition? Either way, there was no doubt in Jack's mind – Mr. Powell was at Stormont and Jack's mission was to secure an audience with the great man.

The grounds were calm, everything clean and orderly. He saw nattily dressed politicians, mothers with toddlers, and young men scurrying, perhaps eager to find their place in the world of politics.

As usual, Jack was overcome with emotion. The familial joy welled up from within, the sense of kinship. Of belonging. Even in Belfast. He was among his people, ensconced in his native habitat, when it was still unspoiled by globalist muckrakers.

He gazed at the Parliament Buildings, majestic and stately on this bright sunny day, Stormont's centrepiece atop the hill. They conjured images of England's rich monarchial history.

Despite the tranquility, Belfast was not all sunshine and roses at the time. Not by a longshot. Sure, there was no scourge of alien newcomers (though some Irish may characterize the English thusly), but *The Troubles* were in full vigour. To Jack's mind, they were a quarrel among the people of the British Isles. A family squabble among nations comprised of near-indistinguishable ethnic stock, though that characterization alone would trigger a mighty skirmish in some quarters.

Such a tragic waste for the Poms and Paddies. On the one hand, understandable considering the Irish had been fending off the English for 800 years. Insanity on the other, when you see a few short decades hence, both nations devasted by third-world hordes – first England, and Ireland soon to follow. In retrospect, *The Troubles* were a pointless piece of history.

Nevertheless, they were in full swing and terror threats were a constant concern. Security surrounding public officials was stringent. MPs from both sides of the aisle were targets of the IRA, the UDA, and other paramilitary factions. Politicians were assigned protection by the Royal Ulster Constabulary and they took precautions, varying routes and travelling in unmarked vehicles.

There was less fanfare around Mr. Powell than in the wake of *Rivers of Blood*, but he too was closely guarded, making Jack's job difficult. Random networking in a pub would be a poor strategy. Jack considered bribery, perhaps posing as a wealthy supporter, but discarded the notion. Ethics were too strong back then.

The ruse he settled on was to pose as a reporter and make an impression on Mr. Powell, enough to secure a private audience with the legendary figure. *Ha*, nothing to it.

Things started out well. Jack was granted admission to the Stormont Pavilion, flashing phony press credentials and waltzing past security with an air of confidence. He had crafted an impeccable replica using AI and Photoshop, mimicking imagery he'd found online. No chance a 1974 official would question their authenticity. No colour copiers back then.

But it would take more than credentials. Not to be vulgar, but it would take balls, and Jack had 'em. After twenty years in corporate banking, he knew how to look the part. How to stay cool and dry under pressure. It was a required skill for any executive.

Of course, gaining access was only the start. Now came the hard part – *making contact.* The Pavilion was a place for social gatherings, but it also supported the occasional press conference. It was intimate and well-suited to a friendly line of questions, which was the expectation of the day. Perhaps a dozen reporters milled about, plus camera crews, assorted assistants, secretaries. Most clearly knew each other, but no one questioned Jack's presence – so far.

Mr. Powell's address was short. He remarked on local issues, made several promises, and expressed gratitude. He opened the floor to questions. A gangly fellow approached the mic and enquired on parliamentary proceedings returning to Stormont. Enoch's answer was eloquent and non-committal. He *was* a politician after all. Next, a similarly banal question about the VAT – an unpopular *goods and services* tax. Again, a perfectly satisfactory answer from Enoch.

Then it was Jack's turn, and he went straight to the heart of the matter. "Good afternoon, Mr. Powell. Max Montgomery with the Irish Times." Jack elected to use an alias. Not part of any master plan, just seemed a good idea. "I'm planning a three-part series on your arrival into Northern Ireland politics. Will you bring the same firebrand energy to Belfast that you did to London? Will you deliver a *Rivers of Blood* speech to denounce the IRA?"

It was an incredibly provocative question, particularly from a man representing the Irish Times, a paper whose editorial leaning favoured Irish constitutional nationalism. Everyone knew this, and that was Jack's trump card – his way of making an impression.

The question brought a smile to Enoch's face. "My good man, your paper is not known for its pro-loyalist stance."

To be taken seriously, never hesitate. Show no fear. "I'm out to change that, Mr. Powell. I'm a man on a mission."

"I confess, I've not seen your name. You say you're with the Irish Times?"

Jack smiled brightly. "I'm new to politics, sir. Also, new to Belfast. Just over from Manchester – had an Opinion Column there for five years. Great fun, but I needed a change."

With no internet, an immediate check on this fictional past was impossible. Jack figured the ruse was good for a few hours, even if it was certifiably insane. Anyone pushing a Loyalist position for the Irish Times in 1974 would have a price on his head.

"You may get more than you bargained for, Mr. Montgomery."

"I'll speak the truth as I see it. If the majority of Northern Ireland's population is Unionist and Protestant, if they identify as British and wish to remain that way, so be it."

"The IRA will take issue."

"Is it not our democratic duty to respect the preference of the majority?"

"A Republican might ask why the population is thus skewed. He might also demand unification, and anyone who didn't like it could jump in the Irish Sea."

Or get thrown in it, came a random voice from the crowd, prompting gales of laughter. Jack didn't let up. It was a confidence game, and he had to go all in. "I'm writing the piece one way or the other. I suggest it's in your interests to participate."

Enoch's face lit up in amusement.

"Might I suggest a short interview this afternoon," Jack continued. "To break the ice."

"I think the ice has been broken."

"All the better," said Jack. "I dare say, this may be the most important interview you've ever conducted."

Enoch was taken aback by the brashness, and respectful of it. "Speak to my secretary. We'll let him decide."

More laughter. And more questions followed, but none dared press Mr. Powell in the manner Jack had. When formalities ended, several reporters approached Jack. His antics had stolen the show, and there was curiosity, perhaps even a hint of suspicion, around the dashing newcomer.

In due course a fastidious young man introduced himself as Mr. Powell's secretary. He asked several probing questions, assessing Jack's worthiness. Jack handled them with just enough charisma to get the job done.

A private tête-à-tête was arranged.

Boom.

Ask and you shall receive.

28. Enoch Powell

Thirty minutes later, Mr. Powell's secretary, with the help of a brawny security guard, escorted Jack through a series of corridors. When they arrived at the legendary man's office, the secretary escorted Jack in.

Enoch Powell, in the flesh, was seated behind an enormous desk, his piercing gaze conveying deep intelligence. He evaluated Jack with interest, and a hint of amusement.

Jack was momentarily flustered, almost intimidated. This was a formidable figure in British history. Controversial to establishment machinery, but a hero to any English patriot.

Mr. Powell stood to shake hands, and Jack marvelled at his distinguished appearance. Exactly as he'd seen in photos and video. Why would it be different? His hair was dark with silvery patches and immaculately combed. His demeanour serious, almost austere. He was dressed in a finely tailored suit befitting a politician of the era. Jack suspected he wore such a suit every day of his life.

He had a slim build and was several inches shorter than Jack. But he was a towering figure in Jack's mind. The eye contact was steady as they shook hands and made introductions. Jack almost stated his real name but caught himself in time.

"You're a persuasive man, Mr. Montgomery."

"I can be, for a just cause."

"And speaking with me, that meets the bar?"

"You're a famous man, Mr. Powell. People still speak of *Rivers of Blood*."

Enoch lowered his gaze. "I'd prefer to discuss issues of the day here in South Down rather than rehash a talk I delivered six years ago."

"Right, splendid," said Jack. "But what if issues of the day are precisely what you spoke of on April 20, 1968?"

Enoch displayed a wry smile. "That's not the case, sir. Not in my district, nor any part of this fair land. I've spent considerable time this side of the Irish Sea, and I can scarcely recall seeing a single non-white person."

"I believe you," Jack said calmly. "But if I asked a London MP the same question twenty-five years ago, he'd have said the same."

"It's a fair point. The country was essentially monoracial at that time."

"And look at London now. Look at your previous constituency, Wolverhampton. Your place of birth, Birmingham."

"Another fair point."

"It will get worse, Mr. Powell. Much worse. You of all people know that."

"Are you here to discuss the Sunningdale Agreement?"

"I'm here to tell you the Sunningdale Agreement is a pointless distraction when the English will soon be a minority in London, *and in all of Britain.*"

"This was my warning, though of course the outcomes you describe would take a very long time. I still have faith good sense will prevail, and we'll reverse course."

"And I'm telling you there won't be a course correction. The problem will get worse. In a few decades, it will hit this very island," Jack pointed at the ground for emphasis, "*north and south.*"

Enoch's smile vanished. "I find that hard to believe. The Irish have resisted occupation for centuries. They don't take kindly to strangers, you may have noticed."

"Let me tell you my predictions."

Enoch shrugged. "If you must."

Jack unleashed a prepared diatribe. He described the annual influx of foreign peoples by decade. In the '70s, 100,000 annually. By the '90s, 250,000. Mid-2000s, up to half a million pouring in from all over Africa and Asia.

"Politicians will occasionally speak out. They'll even write laws to restrict immigration. But the laws will be ineffective and broken."

Jack provided more stats and Mr. Powell listened without interruption, his piercing eyes narrowing as Jack rattled off numbers – *disguised as predictions*. When he was done, Enoch didn't rush to fill the silence.

After several moments: "I must say Mr. Montgomery, the information you've shared is rather specific. You speak in a manner that suggests *knowledge* of the future."

Jack smiled. *He has me sussed.* At sixty-two, Enoch was still vital and sharp. "Perhaps I do have such knowledge."

Enoch's wry smile was back.

An internal debate raged as it had with Charles Winthrop. *Do I show him the phone? Do I come clean?* Of course, the answer was yes. It would be easy in the confines of a private office. No listening devices. No surveillance. Not in 1974.

How would Enoch Powell respond? He was more pragmatic than Charles. Less a dreamer, more a doer.

"Shall I show you the future?"

Enoch raised his eyebrows as if to say *why not?*

Jack withdrew his iPhone and placed it on the desk, icons glowing. He scrolled casually as Enoch stared in astonishment. An identical reaction to that of Charles Winthrop.

"What madness is this?"

"This, Mr. Powell, is the future."

The great man stood in protest. "You'll not waste my time with magic tricks."

"No, no. Not at all Mr. Powell." Jack was surprised by the rejection but rallied swiftly. Powell was born in the horse-and-buggy era. Forget computers – he was around before radio and TV. Perhaps he was resistant to technology.

"Hear me out, sir." Jack held hands up in a pleading gesture. "Give me five minutes. This is no magic trick, I assure you."

Mr. Powell sat down. He perched his glasses on the end of his nose and regarded the device suspiciously, but also curiously.

"Allow me to demonstrate." Jack conducted the same dog-and-pony show he'd given Charles – the timer, the calendar, the calculator.

"What is this machine?" Enoch demanded. "Where did you get it?"

"This is a futuristic device." Jack snapped several photos and showed Enoch. He took a short video. He opened one of Finn's colourful games. Enoch's skepticism was slowly replaced by fascination.

"I feel as if I'm in a Star Trek episode."

Jack smiled. "Look, I don't understand this myself. I don't know why or how I'm here, but I come in earnest. I bring warnings from the future. Dire and urgent. This device is from the future. How it is here, how I am here – I've no idea." Jack fished into his coat pocket. "Here's a newspaper clipping from the year 2025." Jack slapped it on the table. Newsprint was a medium Enoch was familiar with.

"Extraordinary."

"I can tell you the future, Mr. Powell, because *I've seen the future*. You want to know who wins the trifecta at Epsom Downs, I can tell you." He produced a sheet of paper with the results of *tomorrow's* events.

"If you were a greedy man, this could make you very rich." Enoch was a man of high morals, but any man is subject to temptation. "Go to the betting shop. You'll see. This is no parlour trick."

Enoch eyed the sheet skeptically. It was all so fantastically outlandish.

Jack pressed on. "You're in the early days of a malicious mass immigration experiment. Some of my peers call it demographic warfare. Your instincts six years ago were prescient. It will not work out well for Britain. It was never intended to. This is the willful destruction of our people – a trusting, kind, and decent people. The numbers I shared are precisely what will happen unless something – or someone – forces a change. Maybe that's you?"

"How do you know this?" Enoch fixated on the improbability of seeing the future.

Jack brushed off the question: "I bring a warning from fifty years into the future, sir. I've *come* from the future." Jack reached for his mobile and adeptly flipped through the same provocative content he'd shown Charles. He hit hard on the same talking points.

"Stabbings become commonplace. There will also be beheadings, acid attacks, and vehicular attacks."

"Vehicular attacks?"

"One of the Muslims' favourite tricks is to drive vehicles at high speed into crowds – perhaps at a Christmas market. It's horrific. The carnage, beyond comprehension." Jack showed video from the recent Magdeburg massacre in Germany.

"Good Lord."

"Our government – *God love 'em* – they've erected concrete barriers to prevent access by cars. That's how they try to solve the problem." Jack scoffed in disgust. "It's bad in the future, sir. Riots, carnage, rape of our children by the thousands."

"Rape of children?" Jack would never forget the look of horror on Enoch's face.

"By the tens of thousands. The Home Office turns a blind eye. Same goes for the Old Bill."

"I find it difficult to believe our government wouldn't intervene."

"So do I," said Jack. "Then again, you have to see our government in 2025. I present the MP for Newfordshire East speaking after the slaughter of children in his home constituency."

Kwame Mangata was a perpetually angry black man. He spoke in distinctive African tones and in this video, cautioned everyday Brits on the dangers of *protest* following the massacre: "If you eez coming to mosque to protest, you weel get rude awakening." He wagged a finger. "I won't be responsible for de violence you eez suffering. This eez our country, too. You British occupied our lands, *now we are here.* Chickens to roost."

Mangata was from The Congo, but identified so strongly with the Muslim community in England, he converted.

"Good heavens, how was this man elected? He butchers the language. How was he permitted to run? *He's a primitive.*"

Jack gasped for effect. "That comment would get you jail time in my era."

"He threatens the British people. *Extraordinary.*"

"Mr. Powell, your fight here in Northern Ireland may seem admirable from today's perspective. But as the saying goes, you're rearranging deck chairs on the Titanic."

Enoch had not heard the metaphor but appreciated its meaning. "Go on."

"We must have no more brother wars. They've been a great devastation to our people. My God, World War I and II killed millions of fine young British men, and an equal number of Germans."

Enoch took offense. "The Germans were—"

"What did England gain in defeating Germany?" Jack interrupted. "She lost her Empire. She's since lost her identity, *her self-confidence.* Looking back, going to war with Germany had to be one of the worst strategic decisions in history."

Enoch shook his head vehemently, but Jack pressed on. "It's as if these wars were meant to weaken us."

After a lengthy pause: "Is another great war coming?" By now, Enoch seemed convinced of Jack's power to see the future.

"Ha, no. Not in the traditional sense. It's not needed. As I said, in my era, Britain's under attack by *demographic* warfare. She has been since the bloody Windrush docked in '48. Not only Britain, all Western countries, *Germany too.* And this war will do more damage than all other wars combined."

Enoch drew a deep breath, as if realizing all his fears (and then some) would come to pass.

"They come by plane, by boat, by dinghy. Once they outnumber the English in a community, they become arrogant. They lord their dominance over locals. They mock and intimidate, and resort to violence if challenged."

"And no one speaks against it?"

"Speaking against it is criminalized."

"They criminalize speech?"

"Oh yes. They call it hate speech." Air quotes. "Say the wrong thing, they'll imprison you. Of course, most Brits in my day would rather say nothing than be called racist. But the courageous ones, I tell you. When Rishi Sunak was Prime Minister, he—"

"Rishi Sunak?" Astonishment. "An Indian?"

"Yes sir, the UK will have an Indian prime minister."

"From India?"

Jack smiled mirthlessly. "No, born in Southampton. And until recently, the First Minister of Scotland was a Pakistani and Ireland's Taoiseach was a half-Indian homosexual."

"*A homosexual?* And this was publicly known?"

"Sir, if you only knew how bad it will get. Your great speech—"

Enoch scoffed. "My *speech*, as you call it – that was a very long time ago. People rarely mention it these days."

"On the contrary, sir. Fifty years from now *Rivers of Blood* is still talked about by true British patriots. You're a hero in 2025. No exaggeration. Your name is mentioned with reverence and respect."

A smile flashed through Mr. Powell's features. *Ha*, even he was susceptible to flattery. At that precise moment, a wave of nausea rose suddenly in Jack's throat.

Oh no! Am I entering forbidden territory? Is this the resistance? I must press on, nonetheless.

"Mr. Powell, you knew in 1968 what would happen." A tremor appeared in Jack's voice. "You were p-p-prescient and c-courageous, and you still know today." Jack paused to cough. "Yet you've stopped f-f-fighting. You've taken on new b-battles."

"Are you quite alright, Mr. Montgomery?"

"Don't–" Jack paused again to cough – "d-don't w-w-worry about me. I'm worried about you." He adopted a scolding tone, and the resistance worsened. "What happened to you? Why did you not f-f-follow up *Rivers of Blood?* Why did you g-give up? Did you l-l-lose your nerve?"

Enoch regarded Jack carefully, even glancing at the door as if ready to notify the security man. "No, I simply walked away."

With difficulty, Jack withdrew his mobile and retrieved the quote he was looking for.

> "The silencing of Enoch Powell has proved more costly than any other post-war domestic policy in Britain."

"That was written th-th-thirty years from now b-b-by an English philosopher named Sir Roger Scruton." Jack's breathing had become laboured and he felt he may be sick. A film of sweat had formed on his brow.

"Have you become ill?"

Jack hunched forward in an effort to ease the pain. After several sharp inhales of breath: "I'll b-b-be f-fine. Give me a m-m-minute."

"Would you like a glass of water?"

"P-p-please."

Enoch's office was equipped with a kitchenette, and he fulfilled the request. "Ah, you're very kind." After several minutes, Jack's symptoms had eased.

"You must excuse me, Mr. Powell. I'm not sure what came over me." Jack sat up straight to signal a full recovery. "Do you have questions, sir?"

"The immigrants. The foreigners coming in. Are they primarily black? From places like the West Indies?"

"There are plenty of blacks, including full-blooded Africans from places like Nigeria and Ghana. You saw our friend from The Congo earlier. But the real scourge is Asians. Nothing against them personally, but their numbers are endless and they're *not* English. They simply don't belong in our country." The nausea was back, but manageable.

Enoch nodded. "And you say it's not only England?"

"All Western countries go mad with immigration. France, Germany, Sweden. Even tiny Ireland, as I mentioned.

Eventually, you'll walk down O'Connell Street and not see a single Irishman."

"You must be joking."

"I wish I w-was."

Enoch furrowed his brow. He pursed his lips. "The obvious question is *why*. Why does this happen? Why is it *allowed* to happen?"

"The million-dollar question, and I'm afraid it's a c-complicated answer. Obviously, it's not organic. It's orchestrated, top-down. There's a c-c-cabal of individuals – call them globalists – and evidently they hate European nations. They hate *Europeans*, period. That's the only c-conclusion to be drawn. It's like revenge for c-c-colonialism."

"Colonialism?" In Enoch's era, the word hadn't been fully demonized.

Jack nodded. "Where I come from colonialism's evil. On par with slavery."

"British Colonialism *stopped* slavery in some of those godforsaken places."

"Doesn't matter."

"I've heard these arguments, but I maintain," Enoch spoke in his classic form, "the British Empire was a force for good. We introduced democracy. We built roads, hospitals, schools. I'd like to see where they'd be without our help."

"Unfortunately, that's not how history's been written. So now we must accept millions of f-foreigners for the r-r-rest of eternity. Why are they here? Who invited them? There are no g-g-good answers."

"Outrageous."

"And if we so much as r-raise an eyebrow to c-c-c-complain, they come after us."

"Surely the media exposes the malfeasance."

The *resistance* had returned with full measure but Jack swallowed hard and fought on. "The media? The media's c-c-complicit. They l-l-lie on an unimaginable s-scale. Anything to do with...the white man...that's b-bad. For non-whites...everything is g-g-good. It's th-that s-s-simple."

Jack spoke in fragments now. He was squinting through the pain.

"Extraordinary."

"It's still fixable...In m-m-my t-t-time...we've p-p-passed the t-t-tipping point." Jack spoke louder in an effort to overcome the resistance. "It's p-p-probably impossible to r-recover...t-t-to reverse the r-rot." Jack choked the words out.

A light knock, and the security man poked his head in. "Everything quite alright, sir?"

"Just fine, thank you Cyril." He closed the door.

The interruption offered a slight reprieve from the sickness, and Jack didn't rush back to his diatribe. Perhaps he'd said enough already.

"Something you said earlier, Mr. Montgomery. Ireland's Taoiseach was a—"

"Half-Indian homosexual." The nausea had lessened, or perhaps he'd just gotten used to it. "That's correct. In the future, morality is tossed out the window. We live in utter degeneracy. Depravity."

"How so?"

"For one, pornography's rampant. They've n-normalized it. The most shocking m-m-material imaginable. Demonic s-s-stuff. It warps the minds of our young people. It's an absolute s-s-scourge." The sickness was there, but Jack was coping.

"How did it ever get that way?"

He paused to think. "It was baby steps I suppose. They started in the '70s, you're seeing it now with the sexual revolution. With g-gay m-m-marriage."

"Gay?"

"Homosexual." Another mirthless smile. "They've c-commandeered that word...t-t-to mean homosexual."

A puzzled look.

"Homosexuality's entirely normalized...our c-culture celebrates degeneracy. Drag queens and circus f-f-freaks, my friend Ozzie says. The LGBTQ menace."

"LGB...?"

"TQ." Jack attempted to explain the acronym, but it was a bridge too far for Enoch.

"You're telling me that if a man dresses as a woman, people are expected to pretend he's a woman."

"Yes. They'll even let him c-c-compete...in women's s-sports. And everyone p-pretends...it's normal."

"I find that difficult to believe."

Jack shrugged. "It's another symptom of the r-rot...the d-d-debasement of our people."

"Extraordinary."

The *sickness* was back with more fury, but Jack marched on. "In my era, the young p-p-people...are d-demoralized...s-s-sexually confused...they're not getting m-married...they're n-n-not having kids." Pause. "But the f-f-foreigners breed...like rodents...like an invasive s-s-species."

Enoch rubbed his temples. He was at a loss for words.

"I haven't even t-t-talked about...g-grooming yet."

"Grooming?"

Jack hunched forward again. The pain was almost unbearable. "It's m-maybe the worst issue of all...they p-p-prey on our...s-s-schoolgirls."

"Grooming," he repeated.

"It's a euphemism...f-f-for foreign rape g-gangs..."

Enoch was dumbfounded.

"They ply our young g-girls with d-drugs and alcohol...then r-rape and t-t-torture them."

"My God."

"Everyone knows...they w-w-whisper about it. Social w-w-workers, journalists, the p-p-police. They t-turn a blind eye...f-f-for f-fear of being called r-racist."

"Where did this happen?"

"In places like R-Rochdale, Rotherham, T-T-Telford... towns all across the l-l-land...the scale would sh-sh-shock you."

"And no one said anything? No one spoke up?"

"Some did, but they were at-attacked. The entire s-s-system...c-conspired to sweep it...under the r-r-rug."

"Why on earth would they do that?" The sadness in Mr. Powell's eyes was palpable.

"They were afraid of b-being called r-r-racist." Jack paused to catch his breath. "My m-m-mate Ozzie says they should all h-hang. N-no matter their involvement...if they knew even a l-l-little..." Jack made a throat slice gesture.

Anger flashed in Enoch's features. "I don't disagree."

Jack saw something click in Enoch's eyes. In the curl of his lip. A chord had been struck. A decision made. And Jack perceived a monumental shift in the space-time continuum.

Until then, the resistance had been a steady drumbeat, but somehow bearable. However, with this new *shift*, the symptoms spiked massively and Jack doubled over in agony but pressed on anyway. He had to persevere.

"S-s-someone m-m-must d-d-do s-something...b-b-before it..." his speech was slurred. "Before it's..." Jack's voice trailed off.

Enoch nodded solemnly. "I understand," he said, and scrutinized Jack. "You've very unwell, sir."

"I'll be f-f-fine, but I f-feel it's t-time for me to leave."

"Will I see you again? Will I see your three-part series in the Irish Times?"

Jack looked down to express remorse. "I'm n-not a r-r-reporter, Mr. Powell. I don't w-w-work for any n-newspaper."

Enoch smiled. "Perhaps you're a crazy man, and everything you've told me is poppycock."

Jack attempted to return the smile.

"Then again, perhaps it's the truth."

Both men stood and shook hands, and Jack struggled toward the door. The *resistance* was still there and compromising his ambulation. However, by the time he reached the Estate's parkland, the symptoms blessedly subsided. His normal gait returned. In fact, there was a spring in his step and a glint in his eye.

I've created change.

Perhaps not in the *real* world – Anchor Reality, as he'd come to call it – but in some alternate world. Heck, some alternative universe for all he knew.

Either way, Jack was keen to see the results of his handiwork.

29. The Funeral

Jack sat on one of Stormont's many park benches. Others milled about, but there was no clutter, no crowding of people. This was Belfast 1974 and – *ha*, outside of the occasional terror attack – it was very much a First World setting. Civilized and peaceful.

Jack had regained control of his vitals and like magic, the visions appeared. He was getting good at this. He didn't chase them, he simply acknowledged them. Where he was going, he had no idea, but if he had it his way – it would not yet be the sanctity of his bedroom – because evidently once there, any changes, any alterations would all be erased.

Jack was desperate to see a different version of reality – *an alternate reality*. Into the Time Tunnel he went, the scenes flashing by. It never got old. Jack was just as enthralled this go-round as he had been the first.

Then he saw it. A church – a magnificent church – and some deep intuition took over. No conscious thought, no deciding. This was where Jack was supposed to go.

Birmingham. May 22, 1977. Early afternoon, the skies grey and overcast.

The church had a gothic-style architecture – pointed steeple, impressive stonework. The holy structure was at one with the landscape, as if it had stood in this place for centuries, and indeed it had. Stately trees offered parishioners shade, when needed. Church bells chimed. Out back, a tranquil graveyard with weathered headstones, and a freshly dug grave ready to accept a newly fallen.

Jack realized with a start – this was the funeral of Enoch Powell. Not the one that occurred in Jack's *Anchor Reality*, where the great man passed February 8, 1998. No sir. This was an *Alternate World* funeral.

Jack stood apart from the crowd but not out of place. By and by, he strolled toward the entrance, greeting fellow mourners who were slowly shuffling in. He joined the procession and once inside the nave, was struck again by the church's beauty – the vaulted ceilings, the stained glass, attention to detail in every facet imaginable.

Jack scanned the pews and noted a dearth of available seats. Evidently, there was competition for attendance – Enoch was a popular man in Jack's world, and perhaps more so in this alternate world. An open place appeared. Luck or fate, Jack wasn't sure.

"Is this seat taken?"

The man shook his head and slid over. An invitation to sit.

"Max Montgomery." Jack stuck his hand out.

"Good day, sir. Sheldon Cook."

My God, Sheldon Cook again. How very strange. It unnerved Jack, but he recovered quickly. "Sad day it is."

"Indeed."

"Tragic really." Jack was fishing. "Are you privy to the details?"

"Only what I've read in the newspapers."

"Any updates the past couple days?"

Sheldon regarded Jack curiously. "Have you not been watching the news, man?"

"I've been out of touch lately. I'm a tad discombobulated. I travelled a great distance to be here."

The man seemed happy with the explanation. "No particular updates. Scotland Yard's playing it close to the vest. Understandable really, when an MP's assassinated."

"And his killer?"

"Also dead."

Jack nodded solemnly. It confirmed what he'd known in his heart. He'd seen the visions. The government was happy to see Enoch go and almost surely played a part in the execution. *The treachery.* "Were you a friend of Mr. Powell's?"

Sheldon shook his head. "No, just an admirer. He was a hero to our people. A towering figure in my estimation. And you?"

"I met him once, three years ago in Belfast. We had a lovely chat." *My God*, Jack thought. *Three years have elapsed. What has happened since to so drastically alter – and shorten – Mr. Powell's life?*

Their dialogue was interrupted by activity in the sanctuary. The funeral service was set to begin. The vicar stepped forward:

> "Dear friends, family, and parishioners, welcome to this solemn gathering. We are united in this sacred house in the presence of Almighty God to bid farewell to John Enoch Powell, a man who dedicated his life to the service of England and the people of this fair nation. He was a man of duty and integrity, and though we mourn his loss, and the tragic circumstances, we celebrate a life well-lived. A life that reflected the steadfast values of faith, family, and country."

A member of the congregation stepped forward, a bright-eyed lad who looked the embodiment of Englishness. He delivered a reading from Ecclesiastes 3:1-8. The opening line was apt:

> *"There is a time for everything, and a season for every activity under the heavens."*

The scripture comforted and soothed.

The first eulogizer was a well-known political figure, though not quite a household name. A close friend and confidante. A known sympathizer.

> "Today, we honour a man whose courage to challenge the status quo set him apart. John Enoch Powell stands alone as a beacon of integrity in a world dominated by conformity."
>
> "While others prioritized the safe path, the path well-travelled, Mr. Powell dared venture into uncharted territory, championing causes others feared. No man can ever say he played it safe, and it cost him dearly. In the end, it cost him his life."

This weighty remark provoked tears in the family members, and the eulogizer moved swiftly to a summary of Enoch's life:

> "At twenty-six years of age, Enoch was working as a professor of Greek at the University of Sydney. He was a fine scholar and won many awards. He could have carved out a first-class career in academia, but God had other plans. When World War II erupted, duty called and Enoch returned to serve in the British Army. He rose through the ranks to become a Brigadier and was later transferred into military intelligence in North Africa and India. Here, he focused on strategic planning and leveraged his fluency in several languages to translate intercepted messages. He earned recognition for his capabilities and dedication. This was a pattern in Enoch's life – his excellence was recognized everywhere he went."
>
> "After the war, Enoch entered political life and was elected a conservative legislator in 1950, quickly establishing himself as a prominent member of Harold Macmillan's government. Indeed, he was a rising star, and many touted him as a future prime minister. Alas, his infamous speech put a halt to that, and a temporary halt to his political career. It led to his

> removal from the Shadow Cabinet and ended his chances at higher office."

The man paused for dramatic effect.

> "But I will say this…"

He raised an index finger.

> "…and say it with the utmost confidence – Enoch Powell would have made an exceptional prime minister, and our nation would be on firmer footing today had he been one. He was eloquent and erudite – no one can say he was not. Not even his sharpest critics.
>
> "And despite his ostracism, Enoch was well aware the British people were behind him. By his own count, he received over 100,000 letters of support, and we all know, he was a conservative's conservative. Not prone to exaggeration."

Chuckles among the congregation.

> "In the ensuing years, Enoch turned his attention to other matters, but he never repented nor changed his views. He left the Tories in 1974 to join the Unionists in Northern Ireland. But it was a short spell, for unexpectedly, he returned to the immigration issue with a feverish passion. A passion we'd not seen prior. It was a remarkable transformation, and he confided in me that he felt a divine calling. As if he'd had a visit from God.
>
> "Enoch returned to his previous form with a singular dedication, and though he had many critics, he won the hearts and minds of the British people. Of that there can be no question."

> "I challenge you here today, and all the people of England – *heed his message*. They murdered the man. Don't let them murder his message. With your help, Enoch Powell will continue to shape our great nation.
>
> "As we bid farewell, let us honour John Enoch Powell not only in memory but in action. Let us embrace the courage to stand firm in our convictions and work toward a safer and more prosperous Britain.
>
> "Rest in peace, sir. We will not let you down."

The second eulogy was delivered by a family member, and she focused instead on Enoch's private life. She spoke of a kind and loving man who instilled in them a love of literature and a pride in their country and shared history. She recounted stories that showed a softer side, even touching on a comment made to his family the day he delivered *Rivers of Blood*.

> "I think I may have overstepped the mark today."

The audience laughed.

> "It was a light-hearted comment, more for our benefit than his."

She paused.

> "But he most certainly did *not* overstep that day. Enoch knew precisely what he was doing. Even in recent years, when people accused him of fanaticism, of losing his mind.
>
> "People doubted his sanity, but we never did. I will personally attest – his thinking was clear. He was as sane the day he died as he was in 1968."

She was fighting tears now.

> "Yes, he made apocalyptic warnings. Yes, he made fantastical claims of messages from God. I believed every word. His faith was as unfaltering as his unshakable loyalty to family, friends, and nation."

She choked out the final words.

> "We loved him dearly and we will miss him forever."

Applause among the congregation, far more than there'd been for the previous speaker. The vicar hugged her and resumed control, moving swiftly to the next phase. "We will now proceed to the cemetery for the committal. The family invites you to join them in this act of final farewell."

The congregation formed an orderly procession toward the cemetery for prayers, readings, and final committal. Pallbearers set the casket down, ready to be lowered into the grave. Friends and family placed flowers.

On the trek back, Jack found himself walking in step with Sheldon Cook and struck up conversation. Others joined. The congregation seemed in no rush to leave. There was reminiscing to do and stories to share.

Jack was slowly assembling the picture of Enoch Powell's final three years. After their infamous conversation at Stormont, Mr. Powell cast aside his South Down duties and embarked on a speaking tour. He called it a mission from God, and nothing could stop him.

The *Enoch of Old* was back. *Rivers of Blood* Enoch.

Establishment machinery was vehemently opposed and within a couple weeks removed him from office. He couldn't have cared less. The British nation, he said, must act swiftly and decisively. When asked for specifics, he wasn't shy about mentioning race.

The tour lasted several months, and by the end Enoch was anxious to re-enter politics. This time, back in London but not with the Tories. No sir. With a brand-new party. His own party which he dubbed *The National Party.*

It was anti-immigration and anti-communist. It embraced British sovereignty and national identity. The press called it authoritarian. *Fascist* even. Enoch didn't care. *Fascism,* he claimed, *was the best defence against communism.*

It wasn't smooth sailing. There was racial violence, clashes with *antifa,* and plenty of intimidation. Enoch marched on. For him, the threat was no longer speculative. Not some possible world. It was real. Jack had made it real.

Enoch went so hard and so staunch, many believed he'd gone insane. There were rumours he claimed he could see the future, and the press played them up. Jack found this rather amusing.

By and large, the people of Britain responded to Enoch's policies. They hailed his courage. They loved him in the manner MAGA loyalists love Trump. So much so, it appeared Mr. Powell had a genuine shot at assuming residency at 10 Downing Street.

Something had to be done. And something was. Enoch was assassinated. Shot point blank. As if the establishment said, *if we can't beat him, kill him.* It was widely rumoured to be an inside job – and Jack's visions provided hints. Jack couldn't be sure, but he'd have bet money Adam Stern – that rogue at the dinner table – was a key figure in the murder.

The funeral, as Jack could personally attest, was a profoundly moving event. But for a man of Enoch's stature, a relatively muted affair. Not a state or ceremonial funeral. No special session of parliament was convened. The body did not lie in state at Westminster for the public to pay respects. The government didn't want to draw attention to Enoch's cause, and it showed.

It was a similar dynamic with the newspapers. Obituaries acknowledged Mr. Powell's intellect, his eloquence, even his courage. But praise was always accompanied by condemnation – the words *hateful* and *divisive* were used frequently. The skewed coverage was so obvious, the public took umbrage.

By the time Jack departed the mourners, it was half-seven. What a day it had been. He'd seen so much. He'd *learned* so much. He was fascinated and delighted but not satisfied. He had to know more.

How did the assassination affect Britain's trajectory? In the *Alternate World* of course.

These little lab experiments never touched *Anchor Reality*.

Or so it seemed.

30. The Martyr

When the next vision presented, Jack wasn't startled. He was getting to be an old hand at this. This time, he saw modern-day London circa 2015. He could tell by the vehicles.

Momentarily, he entered the Time Tunnel, moving forward from 1977. He watched upheaval through the 80s, 90s, and into the 21st century. He saw Britain under attack from within and without. But he watched a different history unfold. A history where sacrifices large and small were made. And unlike World War I and II, these sacrifices paid big dividends.

Jack descended into an alternate version of modern London. At the corner of Bridge and Parliament, everything was in order. He saw familiar landmarks – the iconic Clock Tower, the Houses of Parliament, the charm and grace of Parliament Square.

It was springtime and the weather was pleasant. Jack was home again. He wandered the square in awe. He heard snatches of conversation, always in his mother tongue, never with some ghastly foreign accent. English as it was meant to be spoken.

He saw statues of Churchill and Sir Robert Peel. But wait...*what's this?* A statue he'd never seen – a statue of John Enoch Powell. It was the grandest effigy of all. This was a different world indeed. Jack noted other differences.

When he arrived at the south side, *my goodness*, the Gandhi and Mandela statues were missing. They didn't exist. Not here.

Evidently, the British saw fit to honour only their own. Or, perhaps in this version of the universe, Gandhi and Mandela never rose to prominence. Who could say? Of course, Jack would soon find out.

For now, he was content to take it all in. He scanned the skyline and noted the London Eye – *ironically* – was nowhere to be seen. It was a major landmark in Jack's era, and frankly not every Londoner's cup of tea. In this alternate reality, it didn't exist. London didn't need it or want it. Jack smiled at the realization.

Something else was amiss. Something significant, and it took a moment to pin down. *Everyone was white.* In modern London, that was unheard of. He was almost moved to tears. This was London as London was meant to be – the landmarks and people both.

This world was far and away the most different he'd encountered yet. If Winthrop's tome took a swipe at the nonsense, Enoch's actions took a sledgehammer. A wrecking ball. Here, common sense prevailed. Here, citizens could speak freely. Here, British men and women stood tall and proud of themselves and their nation, as they should.

My God, Jack realized. *The resistance meant something.*

But how did it all happen? Jack needed to know. He considered seeking out a pub and settling in. He had a feeling fate (or some version of it) might present the right people – perhaps another chap named Sheldon Cook.

Jack had a different idea. An *old school* idea. The library. Not for books, but for computer access. Why not? This was 2015 and the Westminster Reference Library was nearby.

Ten minutes later, he arrived with his state of wonder still intact. A friendly librarian greeted him: "How may I help you, sir?" She was fifty-something, straight from central casting – silver-rimmed glasses, silver hair in a tidy bun, an aura of quiet authority. Jack had no doubt she could navigate the stacks like a pro.

"I'm researching British history. Is there a computer I can use?"

"Certainly, sir." She had him set up in no time – *no library card, not a bother.* But the interface was different. Unfamiliar.

"Sorry, where is Google?" Jack asked awkwardly.

By the way she smiled, Jack knew it was a silly question. "We use *Discover*, sir."

"Ah right, sorry I've been out of the country. Could you show me?"

"Of course, here we are. It's AI-driven. Just type in your question and Discover tells you what you need to know."

"Brilliant, thanks very much."

Such a lovely interaction. And my God, they've got AI already. Ten years ahead of schedule.

The interface was ChatGPT-like. What a pleasant surprise. Jack had been primed for an afternoon of grueling searches and scanning of archives. Nope. *Discover* delivered answers on demand. And unlike the generative AI of Jack's era, this chatbot spoke the truth. No wokeness filters.

Jack unearthed a remarkable series of events. Enoch had courage, Jack knew that going in. But what the man did was the stuff of legend.

In *Rivers of Blood*, he pushed the anti-immigration message with reason and intellect. This alternate version of Enoch pushed the same message but added *religious fervour*. A zealousness to the point of obsession.

Because he was convinced of the moral urgency, he accepted no opposing viewpoint – not the slightest compromise. He dismissed counterarguments with guile and impressive persuasion:

> "Whoever is inflicting these horrors on Britain, we must purge them from our ranks. We must seek them out and destroy them. Who is opening the gates? Who is letting the barbarians in? That person is the enemy of Britain and we must excise them from all political function. And prosecute where appropriate. We need deterrence. Call out anything anti-British and fight it with all your will and worth. Otherwise,

we will lose our country and have no one to blame but ourselves."

This from a speech in parliament three weeks after meeting Jack. During his infamous tour, Enoch sharpened the message. He refined the rhetoric and oratory, and captivated audiences with emotion and force of will. He was on a sacred mission, and he acquired converts rapidly. A devoted following. The people found their collective voice and threw support behind the National Party.

Of course, the enemies of Britain also brought religious fervour – *or was it satanic?* They tried every trick in the book to ruin Enoch. They smeared him, sued him, and threatened him. He didn't care. He had an unwavering faith in his mission.

When asked if he feared for his safety, Enoch replied: "God put me on this path. If I didn't heed His wishes," he pointed skyward, "I would fear for my salvation."

Everything came to an abrupt halt on May 18, 1977. The assassination of Enoch Powell was the biggest news story of the day. England was in shock. The world was in shock. They caught the shooter – a liberal extremist – and an Oswaldian debate raged. Was he the real culprit? Or merely a deep state pawn?

But amidst the churn and spin, something remarkable happened. The National Party lived on. Enoch's second-in-command, a bright and fiery lad named John Smart took the baton and ran with it. Unlike modern-day England, where a traitor would have been planted to infiltrate and destroy, Smart was the real deal. A trusted patriot, with enough charisma to maintain momentum.

Before long, everyone was a National Party supporter. Slogans appeared and became rallying points. "A vote for me is a vote for Enoch Powell," was one of Smart's classic lines. Opinion polls showed they were working.

At campaign rallies, televised debates, grassroots events, Smart proved a compelling figure in his own right. His message was identical to Enoch's, and that was enough for the people. There was no internet and no social media – the public square was pubs and football pitches and watercoolers. Here, the people's support was galvanized.

If the goal of the assassination was to quell the movement, it backfired. Instead, it created a paradigm shift in the electorate. In the 1978 General Election, the National Party won in a landslide. In his inaugural address, Prime Minister Smart acknowledged he was a proxy for their fallen founder. "Enoch Powell was our one and only true leader and is forever a martyr for our cause. We will not forget him."

In time, the enemies that orchestrated Enoch's assassination were rooted out and prosecuted. The extent of their treachery was laid bare in a court of law. Adam Stern's connection was proven, and he was charged with high treason. He eventually died in prison at the age of seventy-four.

In this alternate world, Enoch Powell's name would live for eternity. He placed England on the path to salvation. However, an equally fascinating outcome was that the Nationalist spirit did not catch fire elsewhere in the global political landscape. Other nations tracked essentially the same path as in Jack's anchor world. America still went woke, and it appeared they got there even sooner.

Incredible.

This made for interesting dynamics on the global stage. For one, America was no longer a British ally. Nor Canada, Australia, and most of Western Europe. Nor Israel, ironically, a country essentially founded on British support as expressed in the Balfour Declaration of 1917.

Despite the UK's lack of Western friends, it remained a global power. They had no empire, and they didn't want one. They found allegiance with the *Chinas* and *Russias* of the world. Curiously, many of England's former colonies came to idolize and respect Britain, which made sense to Jack. People respect strength. That's human nature.

Jack went down a few other rabbit holes. Obviously, AI had already hit the mainstream (he was using it), and Britain was at the forefront. Indeed, Britain was at the forefront of a lot of innovation. The Saxon Man was proud again, sharing brilliance with the world, as he did centuries prior.

"Excuse me, sir." It was the librarian. "Sorry to bother you, but the library is closing in ten minutes."

Jack nodded politely and noted the time. *Ten to eight. Crikey, I've been at this nearly four hours, and I could go another ten. In fact, I could spend months dissecting the history of this fantastic version of Earth. Perhaps the disruption is a blessing.*

A thought dawned. *My God, I could live the rest of my days here and be forever happy.*

Of course it wasn't true. He could hardly desert Lily and the kids. Nor Ozzie and the lads. Nor England itself, for that matter, what was left of it. *To even entertain the thought.* A wave of guilt washed over him. And a hint of alarm. These were major changes. More invasive than anything Charles Winthrop did.

What if I've affected anchor time? What if I've disrupted the ecosystem?

The thought left him panicky. It was high time to head home. Time to see his kids. And Lily. Time to face the music. The grim reality of *actual* modern-day England.

Out on St. Martin's, Jack glanced about – a few pedestrians, a few vehicles. Even in his agitated state, he noted the lack of bollards and remembered again the lunacy he lived in.

Conveniently, he found a bench and settled himself. Relaxing mind and body came easily. Panic was replaced by calm. The sensations commenced – the weightlessness, the clarity, the bright light...and...*into the Time Tunnel.*

There were no visions this time, only an intense desire to go home – and the experience was different. To say it was a quick trip wasn't accurate. It was more teleportation than transit. As if he'd been instantaneously transported home. To his house. The master bedroom, precisely the place from which he departed what seemed an eternity ago.

Incredible.

Jack took inventory. Everything was in order. The framed family photo – Lily and the kids. The telly still on – he heard the posh voice of Downton Abbey's Matthew

Crawley going on about his inheritance, or some such thing.

He said a prayer of thanks. But what about the rest of the world? He snatched his phone and scoured several news sites.

Sigh.

The outside world hadn't changed, either. Newfordshire was still front and centre. Bloodworth, still PM. And *blast*, Liverpool still lost 2-1 to Aston Villa.

But what a trip it had been. An adventure for the ages. And if Jack had his way, there'd be many more. A thrilling sensation ran through him but was quickly shot down by more sensible thoughts. *For what purpose will I take these trips? Is it simply for my amusement? There has to be more.*

There must be!

Perhaps it's to learn, as he'd earlier surmised. *A laboratory to demonstrate how actions in the present trigger changes in the future.*

Jack wasn't convinced. There had to be more. This was a superpower.

Another realization hit. Jack wasn't tapping the full power. He was still an amateur, with much to learn. He drew a breath. *Patience,* he preached. And like magic, a biblical passage sprung to mind. The Book of Luke, Chapter 12, Verse 2:

> *Everything that is hidden will be shown, and everything that is secret will be made known.*

The passage came fully formed, and was apt. It was a clear sign. It had to be – a confirmation that this *gift* was indeed God-given.

31. Chaos in Newfordshire

The following day was a Sunday, and Jack relished the familiar routines of fatherhood. Finn and Lucy were noisy rascals, and as usual there was much shouting and squealing and banging. The telly was a Godsend, and sometimes the only way to temper the chaos while preparing one of his classic breakfasts.

Lily padded into the kitchen in her dressing gown, rubbing her eyes. "Mornin' love," Jack said cheerfully. "Perfect timing, coffee's brewed."

"I have the *best* husband." She smiled brightly and gave him a hug and kiss. "How are the little monsters?" She glanced in at the children with a grin.

"No tantrums to speak of."

"Yay." Lily raised her arms in celebration. "Here's to ten minutes of peace and quiet before the madness resumes."

"You're an optimist."

They shared a laugh, and the playful banter continued throughout breakfast. Once seated at the table, the giggling and antics ramped up between Finn and Lucy. Unless required, Jack and Lily didn't aggressively discipline their children. It usually wasn't needed, thank goodness.

With breakfast done, onto the next phase: "Alright you two. Football kits are laid out on your beds." He motioned upstairs. "Twenty minutes until we leave. And…*go!*"

They dashed off as if a race had been declared. The day was officially underway. Unfortunately, Jack had other things on his mind. He didn't make a habit of mobile use while with the family, but he'd had a glance or two at the news that morning. The statements out of Newfordshire were ominous.

> "All over the country, police are preparing for a contentious day of far-right anti-immigrant, anti-Muslim protests. Bristol, Belfast, Liverpool, Manchester, and London. But nowhere more than Newfordshire, where legions of protesters have descended.
>
> 'We're taking this very seriously,' said a spokesman for the Newfordshire Police. 'There's high potential things could take a turn for the worse, and we'll be ready if they do.'
>
> "Prime Minister Bloodworth didn't mince words: 'Police have our full backing to keep the streets safe and take whatever measures necessary to protect the public from those wishing to sow hate.'"

Later at Lucy's match, Jack chatted with one of the fathers, a fellow he'd come to trust. Together, they kept a watchful eye on the reports. During an hour of girl's football, the situation descended, as described in the latest from BBC:

> "In Newfordshire, we're getting reports of far-right protestors throwing bricks and bottles at police. There have also been clashes and skirmishes between the far-right protesters and anti-racism groups."

By end of game, joviality among the parents and kids was conspicuously absent. Parents from both sides were aware of the happenings across their once-peaceful nation.

With memories of Southport still fresh, the collective mood was sombre.

It continued on the drive home and young Lucy was perceptive. "What's the matter, Daddy?"

"Nothing, sweetheart. Daddy's just got a lot on his mind."

She pressed no further. By the time they arrived home, things had worsened according to the latest anchorperson:

> *"The situation in Newfordshire has deteriorated. Let's go to John for a live report. John?"*
>
> *"That's right Amy, things have gone from bad to worse here in Newfordshire. Prime Minister Bloodworth has promised to deploy hundreds more officers onto the streets, many in riot gear. He's vowed to do whatever it takes to preserve order."*

Raw footage of the melees looked horrific. Jack's picturesque hometown was like a war zone. He and Lily watched in disbelief. Ozzie was no doubt in the thick of it, and that multiplied their concern.

At half-four, Jack's phone lit up. *Ozzie.*

"What the hell is going on?" Jack demanded. "You okay, mate?"

"Oi, it's mayhem Jack." There was tremendous noise and chaos in the background. "They got us pinned in, the bastards. The Old Bill on one side, Muzzies on the other."

"Jesus. How'd that happen?"

"Don't know, brother. Started fine. By the time we arrived, we were a few hundred strong. We were feeling good, lots of the football lads, ya know. An' I told 'em, this is bigger than football. We have to come together as *Englishmen.*"

"Right. Then what?"

"Ah, we were peaceful Jack. We laid wreaths for the poor slaughtered wee ones. We said a few prayers. We're here to be seen and heard. To get our message out. No more!"

"Fair enough."

"The coppers started getting aggressive, herding us into the school grounds. And what do ya know, there's a troop of Muzzies waiting. And they're still bloody well there, the cunts. They got us surrounded."

"If there's a few hundred o' you, you'll be fine, right? Just wait it out, Ozzie." Jack was shouting, and Lily shooed the kids away.

"Ah no, mate. There's maybe thirty of us where I'm at. *If that.* And they're swinging bloody machetes at us. It's getting bad, man. It's getting real bad."

"Stand your ground, man. Common sense will prevail."

"I hope so, there's a bloody army of 'em, I tell ya. Armed to the teeth they are. And us, just everyday lads with families and jobs. *Hey fuck off, Osama.*" Ozzie yelled at top volume. "*You're asking for trouble.*"

The chaos continued to escalate, and Ozzie continued to curse. After a few more seconds: "Ah, they're throwing bricks now, the cunts. I gotta go, mate. Gotta defend meself, and the lads."

Christ, what a way to end the call.

"Is he alright?" Lily asked.

Jack shook his head. "Not really. I mean, if anyone can get out of this, Ozzie can. But it didn't sound good."

Lily gave Jack's shoulder a loving stroke. "Shall I put the kettle on?"

Jack shook his head and reached for the gin. Sometimes a cup of tea just wasn't enough.

32. Punishing Dissent

As the violence escalated, the media made it amply clear who the bad guys were – racist white Brits, of course. There was not a trace of nuance.

Prime Minister Bloodworth was done with the slaughter of young innocents. That was old news. The real problem was far-right hatred rearing its ugly head. At half-six, he went live on national television to deliver an Emergency Address:

> *"My fellow Britons, I come to you with a heavy heart."*

Lily scoffed. "I can't stand the sight of him. Such a ghastly man."

> *"There is no place for the despicable behaviour we've witnessed from the far-right today all over Britain, and in particular, Newfordshire. These heinous acts disrupt the lives of law-abiding members of the public, and they will not be tolerated."*

> *"We've watched them attack our fellow citizens in the Muslim community, and even our heroic police*

> *officers. They've destroyed property. They've set vehicles on fire. We even have reports of looting."*

Jack snorted in disgust. "What a load of bollocks. There was no bloody looting done by Brits I guarantee it."

> *"Make no mistake, the perpetrators will be held to account, that I promise you. These terrorists don't care about the children or the teachers. This is simply an opportunity to spread their message of hate."*

> *"We'll not stand for it. We'll hunt them down, and they'll pay dearly for their crimes. We've empowered police with the resources they need to stop this breakdown in law and order. And once we end this mayhem, we'll run our courts 24-7 if need be, whatever it takes. If we run out of prison space, we'll find more. Let this be a message to the British people. We're watching you."*

Holy fuck! A message to the British people? Jack was appalled. What an abomination. Ozzie and the lads did nothing wrong. They protested, as they have every right to. And they defended themselves.

"Do you think they'll arrest Ozzie?" Lily asked.

"I'd say they already have. If he's still alive, that is."

"Did you try calling?"

"Multiple times. Straight to voicemail." Sigh. "Nah, if he's not dead they've got old Ozzie locked up tight. You heard our fuckwit PM – pardon my language, darling – *we're coming for you.* You know who he's talking about. Indigenous Brits, especially the ones like Ozzie who haven't been tamed."

Lily started a response but pulled back. She was a dyed-in-the-wool liberal, like most white females, but she recognized the injustice.

"I'll tell you something else," Jack continued, "they're gonna lock poor Ozzie up for a very long time."

Bloodworth's ominous words kept ringing in Jack's ears: *We're coming for you.*

By 8:00 p.m., hundreds of arrests were touted, with more expected. Prisoners were remanded in custody in various facilities while they awaited sentencing. It wasn't the first time down this path for Britain – Southport was the blueprint. The media was happy to assure viewers that this time, the authorities had ample space to accommodate the influx.

This update from an Indian news anchor sent a chill down Jack's spine:

> *"We're getting reports of serious injuries to some of the protesters, and at least one unconfirmed death. We'll have more at eleven."*

They cut to a hastily assembled panel, a motley crew of far-left commentators. *Good Lord*, it was the DEI lady – Chantelle Williams – looking even more cartoonish if that was possible. Predictably, she was disgusted by the *abhorrent behaviour of the far-right racists. England has always been a nation of immigrants*, she declared.

Jack felt sick. She was an imbecile. An insult to the British public. Jack turned the telly off and headed for bed, where Lily was there to comfort him, thank God.

33. Update From the Lawyer

The following day, Jack worked from home and the word *work* was used loosely. The newspapers were in *name-and-shame* mode, publishing mugshots of as many white British men as possible. There were hundreds, practically all family men. Working men. Heart and soul guys. Jack could tell by looking at them. It was treachery of the highest order.

Try as he might, Jack couldn't find Ozzie's son Bryan. On the other hand, Ozzie's mugshot was front page, his expression defiant. God love him.

Not long ago, Jack had respect for journalists. Politicians, too. Such naivety was long gone. They were no better than criminals. Cartel members.

As Jack grimly scanned the faces of his brethren, he received a call from Ozzie's lawyer. The man got straight down to business. "Mr. Campbell, Oswald Fletcher requested I contact you. First of all, he wants you to know he's fine."

"That's good to hear, thank you. Where is he exactly?"

"He's been remanded in custody. They're holding him in a temporary facility in Newfordshire."

"There's no prisons in Newfordshire."

The lawyer chuckled mirthlessly. "I'm afraid there are prisons everywhere these days. They'll repurpose anything. This particular facility, I'm told, was once a fish processing plant."

"Whittington."

"Whittington?"

"It's the name of the plant."

"Ah righto. Well then, there's talk of moving Mr. Fletcher to Thameside. Nothing confirmed, mind you."

"You can't get him out on bail?"

More chuckling. "No chance, I'm afraid. This government seems rather determined to make an example of these men. Oswald's case is particularly grim. He's accused of assaulting a police officer."

"I call bollocks."

"It's in their report."

Jack snorted. "I still call bollocks. They hate Brits. That's the only reason he's locked up."

"Ah right, yes. Well...be that as it may, we should focus on the details at hand."

"Agreed."

"Oswald has a court date scheduled for Monday week. We'll see how it goes, but I wouldn't get your hopes up."

"Can I visit him?"

"I'm working on that. I'll be there tomorrow myself. Hopefully we can tee something up for Wednesday or Thursday. He's requested you come."

Jack nodded forcefully. "Once I get the green light, I'm there. Let him know."

"I shall."

"Oh, one more thing. What about Ozzie's son, Bryan? I couldn't see his name in the arrests."

There was a long pause. "Yes, well. I'm afraid young Bryan – this is not good news Mr. Campbell. I'm afraid he was beaten rather badly. He was rushed to Merseyside and pronounced dead on arrival."

Jack gasped. It was too much to bear.

"Oswald doesn't know this yet."

"He'll be devasted," Jack barked. "It'll kill him. Bryan was the light of his life."

"Yes, it's a very difficult situation. Very sad. I'll have to share the news with him tomorrow."

Jack said nothing. He was processing the atrocious news.

"Look, I'll be in touch to confirm visitation details."

"Thank you."

Jack sat in stunned silence. Ozzie was an easygoing lad. He rolled with the punches and never got too bent out of shape. Except when it came to traitorous politicians selling out his ancestral homeland – to that, he took exception. But this was a different kettle of fish. Ozzie was facing prison time and his favourite son was dead.

Jack was at a loss. He had to talk to someone. He couldn't bear this on his own. He thought to ring Lily but found himself dialling Steady Eddie. "They've got Ozzie locked up."

"I see that." Eddie's tone was sombre.

"You gonna say I told you so?"

"No, Jack. Not at all." Despite differences, Eddie was immensely fond of Ozzie. "I may disagree with him. I may even think he's off his trolley sometimes. But he doesn't deserve this."

"They're saying he hit a copper."

"Is it true?"

"If he did, it was self-defence. I promise you that."

"I don't believe it, either. He's not one to lash out violently, unless provoked."

"And then, of course, all bets are off."

"Ah, quite right."

"There's more bad news, I'm afraid."

"Oh goodness." Eddie paused.

"Bryan's dead."

"*What?*"

Jack explained what little he knew. "I still can't believe it. It's so...*unfair*. He was so young, so full of life."

"He really shouldn't have been there, but he didn't deserve to—"

"He wanted to go, Eddie. He was nearly twenty years of age. Basically, a grown man."

"Ozzie had influence, I'm sure but..."

"It's such a nightmare."

"This could kill Ozzie, too. Bryan was his golden boy. You could see it in Ozzie's face whenever he talked about Bryan."

"Jesus, prison may kill Ozzie. From what I hear, he could be in for a long stint."

"Will you visit?"

"Definitely. I'm going this week. Wednesday, I hope."

"I'll have Ruth check on Ozzie's ex. And his other lad...what's the name?"

"Jonathon." Jack wiped a tear. "Yes, I should call Jonathon. I'll do it after I see Ozzie."

"I don't envy you."

"I don't envy Ozzie."

They agreed to gather at the pub the following day with a few of the lads.

34. Sad Times

Jack took the entire week off. He needed to digest the horrors, from which there was no escape. The media cycled the story 24-7. The newspapers published editorial after editorial, bashing far-right *Nazis* and calling the Newfordshire *riots* a disgusting display.

Jack knew in his heart it was bullshit. Tuesday afternoon, he popped into the pub to see Eddie and the lads. The mood was sombre, but as pints flowed boisterousness increased. Ozzie was a legend, and there were many stories and passionate speeches about the grave injustice of locking him up and killing his kid to boot.

Some of the younger lads took turns holding court, telling stories of young Bryan, and Jack learned a thing or two about Ozzie's youngest. Bryan was a chip off the old block, so he was. And now gone forever. A tragic loss. And these poor young lads, they never knew England when it was still *England*. They'd been living their entire existence in the ruins of a once great society.

Despite the bravado, there was an air of impotence about the gathering. Here they were, angry and justifiably so, but neutered against the powerful machine intent on their destruction. A fresh wave of sadness hit. At least Eddie was respectful. He didn't make a single critical statement about the circumstances. Perhaps he sensed his lefty views might not be well-received.

That evening, Lily prepared a classic English feast – roast beef with crisp roasted potatoes, Yorkshire pudding, veggies galore, and boatloads of gravy. Fit for royalty.

"In honour of Ozzie," she announced. Ozzie wasn't always her favourite – he tended to offend females – but after all these years she genuinely loved him.

"Where *is* Uncle Ozzie?" Finn asked. Both children sensed something strange had happened and were on best behaviour.

"He's gonna be busy for a while."

"How long?"

"Ah, we're not sure yet."

Finn started another question, but Jack cut him off. "I'm visiting him tomorrow. Maybe you two can make him a nice card, yeah?"

"We will," said Lucy.

Jack turned to Lily. "The dinner's delicious, darling. I wish I could take a plate for Ozzie. Guess I'll just have to tell him about it." He laughed a little too hard at the small joke. He was putting on a cheerful air and it wasn't easy. Bryan was gone and Ozzie may never again see the light of day. Things were bleak.

Later that night, with the children off to bed, Jack and Lily attempted to enjoy a peaceful night. They left the telly off. They sipped tea. They chatted. They read their books. Jack had planned to tell her about the *time travel* thing. It was, after all, a rather significant development, and she ought to know about it.

He hated secrets. Good or bad, he tried to share everything and he'd vowed to tell her. But the Ozzie tumult sort of took over. *Not tonight*, he reasoned. *Wait 'til after I've seen Ozzie.*

He felt another pang of guilt.

35. This Thing is Real!

Wednesday arrived and Jack rose early to see Lily and the kids off. He hugged them a little tighter than usual. The recent events were taking a toll. He promised Lily he'd be back by bedtime. He told her he loved her repeatedly, same goes for the kids. His emotions were off the charts, but he'd get them under control. He had to. It was a day for Ozzie.

The lawyer had no updates on the court date, and Ozzie hadn't been moved. Evidently, the system was moving slower than anticipated. At least the jailhouse visit was still a go. It was scheduled for 2:00 p.m., so Jack had time to kill before hitting the highway.

He brewed more coffee and casually perused the news. The usual shite, but a headline mentioning Enoch Powell caught Jack's eye. It was a garden variety *Enoch Powell was Wrong* piece, written by someone with a non-British name.

Lovely.

It went on to excoriate Newfordshire rioters – *rioters, says the lying cunt* – and compare them to relics of a dark and distant past. Then Jack read the closing line. "Since Enoch Powell's death on March 10, 1987 he has..."

Wait just one second!

Jack Googled Enoch Powell and...*there it was*. Wikipedia reported the day of Mr. Powell's passing – March 10, 1987. Same as the bloody article. It wasn't a typo, nor an error. It was a fact. The great man died March 10, 1987.

But the date was wrong. At least wrong in the world Jack grew up in. In that place, Enoch Powell died February 8, 1998. There was no trace of doubt in Jack's mind.

He scanned the Wikipedia entry and spotted another error.

> *Powell returned to Parliament in 1974 as an MP for South Down in Northern Ireland but served less than one year due to personal reasons.*

Bullshit.

That's not what happened. The man served until 1987. What the hell is going on? Cause of death – he unexpectedly passed away in his sleep of unknown causes. *More bullshit.* He died of complications due to Parkinson's Disease.

Yet, that was not the case.

Not anymore.

What is happening?

Was Jack in a different world? No. This was his world. Exactly where he was supposed to be. But his world was different now. How different? Jack had no idea. But insofar as Enoch Powell's life was concerned, *very* different.

This obviously had everything to do with Jack's Stormont visit. Jack noted further inconsistencies. After 1974, Mr. Powell's life was entirely different. He went back hard on the immigration soapbox. He made attempts at *Rivers of Blood* glory but never achieved the same prominence. Was that *actually* true? Hard to say. Wikipedia wasn't the most trustworthy source.

Regardless, I changed the man's life. I changed his place in history.

Curiously, everything else about Britain seemed essentially the same. Maybe the differences were too subtle to notice? A new thought struck like a lightning bolt. *What about the writer, Charles Winthrop?*

Jack scrutinized that man's Wikipedia page and it took effort to find discrepancies. He'd already confirmed *The Great Replacement* was never written, but he never did study the page in detail. Sure enough, he found something.

It was the writing – the body of work. It was markedly less political. Instead, he found a plethora of Sci-Fi novels. On the cover of one, a leading-man caricature held what looked to be an iPhone.

Incredible.

In Jack's old world, Winthrop wrote political thrillers. However, the dust jacket of one novel proclaimed: "From the prophetic master of tech wizardry and social commentary…"

My God, Winthrop had become a different guy writing in a different genre. I changed his life, too.

What else had changed? How could Jack begin to assess? This was a disturbing discovery, and an exciting one. He was shaking with nervous energy.

He checked the time – almost ten. *Bloody heck Nora, time to hit the road.*

36. How Does It Work?

Jack navigated his 7 Series onto the motorway. Springtime in England meant a little of everything weather-wise. Rain, cloud, wind, even the occasional ray of sun. The adage *four seasons in a single day* was apt.

At the moment, rain poured down in a great deluge, and Jack resolved to take his time. No rush. It was a two-hour drive to Newfordshire, and he'd allowed ample slack. The countryside was beautiful as ever, as were the ever-quaint towns and villages along the way. Jack scarcely noticed.

He had too much on his mind, and for the moment, it wasn't Ozzie. This *power* he'd been bestowed with – this *time travel* gift. It had become a lot more *real* in a hurry. He wasn't playing anymore. This was serious business and Jack tried to wrap his head around it.

Let's start with the obvious – I get visions. They come outta nowhere, powerful and full of detail. Then, through some bizarre glitch in the matrix, I'm magically transported to a past world, where I'm an active participant.

I can bring things, like my phone or money. I can also bring things back. A new thought emerged: Can I bring people? The mind-bending logic escalated, and he gave his head a shake. The whole notion was insane. Yet it was happening. It was real. I enter this Time Tunnel thing and simultaneously assume a new state of consciousness.

The entry has nothing to do with mirrors – contrary to earlier thoughts. So, what is the trigger? Hard to say. Hard to name. I just go into Time Tunnel Mode. It happens magically. Everything's heightened several orders of magnitude – my knowledge, my intellect. And I seem to keep that intellectual horsepower throughout the entire adventure, which is bloody convenient. My IQ shoots up at least fifty points. I speak with clarity on so many issues. And not to brag, I'm no dummy to start with. Heck, maybe even my physical abilities are extended.

Perhaps I'm just unlocking what I already possess. What's that thing Einstein said – we only use ten percent of our brain. I've heard that's rubbish, but who knows?

Coming back through the Time Tunnel – now that's a trip, especially the stops along the way. I get to see effects of my actions. I witness monumental changes in – what shall I call them – Alternate Worlds. Possible Worlds. Hypothetical worlds. Like the impact of Winthrop's epic tome. Or Enoch's martyrdom saving Britain from woke madness and mass immigration.

What are these places? Simulations? Or are they real? Just as real as my own Anchor World, but sitting in some other plane in the multi-verse of infinite dimensions?

Crikey, that's deep! For now, I shall think of them as lost alternate timelines. Fragments. Fascinating, yes and perhaps real for the people in them, whoever they are. But for me, ultimately meaningless. They might as well be dreams.

I only care about my own world. My Anchor World.

And the visions – do they determine where I go? So far, yes. But is that written in stone? Maybe they're only possibilities. Suggestions. What about spontaneity and free will in the Time Tunnel?

And what of Anchor Time itself? Anchor Reality. I can change those fake Alternate Realities – that's easy. I can change them massively. Anchor Time, however, that's a different cup of tea. Heck, until an hour ago, I thought changes to Anchor Time were impossible.

Evidently, not true. However, changes to Anchor Time were certainly less pronounced. Perhaps harder to achieve? Harder to control? A litany of questions sprung forth.

There is but one actual reality. That's my working assumption. And that reality is right here – me driving up the M5 to visit Ozzie on a rainy Wednesday. 12:27 p.m. on June 4, 2025.

And Anchor Time – or Actual Time – moves forward linearly. These I will consider immutable facts. They have to be, right?

So what happens to Anchor Time while I'm off gallivanting in the past? Evidently, it stands still. Does that mean I'm getting free time? As in, I could spend a month in the 1970s and come back not having aged a single minute?

That doesn't make sense. Then again, aging a month while time stands still doesn't make sense either. Maybe this so-called Time Travel happens entirely inside my own head. But that can't be. I've changed lives. Case in point – Enoch and Charles. This thing's definitely happening in places outside my own cranium.

Of course, the changes to Anchor Reality are limited. Maybe Enoch tried to be the big hero and got shut down? Quite possible. History books, as usual, would be unreliable narrators.

Perhaps the disruptions I introduce cause changes that are hyper-focused on the person's life, while the world around them seeks to stay the same. Interesting. Not a bad working theory.

And what of the resistance? The sickness I feel? I'm guessing it happens precisely when changes are being made. The more I feel, the greater the change.

Interesting.

When I became deathly ill with Enoch Powell, perhaps that's when I was tipping the scales of Anchor Time.

Deeper questions lurked.

What if I spoke to my father before I was born? Or to an earlier version of myself? Jack had read enough Sci-Fi to know these were paradoxes and they were dangerous, at least according to the writers.

What if I died on one of my adventures? Would I die in the Real World? Would the old wives' tale come true – die in your dream, die in real life.

Ah, so many mysteries. So many enigmas. Some instinct told Jack it was best to give the paradoxes a wide berth.

Thus far, there'd been no great price to pay for his shenanigans, and he preferred to keep it that way.

In this regard, something else was on his mind. Perhaps the most profound question of all. *What is the source of this special power? Is it divinely bestowed? Or some random act of science and nature?*

For Jack's money, it had to be God-given. And with that assumption, he felt a great burden – a responsibility – to use the power wisely and fairly. He was a Christian man, after all, raised in the Church of England. A believer.

Then a new spine-tingling thought slipped into his head. *What if there are others? The likelihood of other time travellers must be high, yeah? Why would it be just me? Surely there are many of us time travelling interlopers.*

Again, Jack acknowledged, some mysteries may never be solved. *It's a learning experience. I can't be an expert all at once. I've taken three trips so far, and there will be more, and I shall experiment and learn.* He smiled at the thought of it.

Alas, he would ponder further another day, because presently he was entering the outskirts of Newfordshire. Time to operate in the Real World. Time to focus on Oswald Fletcher and the evil regime now running the nation of his heritage.

The town's salty air triggered the usual blast of nostalgia. The rocky cliffs to his left dropped hundreds of feet to a pristine beach where waves crashed all day every day and would for eternity. Jack and his family spent many a pleasant summer day at that beach. Carefree times – swimming, exploring, picnicking.

The town hadn't changed much, really. It was still the epitome of Englishness. Even the people were the epitome of Englishness. It was one of the few pristine hamlets left.

But it was only a matter of time.

37. The Fish Plant

Whittington was once Newfordshire's pre-eminent Fish Processing Plant, employing a sizeable percentage of the townsfolk, including Jack's own father and grandfather. Jack himself even worked there for a spell and was familiar with the facility's layout. The plant had stood idle the best part of two decades. Until now that is, when the tyrants running the once-great nation of Britain found a new and grotesque purpose for it.

Jack pulled up to a makeshift security gate at the entrance to the car park, and a female guard quizzed him on the purpose of his visit, and a lot of other pointless nonsense. Once parked, he endured a similar ordeal at the main entrance. He was also searched, and they took temporary possession of his iPhone and wallet. *The bastards.*

With recent events, rumours had reached fever pitch in the town of Newfordshire, and the goings-on at Whittington were top of the list. Some speculated over fifty men were being held. True or otherwise, the waiting room wasn't exactly packed – eight souls sat quietly, anxiously awaiting their turn.

Wouldn't you know it, Jack saw someone he knew. He couldn't go anywhere in Newfordshire without that happening. People from small towns know the phenomenon well. Mrs. Walker was one of his primary teachers, a lovely lady, and he nodded a polite hello.

Was small talk appropriate? Mrs. Walker jumped in without hesitation. "Jack Campbell, so nice to see you. You must be wondering what I'm doing here." Evidently, she was embarrassed. "I'm afraid my son got caught up in the...you know...the troubles," she announced.

"I'm very sorry to hear that."

"He's never seen a spot of trouble, Jack. Not since he was a wee lad." She wiped a tear. "Now he's a grown man with a family." She let out a small sob. "It's been very hard for all of us."

"I understand, Mrs. Walker." Jack reassured her and summarized the reason for his own presence. The conversation drifted to more pleasant subjects, which suited them both. Momentarily, a prison guard stepped in and called Mrs. Walker's name.

"Nice catching up, Jack," she said, minus the twinkle that usually accompanies such a remark.

Jack glanced around. No one seemed eager to make eye contact. Without their mobiles, they were left to their own thoughts, and the thoughts were not pleasant. When Jack's mind wandered back to *time travel* and his *special powers*, he scolded himself. *This is about Ozzie.*

That's when the vision hit.

And it hit like a freight train, the images as palpably real as the day is long.

London. Late 1990s. A night on the town.

Crowds of people circulating – mixing, mingling, smoking, conversing. Pubs galore, the vibe youthful and buzzing. The people were diverse, but more in the fashion than the racial sense. Non-whites were sprinkled about, but sparingly. The dominant variations were in style and dress, with a host of eclectic forms represented. Mods, skinheads, yuppies. Techno-freaks, Rastafarians, house clubbers. Even the odd transgender.

They mixed easily with each other. There was no tension. It was like a scene from a David Attenborough documentary. It wasn't all kids either. In England, forty and fifty-somethings enjoy a night on the lash as much as youngsters. And speaking of kids, some of the girls were shockingly young. They could not have been of age, though British culture didn't take age restrictions seriously at that time.

Then Jack saw them. A throng of Pakistanis, four or five. Lurking. The vision morphed unexpectedly. A much smaller English borough, a scale model version of the nightlife presented earlier. A muted version of the London scene – less people, less glamour, less diversity. Still, undeniably British. In fact, all the more British.

Again, there they were. The same Pakistanis. Loitering, leering, staring. Totally out of place. Foreign. A glaring discontinuity in the landscape. They spoke to each other in their native Urdu, but a British voice soon rose above.

Oi, keep an eye on that bloody lot. You know what they're up to, the Paki paedos. Everyone knows.

With that, the vision terminated. Jack was back in the waiting room. He darted his eyes to-and-fro. Some of the people were staring at him. He drew several breaths to calm himself.

What did those visions mean? And whose voice was that? It was vaguely familiar.

Jack didn't have time to ruminate, as the guard popped in and called his name.

Time to see Ozzie.

38. Prisoner of War

Jack followed the guard down a familiar corridor, passing an entrance to an area once known as the Cutting Room. Where the dirty work was done. A few doors down, another entrance, this time the former Packing Room. The guard entered a code on a keypad, and a sturdy steel door magically opened.

Substantial renos had been done. The area, once an open concept, was partitioned into a maze of cells. In the entryway, a second guard consulted his tablet and asked several questions. He executed another rudimentary search of Jack's person. "Sorry, sir. Protocol."

Jack offered no resistance.

"He's all clear. Prisoner's in 17A."

"Very good," said Guard #1. "Right this way, sir." Nice to see British civility alive and well in the facility. Into the maze they went, and before long the guard was unlocking 17A. "You have 45 minutes."

Jack entered and there sat Oswald Fletcher. He'd been in lock-up three days and was looking worse for wear. He needed a shave. His eyes were bloodshot. His clothes, rumpled.

"Blimey, look at the state of you."

"Bout bloody time you showed up." Ah, Ozzie was still Ozzie.

Jack grinned. "I came as quick as I could."

Ozzie smirked. "Did you walk up from London, then?"

Jack's grin widened. "Where's your prison garb?"

"It's on order. They didn't have my size. Or my colour."

"How are you, Ozzie?" Jack came in for a hug, which Ozzie gratefully accepted.

"They told me about Bryan."

"I know, mate. I know." Jack gave Ozzie's shoulders a manly squeeze. "Can't imagine what you're going through."

"Neither can I." Ozzie chuckled mirthlessly. "It's a lot."

"I just wish there was—"

"Bryan was my boy..." For a second, it appeared Ozzie may burst into tears. "He was the one for me."

"I know, Ozzie. Bryan was something else." It was all the more horrid considering Ozzie didn't care for his older lad. *A libtard,* he called him. "If there's anything I can do."

"No, mate. I gotta get..." his voice caught. "Gotta get through this on my own. I've thought about giving up. Thought about that a lot."

"I wouldn't let ya, mate. Not on my watch."

"It's not easy, especially with all this..." his voice trailed off.

"Let's see what happens." They were speaking of Ozzie's legal woes. "For now, you keep on bloody going. One foot in front of the other, even if it feels like you're dragging a boulder."

Ozzie nodded firmly. "I won't give up. I wouldn't let Bryan down like that. He died fighting for his country."

"He did."

"He's a hero in my books, and I'll keep him here forever." Ozzie pounded his chest.

Jack nodded approvingly. "He'll always be a hero. That's his legacy."

"Will you make bloody sure he gets a good sendoff?"

Jack gestured emphatically. "It shall be done."

"Sorry I'm gonna miss it."

"Me too." Jack drew a deep breath. "How are you, Ozzie. Y'know, otherwise?"

"Ah, never better."

"Right."

"Suppose I'm in a spot of bother, am I? A bit o' barney, yeah?"

"That's what the lawyer says."

"Fire that man. Get me a better one." The old Ozzie – the feisty take-all-comers – was still there, but Jack could see it was a struggle. The mirth in his eyes was absent.

"Take me through it, Ozzie? I mean, *good Lord*, what the hell happened the other day?"

"You know we're being monitored?"

"Oh shit."

Ozzie nodded at the camera and grinned. "One of the guards told me they're watching but not listening. Don't know if I believe the plonker." He shrugged. "That's okay either way, I can tell ya."

"Keep it above board, mate," Jack cautioned.

"Fuck them, what do I care? What're they gonna do to me? They already killed my kid."

Jack frowned. Unfortunately, there was a lot they could do to him.

Ozzie leaned in close and lowered his voice. "We did nothing wrong. We were well-meaning patriots, that's all. I tell ya, the camaraderie was brilliant. All for one, one for all. That alone was enough to piss off the pricks." He shook his head. "The rozzers had it in for us. You could feel it."

Jack nodded.

"We didn't start anything. We were just protesting. Yeah, we want our fucking country back. What of it? We've every right to protest that murderous rampage. But yeah, the Old Bill made us out to be racist hooligans from the start...provoking us, just looking for a scrap."

"Then what?"

Ozzie was whispering now. "Some of our lads pushed back, verbally. Nothing wrong with that, yeah? Then they start threatening us, shoving us, herding us around. Before ya know it, we got fucking Muzzie bastards on one side and coppers on the other. Was getting hairy, mate. I mean, we had numbers, but those Pakis were swinging bloody machetes. Not a bother for them, ya hear? We tried to stick together, but the coppers got in amongst us, and a few of the lads got separated from the pack."

Ozzie rubbed his eyes. "I saw one poor lad, Willie Blackmore's kid if you know 'im. The Pakis laid a beating on him. Happened to a few of us. Including–" his voice broke. "Including Bryan. I didn't see it, thank heavens."

Jack shook his head. There was nothing to say.

"Yeah mate, we didn't stand a chance. And the goddamn PM – Mr. Blood-On-His-Hands, the treasonous rat – he made his orders. Anything we did – anything I did – it was bloody self-defence. We were fighting for our lives. By the end of the day, what I hear, gangs of Muzzies with swords and machetes were roaming about looking for English people to fuck with."

"Jesus."

"I only wish I could've protected him." Ozzie let out a small sob, and for a few moments broke down entirely. When he gathered himself: "Bryan had his whole life ahead of him. It's not fair." He slammed a fist on the table. "It's not right what they're doing to us."

"No, it's not."

"It's a travesty."

Jack nodded.

Ozzie sighed deeply. "I'll be alright, mate."

"I know you will."

"Guess I needed to get that outta my system."

"Course you did." Jack nodded and switched gears. "What's the latest from your lawyer? Any news?"

"My court date's Monday. Old fucking Bailey."

"Whoa."

"Yeah, mate. They're pushing me to plead guilty on a whole heap o' shite."

"What's the lawyer say?"

"Every option he gives me sounds terrible. If I plead guilty, I get fucked. Go to trial, I probably get fucked worse. I can kiss my life good-bye."

"Wait and see, mate. Never forget, you're innocent. You did nothing wrong."

"You think that matters? They're gonna railroad me no matter what."

After that weighty declaration, they sat in silence for a spell. "Why's it like this?" Jack asked. "My God, why are they so traitorous?"

Ozzie scoffed. "God only knows, mate. But I tell ya, the people in charge have one job." He lowered his voice further. "Destroy Britain and its people."

Jack nodded meekly. He'd heard it all before.

"I know Muzzies charged years ago, and the courts still haven't gotten round to 'em. They're out walking the streets."

Another nod.

"I used to say *they can't put us all in jail.* Suppose I was wrong, yeah? Christ, look at this place." Ozzie leaned back in his chair and for a split second, looked like an old man, beaten and withered. "I don't know what's ahead of me, Jack. I never expected much outta life. Never expected a knighthood for Christ sakes. *But this?* Facing years in prison."

"Steady on, mate. They haven't condemned you yet."

Ozzie scoffed, louder this time. "Y'know the outfit I been working for?"

"Yeah."

"They ditched me. That's another charming bit o' news from the lawyer."

A firm knock and the guard poked his head in. "Five minutes, lads."

Ozzie nodded toward the door. "He's one of the good ones. Leastways I think so."

It's so unfair, thought Jack. *The entire machine's coming down on poor Ozzie.*

"They say I'm radicalized," said Ozzie, as if reading Jack's mind. "Bollocks. I'm de-programmed, that's all. I see the world as it is. I'm no bloody criminal. I'm a patriot whose had enough."

"Always shocks me that police follow orders in these situations."

Ozzie nodded. "Not that surprising. They gotta put food on the table. In fairness, you're no better, Jack. You sell your soul to the corporate world."

"Ouch."

"Pfft." Ozzie made a dismissive gesture. "Don't sweat it. I understand, mate. You'd be in here with me if you'd come along."

"It's bullshit, Ozzie. You're a political prisoner, no doubt."

"Prisoner of war more like it."

"The next phase is public shaming," Jack joked. "Then of course the show trial."

"Something to look forward to," said Ozzie grimly.

Another knock. "Wrap it up, lads."

"Time's up." Jack stood and nodded. "I'll check in with your lawyer. I'll be back to see you soon."

"Will you now?" Ozzie said it with a grin. He was putting on an air of confidence, bless him.

"Damn right." Jack stepped forward. "Now give me a hug, ya muppet."

The moment they came together, the familiar surge ran through Jack's nervous system, with vastly more force than usual. Then the weightlessness, the clarity of thought, the bright light.

My God, I'm in the Time Tunnel.

And he was.

Traversing time and space, observing historical events, perceiving them in infinite detail.

However.

This time.

He wasn't alone.

He had an arm draped over Ozzie's shoulder and he glanced over at his best friend.

Ozzie was staring back as though he'd seen a ghost.

39. The Stowaway

"What the hell's going on?" Ozzie's eyes were wide with fear.

"All is well, Ozzie." Jack smiled calmly. "We're going on a little trip."

"What the fuck, Campbell? You're scaring me."

Jack motioned toward the passing imagery. Boris Johnson talking shite about Brexit. Theresa May calling a snap election. David Cameron waxing on about an immigration cap – the usual lies and hypocrisy.

Everything playing out in high fidelity, and Jack perceived everything with perfect understanding. Incredibly, he was also able to focus on Ozzie.

"Can you not see that?"

"What the devil are you talkin' about? I see nothing."

"It's all around us, mate. It's England. It's our history."

"What're ya talking about? I see you. Beyond that I see nothing. Nothing at all. Where the fuck are we?"

"Where do I begin?"

"Just tell me, mate."

Jack went straight to the point. "This is gonna sound crazy, but we're going back in time, Ozzie."

Scoff. "Pull the other one, mate. It's got bells on."

Jack observed the latter stages of Tony Blair's horrid Premiership, a traitorous war criminal is how Ozzie described the man. Simultaneously, Jack pressed on with the explanation. "I've been bestowed with this power."

"What the hell did you say? *Back in time...*"

"Hear me out. I'm in earnest. This is really happening, Ozzie. At the moment, we're in a *Time Tunnel* travelling back in time. Sit back and enjoy the ride. We'll soon be hanging out in 1990s London. You hear me?"

"This is crazy, mate. Are you on drugs?"

"No, mate."

"Am I on drugs? Did you slip me something?"

Jack laughed. "This is better than drugs."

"How do you do it?"

Shrug: "I switch my mind off and something takes over. Some force. Some sort of gift from God. I had no idea I could take someone with me."

Ozzie was aghast. "How long you been doing this?"

Jack smiled. "Not long. This'll be my fourth trip."

"Can you go into the future, too?"

"Geez I don't know. So far, no."

"And what happens while we're uh...gone? What's happening, y'know...back in that godforsaken Fish Plant?"

"Nothing's happening there."

"Nothing?"

"Nothing at all. While we're gone, time stands still."

"Jesus."

"Yeah."

"Why didn't you bring me back before?"

"Didn't know I could."

"So you didn't plan this?"

Jack shook his head. "I had a sense something was coming." Trying to explain the visions would be too confusing.

"And we're going where?"

"London. 1990s."

"Are we gonna be in our twenties?"

"Ha, I wish. No mate, we are who we are. Forty-somethings."

"Where've you been so far? Or should I say when?"

Jack grinned widely. "I've had some grand adventures. Spent time with one of your heroes."

"George Best?"

"No, mate. *Enoch Powell.*"

Ozzie's jaw dropped. "Fuck off."

"Oh yeah."

Ozzie was blown away. "This is insane, mate."

"I know."

"So, did you tell him he was right? Did you tell him bad things are now?"

"I told him all that."

"And he couldn't...uh...like uh..."

"Change the future?"

"Yeah, why didn't he uh...."

"It's complicated. Ozzie. I'm not totally sure how it all works."

While Ozzie ran that through his noodle, their journey in the *Time Tunnel* continued, as did imagery from historical events. Jack zeroed in on the 7/7 bombing. My God, there'd been so many horrors, he'd almost forgotten about that one. Three bombs in the London Underground, then a fourth on a double-decker at Tavistock Square. Fifty-two dead. Hundreds injured. Life-changing injuries. Amputations. Burns. The attackers? Three Pakistanis and a Jamaican. Islamic extremists inspired by al-Qaeda.

Jack glanced at Ozzie. Evidently, he was starting to accept the time travel premise. He was getting used to the idea.

"They can't hear us talking now, yeah?"

"No, mate. You may speak freely. Whatever's on your mind."

Ozzie sighed happily. "Whatever the fuck this is, I'm mighty glad you got me outta that place. I was going stir crazy."

"I bet."

"Sitting there all day every day."

"This is like a day pass."

"And whatever renos they've done at Whittington, I swear to God, there's still a smell o' fish in the air."

Jack laughed.

"Tell ya something else. Going back in time – that might be the only way to fix things in Jolly Old England. We're too far gone, mate."

"We'll see," said Jack.

"Nah, mate. Even Orwell never dreamed this shite up. We can't even fight back. I tried and look what happened. They locked me up and killed my kid, the bastards. Now they're arresting anyone and everyone for mean tweets."

"They've certainly removed the mask."

"*Pfft*, even a sniff o' resistance is rooted out. It's full totalitarian. The technology lets 'em reach down and squash dissent like a bug. They're gonna squash me, Jack. I've come to accept it."

"Wait and see."

Ozzie waved him off. "My life's done. And what do I care, they killed my boy."

Jack shrugged.

"I just wish there was a way we could fix it," Ozzie said wistfully, then laughed out loud.

"What's so funny?"

"I was about to say, *I wish we could turn back time.*"

Jack laughed. "We're going back to the 90s, mate. But I can go back as far as I want."

"Yeah?"

Jack nodded confidently, though he wasn't entirely sure he could. "We've a lot of heroes in our past."

"Mr. Powell, for one."

Jack nodded. "And—"

"Don't you dare say Winston Churchill."

"I won't." Grin. "I was in 1968 recently and I told a roomful of politicians he was shite."

"Get out of it."

"Called him an obese drunk. Said his legacy was rubbish."

"Which it is."

"Not if you ask Eddie."

Scoff. "People like Eddie have blinders on." Ozzie mimicked a pompous tone. "*Just ignore the dystopian hellscape all around us.*"

Jack chuckled in appreciation. "He lives in a bubble, no doubt."

"I'd love to meet a guy like Cecil Rhodes," Ozzie declared.

"Your Uncle Chester knew him, right?"

"Too right. I tell ya, they had something special down in Rhodesia 'til the bloody commies took over." Ozzie pondered that for a split second. "We could go back a hundred years and hang out with the fellas in charge of the Empire."

"Make it two hundred to be safe," Jack added.

"They were the glory days for us Brits. Gets me a little sentimental to be honest."

"Not you, Ozzie."

"It happens." Big grin. "Don't tell anyone."

"We've got glory in our future, mate."

"I hope you're right."

"We just need courageous men. Great men willing to risk everything."

"I'm a great man." Ozzie puffed up his chest.

"Why don't you run for office."

"Well, besides the fact that I'm in lockup, we'll not be voting our way out of this mess. Even you know that."

"What about Reform?"

"Fuck Reform. Just more goblins and ghouls. We need a bloody revolution."

"You just said revolution's not possible."

Ozzie sighed, and they sat in silence. Jack watched recent history pass. It was way more fun sharing *time travel* with his best friend. Ozzie was sound as a pound, he was.

"This *time travel* thing, assuming it's real...and I'm not saying it is." Ozzie guffawed. "But are we there yet?" In the tone of a youngster in the back seat.

"Soon."

Journeying through the Time Tunnel with Ozzie certainly had a different vibe. But indeed, they were almost there. The *destination vision* abruptly flashed – the streets of London, the same voiceover. It suddenly dawned. *That was Ozzie's voice.* How did Jack not know? The exit moment was near, even Ozzie sensed it. Jack took him by the arm. The street was in view as was the pub – *The Highgate*. Jack zeroed in and they descended gracefully.

May 31, 1997. Saturday night on the town.

Glorious.

Crowds of people mixing and mingling. Vibrancy in the air.

A sense of fun and frivolity. Not a trace of angst or danger.

All the same characters – the mods, the skinheads, the punks, the ravers, the Rastafarians. The young, the old, and almost entirely – the white.

Almost.

Ozzie was chuffed. Grinning ear to ear, wider than Jack had ever seen, which was saying something.

"This beats the bloody Fish Plant."

"You're still there, technically."

"Whatever." Ozzie's grin didn't dampen. "You, mate, are the absolute guv'na."

40. Vigilante Justice

They were on Portobello Road in Notting Hill, an area Ozzie and Jack had once frequented. They were slightly underdressed but fit in well enough. Thank God Ozzie hadn't been issued prison garb. Out of habit, Jack reached for his mobile and...*oh no, the guards took it.* Such an empty feeling.

He accepted the temporary fate. Heck, no one else had one. Correction, a few did. *Actual* phones. No internet, no social. Texting wasn't yet widespread, but it was catching on fast.

This was clearly a different era. A lighter, happier time with more smiles and joy in people's faces. They spoke to each other. Women dressed more modestly. When you did see skin, it wasn't marred by tattoos, though that was also ramping up.

"Look at all the white people," Ozzie said, grinning like a madman. Jack watched him take it all in. To be among your own was a soothing experience. It struck deep to the core.

Nonetheless, Ozzie adjusted quickly. "Shall we hit the boozer, then?"

"We shall."

"Follow me, mate."

They waltzed in like they owned the place. The Highgate was busy enough, but they found a table. Coincidence?

Somehow, things always worked out for Jack on these junkets.

Or do they? *What about money?* Jack reached for his wallet, but it wasn't there. "I don't suppose you've any cash?"

"Oh shit."

Jack scanned his pockets and what do you know, he retrieved a crumpled ten-quid note that somehow evaded the search. Issue date, 1974. He passed it to Ozzie with a grin.

"Brilliant mate. Where'd you get that?"

"One of my recent adventures. Think they'll accept it?"

"They have to, it's legal tender." He was grinning ear to ear. "This'll cover us for awhile. Beer's cheap as chips in 1997."

"In that case, grab a couple pints, would ya?"

"Aye aye, Captain." Ozzie strutted off, a man on a mission.

What a joy. I must bring Ozzie back more often.

Jack marvelled again at the flamboyant styles. This was the London he missed. Eclectic but not sketchy. Nor dangerous. It was iconic Britishness, but unfortunately, Britishness in decline. The glowing embers of a once-raging fire.

As if to emphasize the point, Jack spotted them. A throng of Pakistanis lurking and leering from a nearby alcove. As much as Jack trusted the visions, the scenario took him by surprise, such was the overwhelming bonhomie he'd been feeling. His goodwill took a dent. These men represented a discontinuity. A blight on the Britishness of the tranquil scene.

A flash of nausea washed over him. It came straight out of the blue. *What the heck?* Nothing to do with the Pakistanis, right? It passed quickly, thank God. Ozzie was on his way back, pints in hand.

"I know the bartender."

"Get out."

Ozzie nodded. "He didn't recognize me, o' course, but I had a bit of fun with him."

"You didn't say anything stupid I hope."

"Who me?"

Crikey, was that the source of the nausea?

Jack had little time to consider further because Ozzie noticed the foreigners, and a snarl replaced his grin. "Look at these chancers. What the fuck are they doing here? The bastards shouldn't be on British soil, much less in this pub."

Jack nodded, his mindset cast back thirty years, when resentment of unwelcome newcomers was still expressed in some quarters. At the time, grooming gangs were in full force. They'd set up shop all over England, but the horrors weren't widely known, and coverups were in full swing.

Jack and Ozzie knew, though. They had a modern-day perspective. "Look at the wretched cunts. Loitering, just like they loiter outside our schools."

Jack tried to diffuse the situation. "Let's not ruin our night, mate." Jack held up his pint. "Cheers to the good old days."

"Ah right, cheers mate." Ozzie gulped a few swallows. "But these wankers, they're the bloody end of the good old days."

At that moment, a gaggle of girls wandered through the vicinity. Impossibly young and cute. They didn't check ID much in those days and these lasses were almost certainly underage.

With the Pakistanis, it was classic predator-prey. The main fellow was a handsome specimen, with perfect hair and the gift of the gab. He was probably thirty, and in no time flat, was chatting up the youngsters. He zeroed in on the tall blonde. Not the best looker of the bunch, and she was clearly enamoured with the attention. Ripe for the taking.

The handsome fellow draped an arm across her shoulder, while one of his buddies snapped photos. Some of the girls moved on, but this chap was possessive of the blonde. He fawned over her.

"That's how they do it, mate," Ozzie whispered. "They butter 'em up, gain their trust. Then they drug 'em and the nightmare begins." He scoffed loudly. "The Quran permits all of it."

The waiting room vision flashed in Jack's frontal lobe, and a distant memory came to the fore. There was backstory in Ozzie's family. A cousin in Rotherham. Lured in at sixteen years of age and passed around the rape gangs. She was never the same and the poor girl eventually succumbed to drugs.

Ozzie spoke of it seldomly. A mention here and there over the years. It had faded from Jack's memory, only to resurface this very moment. Ozzie's ire was up. His protective instincts on fire. He wasn't about to stand idly by.

"How about we deal with these fuckers, yeah?"

Jack wasn't sure. He wasn't a big fighter, he had a more gentlemanly leaning. More inclined to discuss a solution than impose one through violence. Ozzie, not so much. He wasn't gonna let this go.

"I'm gonna wipe the smirk off that bloke's face."

Jack took stock. They were outnumbered five two. However, they had the element of surprise. These arrogant foreigners knew in their hearts an Englishman wouldn't dare challenge them. And they weren't big men. In a fair fight, Jack and Ozzie would probably wipe the floor with them. But if they produced weapons. Knives. Even guns. *Shit!* It was a possibility. Perhaps, a likelihood.

Ozzie was throwing caution to the wind. He never lacked courage. Once in motion, there was no stopping him. He took a few bold steps. "Oi mate, she's a little young for you, yeah?"

The looks of surprise quickly morphed into amusement. Then irritation. Imagine a Brit challenging us – an old fella to boot. They exchanged jokes with each other before the leading man, arm draped over the blonde, replied cheekily. "What's it to you, gammon?" He spoke English fluently. Second generation, apparently.

Ozzie ignored the slur and stayed on point. "You're a disgrace, mate. That's what it is to me."

More arrogant laughter, but also a posture of aggression. He removed his arm from the blonde and faced Ozzie. "Look at this ancient prick. You're too old to be messing, mate." The Muzzie's friends laughed uproariously.

"I don't need your help," the blonde added, throwing her hat in the ring. "You can just leave us alone."

"Aye love," Ozzie spoke tenderly. "You don't know what you're mucking with. You want no part o' this lot."

"Oi fuck off, ya chalky prick. This bird needs a real man." He made a lewd gesture, and the blonde thought it hilarious. "Just pay your bloody taxes and watch your bloody football. We'll take care of the ladies, yeah?" Another lewd gesture. "We know what they want."

Ozzie smiled a reckless smile, aimed first at the Pakistani, then at Jack. "You believe this guy?" He spoke threateningly. "I've never seen such a vile specimen in me life. I think he needs to be taught a lesson, yeah?"

Ozzie's working-class roots were showing. He was dropping his Ts, a real Tommy Robinson brogue.

"Oi, bruv, look at the bloody gammon. He's right fuming. He's changing colour." Laughter. "Looks like a full English breakfast to me, mate."

"Funny stuff, lads. Good times, yeah?"

The Pakistani tapped his watch. "Isn't the football coming on, bruv? Time to sit your fat ass down, yeah?"

Ozzie turned to Jack. "Cheeky sods, aren't they?"

Jack nodded. His own ire had also risen, and he spotted a glimmer of fear in the supporting cast. Jack was a big man, and Ozzie was clearly crazy. Amir, the lead man, was still spouting off.

"Hey old man, we're taking your country and your girls, yeah?" He pinched the blonde's ass for emphasis, and she squealed with bawdy delight.

"Don't think so, mate." Ozzie said it with unnerving deliberateness and stepped into the man's range. "I don't think you've got what it takes." It was a dare.

"Don't try me, bruv." He tapped his coat pocket, indicating a weapon. "You'll get more than you bargained for."

"Aye, you're right, mate." They were eye to eye. "Be a real shame if someone got...*hurt*."

On that final word, Ozzie tensed neck muscles and lashed forth with a vicious headbutt. It was an ugly thing to watch. Amir's prodigious nose was gutted. Broken and bloodied. Forever mangled. He crumpled like a ragdoll and would not soon recover.

"That's for the kids in Rotherham." Ozzie stood over him, glaring, then focused on the others. "Who's next?"

The companions were rattled by the turn of events but recovered quickly. The largest one withdrew a menacing machete and began waving it. "Now what do you say, gammon."

The blade was eighteen inches – essentially a sword – and would cause devastating injury, even dismemberment, which wasn't unheard of in London. Ozzie took a step back, but his reckless grin didn't falter.

However, with all eyes on Ozzie, Jack had surreptitiously circled the cluster of Pakistanis. He wasted no time once he saw the weapon. He came in hard and fast from the periphery and delivered a surgical sucker punch to the temple. Lights out for that fella.

Two down, three to go. But the remaining men lost their nerve. With terror in their eyes, they entered victim mode. "Help, help, help," one of them yelled hysterically. "They're attacking us. Help."

"Calm down, ladies," Ozzie said.

The confrontation – the headbutt, the sucker punch – had taken all of ten seconds, but was enough to attract the attention of bargoers. The bartender, too, who was frantically waving for a bouncer.

Ozzie was a barfight veteran and knew well it was time to scarper. But this time round, he pulled a new trick from his sleeve. He flipped over the barely-conscious Amir and nicked his wallet.

Ozzie's grin remained wide and menacing, but his thinking was clear. He grabbed Jack's arm. "Let's skedaddle, mate. Before the coppers turn up." On the way out, he feigned a charge at the Pakistanis. It was a taunt, but they fell for it. Their whimpering was music to Ozzie's ears.

A few patrons protested, especially the females. Typical cucks, Ozzie reflected as they made their getaway. Before shit hit the fan, they were in the back seat of a black cab headed for greener pastures.

41. On The Lash

They rode in silence for several blocks, with Ozzie regularly glancing back, presumably to see if the police were in pursuit. Jack eyed him with a mix of shock and awe.

"Did you really need to take his wallet?"

Ozzie made a *shush* gesture and addressed the driver. "Turn that up, bruv. Haven't heard this one in a while." Boombastic by Shaggy.

"No need to tell the driver, yeah?" Ozzie grinned, "I reckon we need the money, mate. If we're gonna party."

"Is that what we're gonna do?"

"Why not?" Ozzie withdrew a stack of bills from the man's wallet. "Well, I'll be damned. This chap was loaded."

"Oh, bloody heck. Now we got assault *and* robbery."

"Don't worry, mate. We're all clear. And that filthy fucking bastard, I woulda pissed on 'im if I'd had the time. Sometimes you gotta play dirty. I learned that a long time ago. Even in rugby."

"Well…"

"I wanna have a few pints, mate. Don't take that away from me."

"You fucked up that bloke right and proper, Ozzie." Jack was raised a gentleman. He favoured fairness. The English way.

Scoff. "You wanna feel sorry for these cunts, go ahead. But you're condoning gangrape. That's why they were there, you know as well as me."

"I suppose."

"Hey man, we saved some girls tonight. And we took out a couple predators. If that's not cause for celebration, I don't know what is."

"You really messed up his face."

"Look who's talking. You KOed the big chap right good yourself."

Jack grinned. "He had a bloomin' sword."

"Oi mate, you fancy a drink or what? A little trip to the rub a dub for a pig's ear?" Ozzie was itching for a night on the lash.

"Yeah?"

"I reckon we should."

"You think that pub had cameras?"

"Ah, you're wreckin' me head, mate. We did what we did. They've no shame or remorse. Why should we?"

"You're right."

"Course I am, and it did me good. I had a fair amount of pent-up anger."

"I noticed."

"That's the way to deal with these bloody foreigners. Vigilante justice. We'd not be in the state we're in if we'd 've smashed 'em to pieces from the start."

"That sounds rather harsh."

Ozzie waved Jack off. He was a happy man. Happier than Jack had seen in years. It was as if his heart had grown three sizes.

"Where we going?"

"Don't worry, mate. I'm taking you for pints. I've a few places in mind." Again, Ozzie flashed the wad. "My treat. I'm paying for the ride, too." Ozzie's enthusiasm was contagious.

He directed the driver down several side streets in the heart of Soho. No Google Maps available, or needed. He paid the cabbie and added a fifty-quid note. "Wait here for us, Shaggy. We're not done with you, mate."

"Aye, boss," the Jamaican said with a happy grin.

With Ozzie at the helm, they visited a handful of pubs, making fast friends, soaking up nostalgia, and knocking back pints. Brits were not known for acts of physical affection, but Ozzie was hugging everyone in sight, including Jack.

They were six pints deep and feeling no pain when they made it back to Shaggy, their journey just beginning. Their next destination? The East End of London. Shoreditch. It was still gritty and post-industrial with abandoned warehouses and factories. But gentrifying fast. Becoming hip and cool, with clubs and nightlife. It was Ozzie's old stomping ground, and he was primed.

For Jack, however, something had come up and it wasn't good. *Nausea*. It came on slowly at first, and he attributed it to the booze. He'd been matching Ozzie pint for pint, which was never smart. By the time Shaggy dropped them, it was clear something else was going on.

Ozzie was oblivious. He paid the driver. "Hey bruv, you gotta fag for me? I'll make it worth your while."

The Jamaican obliged. "Take the whole packet. I'm trying to quit."

"Me Dad always told me, don't be a quitter. Thanks, guv'na." He handed over another bill and glanced at Jack. "You right, mate? You look a little green around the gills."

"Not feeling well."

"Nothing another beer won't fix, yeah? Follow me, mate."

Jack complied and attempted to pull himself together. *Was it the resistance?* He took in the surroundings. This was Ozzie's turf but there was something familiar about it. A vague memory he couldn't quite access. *What happened to my superintelligence?*

"You brought me here before?"

"Bloody right, mate. You were playing rugby with the big boys that year. I showed you how to party like a true Brit."

The memory rushed back. Jack had gotten drunk that night and he and Ozzie bonded. They got on famously straight away, despite the age gap, and the class gap. Jack was a nineteen-year-old upper-crust newbie. Ozzie was a veteran blindside flanker from the East End. They spoke the common language of rugby and had been best mates ever since.

At their first stop, Jack was still fighting the sickness, and it had taken on new qualities. A pain in the head, dark thoughts, a deep foreboding. Ozzie was not so encumbered and wasted no time acquiring pints and striking up conversations. He drained his glass in minutes and, noticing Jack barely touched his, he drained that one, too. Then ordered another.

"You're still green, mate. Follow me, we'll get some fresh air," he motioned to his cigarettes. "Then I got a surprise for ya."

Jack sensed things were not going well. Were they entering dangerous territory? If so, he had no idea how to stop it. He was powerless. Ozzie was driving the bus.

They walked while Ozzie smoked, Jack getting sicker by the minute. The nausea, the dark thoughts, a weird and horrid déjà vu. He scoured his memory but came up empty. The sickness was affecting his intellectual capacity.

Meanwhile, Ozzie maintained a running dialogue. "My people come from East London, mate. Back in the day, nothing but working-class 'round here. Cockney accents. That's what me Dad told me, and me Dad's Dad. Crikey, it looks pretty good here and now, too. Not like where we come from, yeah? Kebab shops and brown people. It's been a complete ethnic cleansing. Disgusting."

Jack tried to take in the surroundings. People milling about. A happy vibe. A more conservative crowd than Notting Hill.

"There she is, mate," Ozzie announced.

Jack spotted a sign but couldn't make it out.

"Come on, Jack. The Gilded Whistle. I took you here back in the day. I owned this bloody pub."

An intense foreboding flooded Jack's nervous system, as if he'd been possessed. "I d-d-don't...I d-don't...."

Ozzie regarded Jack peculiarly. "Relax, bruv. I got this. You sit for a while." Nothing was gonna stop Ozzie.

"When w-w-were we h-h-here?"

"The nineties, mate. Maybe, '97?" Ozzie's face lit up. "Blimey, I just had a thought."

Jack winced as fresh pain flooded through him in crushing, relentless waves. The sickness was seizing him, consuming his entire body.

"Stay here, mate. I'll check back soon. I'm gonna have a look." Ozzie was off to the races. For him, it was all a great lark. Old times. A celebration.

Jack cried out, but no sound came. He was too...*compromise*d. Something was way, way off. *Oh my God, what if Ozzie encounters his earlier self?* Another fierce stab of pain. *Jesus, what if he encounters an earlier version of me?*

This sickness was at a new level and Jack was powerless against it. The foreboding and darkness were overwhelming. His heart thumped madly and he struggled mightily to breathe.

Jack limped over to a quiet spot and parked himself on the curb. He might've passed out otherwise. As it was, consciousness was fading.

Something unprecedented was taking place.

42. The Paradox

Jack was paralyzed by the sickness, and he was entering a new state. A state in which he could detach from himself. Elevate outside his body, watch events unfold, including visions of his past self. And Ozzie's.

Indeed, they'd been at this pub in East London on approximately this date and time. An elite rugby event. That's how they met. Was it precisely this night? What were the odds?

Ozzie had this in mind from the start, the daft prick. The idea of visiting old friends, that alone was close to the mark. But to visit his former self. If Ozzie's forty-something self meets Ozzie's twenty-something self – it would be a paradox of the highest order. If a young version of Jack was there, too.

Oh my God.

This was bad. Very bad. Somehow Jack knew it. The worst possible paradox. And if Jack's present state was any indication, it was probably happening. It surely was.

He regarded his present self, slouched on the curb, sick and panicked. He sensed the nausea, the pain, the darkness plaguing mind and body. Yet he was detached. As if he'd passed out from the resistance. Passersby gave him a wide berth, surely suspecting he'd had too much to drink.

Then things went completely awry. A few raindrops, a gust of wind strong enough to rattle windowpanes. A strange electricity in the air as temperature and pressure dropped. Jack felt it in his bones. His chest and throat tightened. His heart hammered now, and a cold sweat dripped down his neck.

The storm swept in rapidly. Sudden, violent, and highly localized. Wind and rain pulsed like a heartbeat. Streetlights flickered and hummed, lightning and thunder filled the sky. People ducked for cover.

Not Jack. The storm outside was mirrored by a great storm inside himself. He cried out in torment, *what in God's name is happening? What is Ozzie doing? Is he killing me?*

Whatever was happening, the universe was acutely opposed. Was Ozzie affected by any of this? Or immune? Perhaps it only affected time travellers.

Jack held on for dear life as sheets of rain soaked him to the skin. After what felt like an eternity, the rain slowed and the wind settled. Jack was back in his body, his function slowly returning. The pain, the sickness, the nausea – all blessedly lifting.

Meanwhile, people were filing out of the pub. They were alarmed and panicked. Jack scanned the crowd and Ozzie appeared in the distance. At first a shadowy figure. He was running toward Jack full throttle. He too was panicked and fearful. "Jack, Jack...oh man, oh man..."

"What happened?" Jack tried to stay calm. "What did you do?"

"I didn't do anything. I just, I just...oh man, oh man, oh man..."

"Tell me."

"*I saw us.* I mean, I saw you and me, mate. The younger version of us. There we were, with the other lads. Having a pint, having a laugh."

Just as Jack feared.

"It blew my mind, mate. And I was so buzzed, I figured why not have a word, yeah? And then...*oh man.*" He paused to catch his breath. "I was making me way toward the group, then I don't know exactly how or why, but things started happening. Strange things. The lights were acting up. The music, too. Some weird technical glitch or something."

"What'd you do then?"

"At first, I ignored it. Kinda laughed it off. People were kinda smiling at each other, as if to say *what's this all about?* I kept moving, I mean, I was getting close. I was like ten feet from – you know, *us*. Ready for a grand old time. I was keen for it. Then you – *the younger you* – looked straight at me. We made eye contact. And then..."

"Then what."

"Oh fuck, the eye contact was like a lock. I couldn't break it. It was like you were staring into my soul. It freaked me out, mate." He shook his head. "And then...oh man, this is really fucked..."

"Tell me."

"Man...everything went insane. The whole place starts shaking. Bottles tipping off shelves, was like a bloody earthquake. But you – *the younger you* – kept your eyes locked on me. Like some sort of trance. I finally forced myself to break it, then I see the *younger me* – oh man this is so eerie – he was looking at me, too. Locked in on me."

"Oh no." Jack winced.

"There's more, mate." He swallowed hard. "The chaos kept getting worse. It started feeling dangerous, like something supernatural, like in a horror movie. People were panicking, rushing for the exits. I figured I better do likewise. But then..." Ozzie frowned and shook his head.

"Then what."

"I looked back..."

"And?"

"Jesus Jack, I looked back and I couldn't see *us*. I saw the others...but you and me. We weren't there, mate."

"Maybe we left?"

Jack shook his head. "Don't think so."

"Fuck Ozzie, this is a proper mess."

"I was just trying to have a laugh."

"Yeah well..."

"Let's bugger off, mate. I mean, I think maybe I, uh...messed with the universe. Not in a good way."

"You think? *You think?*" Jack's head was clear now, though there was still a hint of nausea.

Ozzie hung his head. "Maybe I wasn't thinking."

"I tried to stop you."

Ozzie nodded. "I know, I ignored you. You were messed up, mate. That should've been my first clue."

"Bloody hell, Ozzie, you left me there."

"Look, we can talk more after. Right now, I feel like we gotta get outta here." Ozzie was spooked. "Let's find Shaggy. Or any old cab'll do. Let's just get outta here."

Jack rubbed his temples. The foreboding was gone, replaced by a real and tangible fear. *What has this done to Anchor Time?* They found another taxi and Jack instructed the driver to head for City Centre.

"What were you thinking, Ozzie?"

"Don't know mate. Guess I was just determined to see what I could get away with."

"When you uh...made eye contact? Tell me more."

"Ah man, do I have to." He hung his head. "It was proper weird mate. Uncanny."

"Tell me."

"It was like *the younger you* was possessed. Like he was seeing something...and chaos was happening all around. Flashes of light, bottles crashing, people panicking. But he was locked on me, mate."

"You weren't supposed to go near the young you and me. You know that, eh?"

"Suppose I do now."

"I haven't been doing this long, and I'm no expert. But that's what's called a paradox. And your bloody shenanigans might have royally fucked up the timeline."

"You should've stopped me, mate."

"I was dying, Ozzie, case you hadn't noticed. I get this sickness. I think it's when changes are happening...you know, to the universe. The bigger the change, the worse the sickness."

"Jesus, mate."

"You didn't feel anything? Nausea, weakness, strange thoughts?"

"Nothing."

Jack pondered the implications. *Christ, that could come in handy one day.*

"Did it rain while I was in the pub? You're drenched, mate."

Jack ran fingers through his rain-soaked hair. "Yeah it came down in buckets. There was chaos outside, too. A freak storm like nothing I've ever seen."

"Blimey. Wish I had a towel for ya."

In spite of himself, Jack grinned at Ozzie. He was such a pure soul.

"I'm sorry, chief. Didn't mean to be a messer."

Ozzie didn't seem to grasp the gravity of the situation. And who's to say Jack did? He was worried sick, nonetheless. There was the unspoken fear of losing his...his...he couldn't bring himself to even think it.

"This is amazing, Jack," Ozzie proclaimed. "The whole experience. Not just seeing our old selves – *I'm gonna leave that alone* – but being back here, when England was England. It's something, man."

Jack nodded. "It's powerful stuff, mate. Takes you back, not just to the memory, but *the feeling*. They were glorious days, Ozzie. Bygone days, unfortunately."

"I felt it deep in here." Ozzie pointed to his guts. "Thanks for bringing me, mate."

Jack grinned. "Don't mention it."

The exchange brightened Jack's mood, but apprehension still lingered, and Ozzie sensed it. "It'll be fine, Jack. Don't worry."

They turned onto Parliament and the Palace of Westminster came into view. Jack tapped the driver. "Drop us up here, mate. Ozzie, pay the man."

On the street, people went about their business. It was Saturday evening and there was a festive vibe. But not for Jack and Ozzie. They'd had their fun. It was time to go home and Jack dreaded what they might find. He was frightened. You might say terrified. And doing his best to hide it from Ozzie. *And himself.*

Ozzie was apprehensive for altogether different reasons. In fairness, his worries were nothing to sneeze at. He was worried for his future. For his freedom. He was dreading being locked up again, possibly for a very long time.

"Not sure I wanna go back, mate."

"We have to."

"What if we don't?"

Jack didn't know the answer to that question. "We have to."

"They're threatening to throw me in with the Muzzies and the blacks."

"Fuck off."

"They play dirty, mate."

"Sorry Ozzie, we have to go back."

"I know. I'll be fine." Ozzie was still drunk and suddenly became emotional. "No matter what happens, I love you man."

Jack looked at his best friend sincerely. "Love you too, brother." He draped an arm over Ozzie and gave him a good manly squeeze. At that instant, the vision appeared. *Whittington.* Formerly, Newfordshire's pre-eminent Fish Processing Plant. Currently, Remand Centre for Brits deemed excessively patriotic.

The vision didn't startle Jack. He'd been expecting something. He'd been *hoping* for something. He acknowledged the vision and humbly accepted it. Presto, they were in the *Time Tunnel* hurtling through space and time, familiar scenes flashing past. A tinge of anxiety sprinkled over Jack's usual calm.

He had no desire to examine passing events, to marvel at history. His only desire was to be home. He desperately missed Lily and the kids. He was worried sick about them, to be honest. The Time Travel machinery seemed to sense his mood – and adjust for it. The transit was more teleportation. There wasn't even time for Ozzie to ask questions.

Jack spotted the Fish Plant and the descent began. It would be the first time Jack would return somewhere other than his master bedroom.

This time, it was a prison.

Or was it?

43. What Now?

Jack and Ozzie landed at the entrance to Whittington. Not inside Ozzie's makeshift cell. Not even inside the facility. It was mid-afternoon, precisely the time Jack had been visiting. Jack surveyed the car park. It was deserted. No security gate. No guard. Just a whole lot of nothingness.

"What the fuck, mate?" Ozzie asked.

They peered inside the glass doors. No front desk. No prison guards. Nothing.

"What the fuck," Ozzie repeated. "Are we in the Twilight Zone?"

Jack sighed. "We might be."

"Looks like I'm a free man," Ozzie declared and did a celebratory dance. "Woohoo, brilliant."

For Jack, though, it was *not* brilliant. It sent a chill down his spine. It was proof his worst fears were not flights of fancy. They were not only possible, they were – to be frank – *likely*. Panic struck.

I need to see Lily. I need to see my kids. Need to see them now. Oh God, oh God, oh God.

"You alright, mate?"

Jack was pacing maniacally.

"*Jack.*" Ozzie seized him by the shoulders. "Calm down."

"Do you realize what this means?"

"What're you on about?"

"Don't you see what's happened? *We've changed everything,* Ozzie. You're not in that prison." He pointed at the facility. "That's not even a prison. Everything's changed."

"What do you mean, *everything?*"

"I mean everything." He emitted a wail of despair. "Hell, I don't know exactly. Shit, how the hell would I know? I don't even know if *we* exist in this place anymore. I mean we're here, but are we supposed to be? I have no idea how bad this is."

"You mean like," Ozzie hesitated. "like...what about Lily and—"

"*I don't fucking know, Ozzie.*" Jack cut him off. He didn't want to voice the possibility. Give it life, give it agency. And so, he buried his worst fear – that in this alternate timeline he might not be married to a beauty named Lily and that he might not have two sweet kids named Finn and Lucy.

Correction. This is not an alternate timeline. This is Anchor Reality. This is where I live. And there's no fixing this.

To think they may have jeopardized their own existence made Jack's head hurt. And his heart. And his soul.

Why oh why did I not warn Ozzie? Why did I not rein him in? I knew to stay away from paradoxes. Ozzie did not. I should have seen this coming.

For the hundredth time, he scolded himself and despair overwhelmed him. He looked around. He looked at Ozzie, who looked back with concern and sympathy.

Jack ignored it. "How we gonna get outta here?" He realized their immediate predicament. They were stuck in the middle of nowhere.

"How far's the town centre?"

"A mile and a half down the road."

Ozzie nodded. "Your parents? They could probably help us."

Another tangled web. Another dagger to the heart. *Would Mum and Dad know me? Do I still exist for them?* He'd consider that later.

"I don't think so."

"Why not?"

"Because I said so."

Ozzie raised his eyebrows. He wasn't used to Jack snapping. "Anyone in Newfordshire that could help?"

"No, mate. We've got to make our way to London."

"Right then. I don't suppose you've your car tucked away somewhere." It was meant as a small joke, but Jack wasn't playing.

He pointed at the empty car park. "You see my fucking Beamer?"

"Perhaps an Uber?" Ozzie pushed back with another joke.

"Yeah, dial one up on your mobile, ya fucking numpty."

"Sorry, mate." Ozzie held both hands up. "No phone."

"Yeah, me neither. No phones, no ID, no car. *Nothing.*"

"I have that Paki's wallet."

Jack nodded. "How much money left?"

"Few hundred, maybe."

"Right. We've enough for train fare."

"Where's the station?"

"Same as the city centre, mate."

"How we gettin' there?"

"Shanks' pony, mate. Follow me."

Off they went, Jack still soaking wet. Ozzie hungover and confused, but thankful for his freedom.

44. Things Aren't What They Used to Be

On the train, Jack attempted to dry his clothing in the loo, with limited success. He'd find new duds in London. Eventually. Other things were top of mind.

Meanwhile, Ozzie ordered them both tea and biscuits. They were famished, especially Ozzie who was feeling the effects of the alcohol. After eating, he promptly nodded off. Typical Ozzie.

Jack found a copy of the Newfordshire Telegraph and studied it eagerly. Nothing on the recent slaughter. Nothing on the riots. Not a mention. Clearly, none of it happened. Not in this world. Right? Jack sighed deeply. It was indeed an altered reality, but it *was* reality. And Jack had best get used to it.

An hour into the trip, he got his hands on a day-old copy of the London Times and zealously searched for clues on...on what, he didn't exactly know. He found nothing to give him peace. The news was *same old, same old*. Bloodworth still Prime Minister. London still a mess. Wokeness, DEI, migrant invasion, and the general degradation of Britain, all still in full vigour.

So, the country's still fucked and as an added bonus, now my life's fucked, too. Nice work, Einstein. You're a time travelling genius. A moment later, Jack scolded himself. *You don't know your life is fucked. Lily and...*he couldn't finish the thought. *Just wait and see, yeah? Wait and see.*

Jack put the paper down and rested his forehead against the cool glass. He studied the reflection staring back at him, and his breath soon fogged up the window. He sat back and watched the countryside drift past – fields and farmhouses and rural England. Everything beautiful and quiet and peaceful. A green and pleasant land.

Periodically, he poked Ozzie when the snoring got out of control. They passed through towns with familiar names. People got on and off the train. The closer they got to London, the more crowded the carriage became. And the more non-white.

As they neared London's outskirts, green fields gave way to the density and industrialization of northern suburbs like Watford, Harrow, and Finsbury Park. They passed rows of terraced housing and modern high-rises. Graffiti became common. They entered Euston Station at 5:47 p.m., passing through gloomy steel and concrete rail infrastructure.

The platform was packed with Londoners rushing to get somewhere. Jack, too, had somewhere to be. Out on Euston Road, the sun shone in the heart of London's transport centre. Taxis and buses were plentiful, but Jack's destination required neither. The British Library was what held his interest. It was only a short hop away and Jack set a brisk pace. Ozzie followed obediently.

"We're running low on dosh, mate." Ozzie announced.

Jack didn't break stride. "I need to make a stop first."

Ozzie pressed no further and within minutes they arrived. They entered through large glass doors leading into a grand foyer with an impressive statue of Sir Isaac Newton. Somehow, it gave Jack comfort.

The place was busy, but Jack found another helpful librarian, a youngster this time, eager to save the world through access to books and the internet. She didn't quite know what to make of the pair, especially with Jack damp and dishevelled. He'd done his best to spruce up but there was only so much he could do.

Ah, bless her, she was determined to help anyway. No identification was a minor hurdle – *I've lost my wallet, Jack explained* – but she bent rules and issued a temporary library card, on the promise he'd bring in ID once reissued. Before you know it, he was parked in front of a computer and went straight to work.

It didn't take much sleuthing to find Lily. One Google search: Lily Burgess (Burgess being the maiden name). In his heart, he knew what was coming. But to have it confirmed was devastation he wasn't prepared for. There she was, looking better than ever, with a different husband, different last name, different children. Three kids this time. All boys.

Crushed and broken, Jack kept searching. His brain trotted out irrational thoughts. *Maybe that wasn't her?* He creeped Lily's Facebook. He found her on LinkedIn. Each new discovery, another devastating blow – further evidence this was the Lily he knew and loved.

Except, she neither knew nor loved him. This version of Lily was living a different life. He studied her face and the face of her new husband. To acknowledge the man filled Jack with jealousy and rage, as if she was cheating on him. But she wasn't. She never would. She wasn't the type.

Jack's kids.

That was an immeasurably darker tale.

At least he could *find* Lily. He could look at her pictures. The same wasn't true of precious, innocent Finn and Lucy. They weren't leading different lives with different parents. Unfortunately, they weren't living period. Jack couldn't find them anywhere (not for lack of trying) and he never would. Somehow, time had folded over on itself and crushed them, erased them from the fabric of reality.

Losing them was like the death of a loved one – *times two* – only far worse. He kept searching obsessively, looking for some scrap of evidence young Finn and Lucy lived. Some sign that *somewhere* they existed.

He found the parents of their classmates and teammates. He recognized the faces of the children Finn and Lucy played with. But no Finn and no Lucy. There never was and there never would be. They didn't exist. They never existed. They weren't real.

But for Jack they were real. They *had* been real. They were his flesh and blood, and they'd been cruelly expunged from the universe. It was too horrid to contemplate. He didn't even have a photo to hold onto. The anguish was unbearable.

Ozzie, meanwhile, found similar results with his own family. His ex-wife married someone else and produced two entirely different offspring. Bryan and Jonathon never existed.

He took the news with less fanfare. It wasn't that Ozzie's heart was made of stone, it was that he didn't love his ex-wife and had already mourned the loss of the only son he truly loved. Sure, he loved the older boy as any father loves a son, but there was no respect. In Ozzie's words, Jonathon was an *insufferable woketard. A bit of a poofter.* They hadn't spoken in years.

By now, Ozzie was aware of Jack's torment. He knew Jack's love of family was above all. He knew, too, there were no words that could comfort. But he had to try.

"It's a tough one, mate." He put a hand on Jack's shoulder. "To say the least."

Jack nodded.

"I'm at a loss meself. Me boys are gone, and me *ex-trouble-and-strife*, God bless her, she married someone else. Me heart's shattered."

For a brief instant, Ozzie detected mirth in Jack's eyes. But he was in no mood for chatter. He didn't so much look *at* Ozzie as he did look *through* Ozzie – the thousand-yard stare of someone suffering trauma. Jack was empty and hollow. "Let's get outta here."

Out on the street, they both hesitated. They'd no place to go and nothing to do. Ozzie took charge. "Come on, mate. I'll buy you a cup of tea."

Once seated with tea in had, Ozzie tried again to offer solace. "I know they're gone, mate. I wish I could tell you something different."

Jack nodded, and Ozzie kept pressing. "What about us then? Do we exist?"

Jack had already considered the question and done some sleuthing in between his other searches. "We *did* exist."

"Did? Past tense?"

Jack nodded. "I looked us up."

"And?"

"I found our obituaries."

"Oh no." Classic deadpan.

"Yeah."

"What did we fall prey to?"

"Don't know. Couldn't find anything. Not even a hint. Other than we died in East London that same day. May 31, 1997."

"Oh sweet Jesus."

"Yeah," Jack nodded aggressively. "Precisely the day you felt like meeting your younger self."

"Hey...I've apologized. You can't keep bringing that up. I feel terrible."

"Yeah, yeah."

"Is there some way we can, like, *undo* what we've done. Or what I've done. I mean—"

"*No Ozzie*, there isn't." But even as he scolded, Jack questioned if it might be possible. *Who am I to say it can't be undone?* He resolved to consider this in the future.

Ozzie switched topics. "So, if we did exist at one time, our parents would know us, yeah?"

"They'd know our *twenty-year-old* selves. But I'm not sure it's the best idea to roll up to my parents' place and interrupt their crosswords and tea and crumpets. Crikey, I'd probably give my Dad a heart attack."

"Right."

"I don't recommend you visit yours either, just saying."

Ozzie nodded obediently.

"We don't exist, Ozzie. We're not supposed to anyway, not in physical form. Not here, not now. We're non-entities. Don't you get it?"

"I suppose I do."

"You better."

"So what are we gonna do? What kind of life we gonna lead?"

"You act like I have all the answers." The severity and strangeness of the predicament was soaking in. *Ozzie's right. What* are *we gonna do? Jesus.* Coupled with the grief and pain of losing his family – the chill of despair escalated to an icy, howling wind.

If God struck Jack down this very moment, he would have considered it a great blessing.

45. Logistics

Jack was so overcome with grief and despair, someone had to take charge. Obviously, it had to be Ozzie. Luckily, he was resourceful and street smart.

"You figure me Nana's still me Nana?"

"You can't visit her."

Ozzie shook his head. "I've a different idea, mate."

Jack was skeptical. "What is it?"

"She's got this thing about banks. Got it from me Grandad." Ozzie was sheepish. "Bottom line, she keeps a lot of cash in the house."

"You want to steal from your Nana?"

"No mate, *borrow*. I'll pay her back. But right now, we need some proper dosh and I know exactly where she keeps it. I also happen to know tomorrow's Sunday and she'll be at church." He grinned widely. "She attends religiously."

The small joke took Jack by surprise and he barely suppressed a chuckle. It was the first light moment they'd had.

"We gotta get on our feet, mate. Sometimes you gotta make tough choices."

Jack nodded. "Fair enough."

That night, they used more of Ozzie's rapidly depleting stash to book shared space in a hostel. The young travellers they bunked with didn't know what to make of them, but Ozzie chatted with them like long lost pals anyway. Jack was just happy to get out of damp clothes, take a shower, and collapse into bed.

The next day, Ozzie took charge again. He was a man on a mission. Step One, take the tube to Upminster and *borrow* money from his Nana. An hour and a few train transfers later, they rocked up to her residence.

The spare key was in its usual hiding spot. "You stay here and keep an eye out."

Jack scoffed. "Fucking dumb and dumber here."

Ozzie grinned. Nice to hear Jack crack a joke. The caper went off without a hitch and quick as a wink, they were on their way, with not so much a nosy neighbour disturbed.

At the train station, Ozzie flashed the new wad. "This ought to last a week or two."

"How much?"

"Fifteen grand, mate."

"Jesus, you robbed her blind."

"Borrowed, mate. And we're gonna need it. London ain't cheap."

"How much does she bloody well have?"

"I ain't saying," Ozzie grinned, "but it's a lot."

Back in East London, Ozzie moved to Step Two – Identification. They couldn't get by without proper ID. Thankfully, Ozzie knew the right people. Unfortunately, they didn't know him. Not a problem. Not for Ozzie. He was a fast and convincing talker. Jack always said, *Ozzie you could've made a fortune in sales.*

There was debate over names. Specifically, did they need new ones? Interesting idea, but they mutually agreed to skip that complexity. Perhaps in the future, but for now *let's keep it simple,* so said Ozzie. Later that day, they received brand-new driver's licences. They could think about passports another day.

Next, off to the National Bank of London where a cheerful foreign teller happily accepted their fake ID (and their cash) and issued prepaid credit cards. Yes sir, they were cooking with gas now. This was followed by a shopping excursion on Oxford Street, which boasted all the top designer outlets and brands. They purchased a small suitcase and filled it rather quickly.

Finally, who could survive without a phone? They got pay-as-you-go models – *burners* – with prepaid SIM cards and a data bundle. No contract required. Perfect for anonymous use.

Overall, a productive day. Like becoming a new citizen. By now, it was past 5:00 p.m. and they were ready for a well-deserved rest. They found acceptable accommodation at a boutique hotel in Shoreditch, and the adjoining pub was to their liking.

"Eventually, we'll need a proper flat," Ozzie announced, "but this'll do for tonight."

"You've it all figured out, do you?"

"Leave it to me, my boy."

"Look where that got us."

"Hey," Ozzie mock-scolded. "Look, I'm off for a swim and a hot tub. Care to join me?"

Jack declined. He had other things on his mind. Important things.

He was going back.

46. A New Reality

After a shower and shave, Jack changed into suitable attire and conjured the desired time and place. East London. May 22, 1997. He wasn't even sure this was possible –temporal excursions thus far had been dictated by impromptu visions. They simply arrived, as if driven by fate.

Fuck that, he thought. *I'm going anyway.* He lay down and relaxed mind and body. His vitals – breathing and heartbeat – followed suit. He neither forced the desired vision nor shied from it – he simply focused on it.

What do you know – *it worked.* He was back in the *Time Tunnel*, drifting through time and space. He ignored distractions along the way – he wasn't interested, not today – and again the special power responded – almost instantaneously he was descending into the same street in the East End of London, the very same day.

Intense déjà vu washed over him. Far more intense than he'd ever experienced. There was something sinister about it. Haunting. Jack disregarded the warning signs.

He had to find out. Was reversal possible? Could he revisit the precise moment Ozzie visited their younger selves, triggering the fateful paradox? Could he somehow, through some wizardry, restore the previous path of history, or write a different path that still involved Lily and the kids? It was convoluted logic to comprehend and decipher.

But he had to try.

The Gilded Whistle was a couple blocks away and Jack commenced a brisk pace. The street was packed with lads and lasses. A happy vibe. But Jack wasn't here to socialize.

Within thirty seconds, the foreboding was back with a vigour. He ignored it. Ten paces on, the nausea and pain hit like a physical blow. He collapsed in a heap. His ambulatory powers gone. His ability to stand, gone. The wind howled and the *sickness* enveloped him. It was as bad as before and worse. He was utterly crippled.

However, as before, he detached from his body and floated above the fracas. Not a willful decision, it just happened. He saw the pub in question. Then he saw something that triggered a shiver down his spine such as he'd never felt.

He saw...*himself.* And Ozzie. Not their younger selves. No. Their *present* selves. It was *them*, on the last trip back. *Sweet mother of God!* In mathematical terms, this was recursion – a function calling itself. A dangerous thing to mess with mathematically, with high potential for infinite loops.

Could I get stuck in an infinite loop, Jack wondered. It was a new type of paradox. And it put the fear of God in his soul. He understood at once – *this is forbidden.* He couldn't go back where he'd been. Why? Because he'd already been there. *And would still be there.* It was a brain-twister, but clearly there could be no *undo* feature. No reversal.

What's done was done. Like entropy. Toothpaste out of the tube. Humpty Dumpty in pieces. It was what it was and would always be that way.

The realization was swift and final. All hope at restoring his previous life evaporated. This recursive paradox was perhaps the most dangerous of all. He retreated from it. Recoiled.

I must leave this place. I must go home.

As full and total acceptance flowed through him, the sickness lifted, and the *Time Tunnel* appeared, as if an escape hatch. Almost instantaneously, he was back at the inn, lying on his bed. Ozzie still gone, leaving Jack to contemplate what had happened. He lay still and one word played in his thoughts.

Acceptance.

His children were gone. They would never be back. Jack had to make peace with it. A strategy came to him. A quasi-solution. He resolved to hold the memory of Finn and Lucy in his heart. Forever. There, he would keep them alive. He would visit them, nurture them, love them. They would forever be a part of him. And wherever they *actually* were, whatever dimension, whatever plane of existence, perhaps they would feel his eternal love.

It gave him comfort.

Another thought arrived. A disturbing thought. A powerful thought. *Perhaps it was not a coincidence the vision ultimately placed them in that precise time and place. Certainly, Ozzie's recklessness triggered the paradox. But the placement made it possible.*

What were the odds they be placed at that precise point in the 4-dimensional infinite coordinate system known as the space-time continuum? Ozzie could have been reckless elsewhere and nothing comes of it.

But no.

They were in the East End precisely on that fateful day. Was it the random hand of fate? Or – *this was a scary thing to contemplate* – was it God's plan?

Jack may never know, but the possibility gave a measure of peace and comfort. Until Ozzie returned, that is, still in swim trunks, towel-drying his hair. Full of beans and chatter. "God, I feel so alive."

"Good on ya."

"Don't forget, not long ago, I was locked up. A prisoner."

"Hmmm."

"You shoulda come, mate. The water was perfect. Exactly what I needed."

"Next time."

"Some lovely lasses, too." Ozzie whistled for emphasis. "Oi mate, absolute ten outta tens. Right proper stunners."

Jack sighed. He wasn't ready to think about other women. He was also aware of Ozzie's tendency to exaggerate.

"I was chatting 'em up, Jack. You'd have been proud of me."

Jack couldn't conceal a grin.

"Right, I'll have a quick shower – then we'll pop to the pub, yeah?"

"I guess."

"You need to eat, mate. And a drink or two would do you no harm."

Ozzie wasn't taking no for answer, and sure enough, they enjoyed a couple pints and a damn decent steak and kidney pie. Was nice to be out. Sure, Jack had been in pubs recently, but this was *Anchor Time*. This was real life.

And real life meant real issues. They didn't dominate conversation, but Jack and Ozzie did reflect on the state of the country, and their own fate.

"So Newfordshire – the attack, the bollocks afterward – none of that happened?"

Jack shook his head. "I've looked high and low for evidence. Nothing whatsoever."

"Amazing."

Jack gestured. "Yep, all out the window."

"Yet Southport happened?"

"Correct. Just as we know it. The same homegrown *Welsh* choirboy." Air quotes. "Same protests, same persecution. Just like what you went through."

"The cunts."

Jack shrugged. "We live in an occupied country with a hostile government. That's how it is."

"So our lives are royally fucked, you and me…"

"Our lives are over, mate."

"And the country's the same as we left it, notwithstanding Newfordshire."

"Precisely. Still overrun with migrants. Still the same bloody PM. Still grooming gangs raping our girls."

"And yet the rise of the far-right, that's the real problem."

Jack sighed.

"Ah, the buggers and their bloody communist claptrap." Ozzie spit out the words angrily. Then changed moods on a dime. His expression brightened and he raised a glass. "On the plus side, I'm out of prison."

Jack joined him and took a healthy swallow. It was the first night of their new life and *crikey*, it was good to be out. Good to not be wallowing.

Nonetheless, Jack pulled the chute early and God blessed him with a peaceful sleep.

Unfortunately, that wouldn't always be the case.

47. Filling Time

Within a week, they found more suitable quarters. Still in Soho, but a larger flat – a suite where they each had their own room. Ozzie did the legwork, and it wasn't far from their old local, The Rose and Thorne. Probably no accident.

Jack was reluctant to check it out, but Ozzie kept the pressure on. "It'll be fun catching up with old mates."

"They don't know us."

"All the better," said Ozzie with a grin.

Jack remained wary. The last thing they needed was another paradox. But the risk was nil. Paradoxes weren't possible in Anchor Time. That was his working theory, and his intuition.

And so, one drizzly Saturday, the pair strolled casually in for the gazillionth time. The experience was strange, but in a good way. It was brand new yet wonderfully familiar, as if the universe was winking at them. Like they were supposed to be here, yet it was a special treat.

The gang was all there, give or take. Certainly, Edward Squire was present, relishing camaraderie and spouting off in his familiar pretentious manner. Ozzie and Jack kept their distance.

"Look at him," Ozzie brayed. "Still a liberal tosser."

"Did you expect any different?"

"I'd have been gravely disappointed with anything different." Ozzie laughed out loud and swilled his pint. "He's the same pompous ass, but with different friends."

"Hey, easy on Eddie. He can't help himself. He's got the patrician sensibilities of the upper class."

"Ah mate, class means nothing in Britain anymore – been gutted by the bloody foreigners. Leastways that's how I see it. Liberals like Eddie, they've the luxury of being far left cause they've enough loot to stay away from the hordes."

"He figures you for a peasant, you know. A crass and vulgar commoner."

"Aye, he's right about that, mate," Ozzie laughed.

"He mocks the way you speak."

"'E really said that? Cor blimey. Tell ya wot, guv'na. I'll give 'im a right ear-bashin', I will." Cockney wasn't a stretch for Ozzie.

Momentarily, Man City potted a beauty against Newcastle – a howitzer from well outside the box. The patrons responded, but Jack and Ozzie barely gave it a glance – neither had a dog in the fight.

They kept to themselves that evening, perfectly acceptable given they were a few tables removed from the crony epicentre. Ozzie was tempted to make an approach, to strike up conversation. The temptation to ridicule Eddie was always high, but he kept his cool. It was enough to be among the gang, to soak up the camaraderie.

And so it went, Jack and Ozzie were finding their feet in the new world. Having fun, having a laugh. Ozzie was drinking too much. Jack, too, for that matter. Ah, why not? They had no job. No wife. No kids. No real friends, though Ozzie was making headway in that department.

Meanwhile, time was passing and Jack was healing. Didn't always feel like it, mind you. He'd made peace with the loss of his children, but no one told his subconscious, and his dreams were occasionally haunting. He saw Finn and Lucy, he heard their laughter, the patter of their small feet. But when he reached out to them, they morphed into ghostly shadows and vanished.

But they always came back, and sometimes they cried out to him. *Daddy, help us...please help us.* Lily was there sometimes. Always indifferent. Always uncaring. It was enough to shatter heart and soul, both. He would awaken with an overwhelming sense of despair. Utter desolation.

Did Finn and Lucy still exist in some other dimension? Some other plane of existence? If so, was there a version of me there to take care of them?

This was Jack's burden to bear. And he suffered the nightmares without complaint. He never said a word to Ozzie. All he could do was pray for the souls of Finn and Lucy and always keep them in his heart. They were gone from this world, however. They never existed. Not here.

Lily was a different story. There was pain there, too, but not as soul-crushing. There was also remorse. Jack never did tell her about the *Time Travel*. He would have gotten round to it, but that ship sailed. And it bothered him. As if it was a betrayal.

He could seek her out in *Anchor Time*. There'd be no paradox. There could, however, be undesirable outcomes. Like, Lily thinking was he was a crazy person. Or Lily notifying the authorities. That sort of thing.

Jack also thought of his parents. He thought of them often. His love for them was alive and well and he desperately wanted to visit. Tell them what happened. Hug them tightly. But it seemed a bad idea. Another cross to bear.

Meanwhile, days turned to weeks. Jack was ready for change. For something to happen. But what?

"How we doing for cash?" Jack asked, not for the first time.

Ozzie shrugged. "Still got some, but it won't last forever."

"No."

"Have you given more thought to the uh..."

"No I have not."

Ever since Jack mentioned the gambling scheme to Ozzie, it was stuck in his head. *It's a no-brainer*, so said he, and he was probably right. Go back a year, maybe two. Bring a list of winners to Ascot. Bet big. Make a fortune.

Nothing to it.

Speaking of *going back*, Jack hadn't since the infamous Recursive Paradox. He'd had visions, mind you. Interesting snapshots from history. He neither ignored them nor acted on them.

Perhaps one day.

48. Making Plans

A month flashed by. Then another. Spring turned to summer, at least what passes for summer in England. The drifter lifestyle was getting old. Jack was getting restless. He needed meaning and purpose.

He'd come to the conclusion that his presence in *Anchor Time* was part of God's Grand Plan. It followed, thus, that the infamous paradox was supposed to happen. God had placed him here for a reason.

Was Ozzie also part of the Plan? Or some strange accident? Jack wasn't sure. Either way, Ozzie was here. Loose end or designated helper. Regardless, the pair were definitely not here to *day drink* at the Rose and Thorne. When he raised this with Ozzie, he got modest agreement. *Aye, we can still enjoy a few pints, yeah?*

No surprises, Ozzie acclimated well to the lifestyle. He was fond of drinking and socializing. He kept fit in the pool and the gym. He was carrying himself with a swagger. However, he also knew deep down it couldn't last forever.

Jack's perspective was philosophical. He was looking deeper into their predicament. He was looking for meaning. Ozzie was more practical. He hadn't changed one iota. "I am who I am. I love my country and I hate to see it destroyed. I'd give me life to save it. Bloody 'eck Nora, I already have. So've you. And our bloody families. Nothing's changed in here, Jack." Ozzie pounded his chest.

Bless him, Ozzie's simple wisdom proved accurate. Their souls were still their souls. They hadn't changed in God's eyes.

Is Ozzie to be my partner in crime? He has his faults, but also his virtues.

With ample time on their hands, they kept tabs on the ongoing destruction of their home and native land. It hardly seemed possible, but Ozzie's political leanings kept moving rightward, and growing more intense. Jack's, too. Understandable, considering the heinous treatment of indigenous Brits.

"The invaders are here to conquer," Ozzie declared, in one of their frequent tête-à-têtes. "But they're not even our worst enemy."

Jack nodded. "It's the people letting them in."

"Bloody right, the traitors. Scum of the earth, they are. If justice is ever served, they'll hang for their betrayal."

"Can't say I disagree."

"The invasion's happening all over Europe. Christ, Germany, Sweden, Belgium, France. They're even onto poor old Ireland. We just happen to be worst of the bunch."

Ozzie was expanding his thinking beyond their own occupied Island. He began referencing *the Indigenous people of Europe.* "They want us weak and sick and vulnerable, mate. They want us gone."

Jack couldn't disagree. The evidence was overwhelming.

"They smear us with propaganda and replace us with aliens. Yet look around." Ozzie was on a roll. "Most of our lads are asleep at the wheel. They do what they're told, they follow the bloody rules. It's a strange thing to witness. A sickening thing."

"They're deferring to power," Jack added.

Ozzie nodded. "Hundred percent, mate. They know damn well what happens if ya don't"

"You sure as hell know."

"Bloody right. You get sacked, smeared, called every name in the book. Then tossed in the slammer."

"If only we could change the zeitgeist. To make it acceptable to stand up for Brits. To make it *the thing* to do."

"Ya know, if that was the case, guys like Steady Eddie would be front o' the line."

"I agree. In a different world, Eddie's a champion for British Nationalism. If that's the common sentiment, he's all over it."

"Exactly. He's a sheep. He'd go full fucking Nazi if the prevailing wind blew in that direction. It's human nature, mate. Follow the power. Most people are like that. Even you," Ozzie added with a chuckle.

"Not anymore."

Shrug. "This is a downer conversation."

Jack nodded in agreement.

"What can we do about it?"

"About what?"

"About England, mate. Can she be salvaged?"

"That's an essay question and I know where you're going with it."

Ozzie had a glimmer in his eye. "Look Jack, what happened *happened*. It's water under the bridge. Time to get back on the horse, yeah?"

Jack shrugged noncommittally.

"You told me about those...what do ya call 'em? *Experiments*. Where you do something and check the effects."

Nod.

"I wouldn't mind trying that."

"Wouldn't you though?"

"Sure, mate. I'd love to see what Britain could've and should've been, if not for traitors and interlopers."

"You know there are limits to this power I have. I still don't fully understand it." Even as he spoke, Jack knew Ozzie was right. It was Jack's purpose now.

As if sensing Jack on the ropes, Ozzie persisted. "I'll be a warrior for ya, mate. Whatever it takes. Beatdowns. Assassinations. Even headbutts."

Jack chuckled.

"We gotta play dirty mate. Fight fire with fire."

Jack raised his eyebrows. "What makes you so invincible?"

Laughter. "They can't kill me. I'm like a cockroach. *And you.* You're a superhero. Saving the world from evil tyrants."

Jack grinned despite himself. He was starting to buy into Ozzie's half-baked decrees.

Then it hit.

An immensely powerful vision, far too big and strong to ignore. As if content had been building, and this was a great release. As if a dam had burst.

49. Rhodesia

This vision wasn't set in England. Nay, it was a land 8,000 km south, yet a land said to be more English than England herself. Nor was it a single vision. 'Twas a great torrent of vivid sight and sound.

First, majestic Victoria Falls and the great Zambezi. Next, a modern first-world city, skyscrapers and automobiles and fashionable city folk. Civilized and safe. Then, a posh Country Club with golf and tennis and bowls, a handful of members savouring cocktails on the verandah, framed by ubiquitous bougainvillea creeper.

There was also business at hand. A farmer in khakis, rifle slung over the shoulder, a loyal Black man at his side. They hastily hop in a Land Rover to rendezvous with a military helicopter. Cut to Prime Minister Ian Smith, steadfast and resolute, committed to his vision.

Jack perceived it all.

1970s Rhodesia. An utter legend of a nation founded by adventurous European colonizers, mostly Brits. In a few short decades, these stalwart souls built a country on par with Canada, Australia, and yes South Africa. An affluent Western mecca.

Surely the world stood in awe of such glorious feats. Surely these fine men were revered and honoured. Right?

No.

Unfortunately, the modern marvels they spawned made the natives look bad, and that didn't sit well with the world's liberals. Nor the emerging globalist cabal pulling the puppet strings. Rhodesia was universally condemned. Deemed disgraceful. The country had to be ripped up by the roots. It started with name calling and threats. Then sanctions. Then bloody war.

Wasn't long before the entire world turned its fury on this daring bunch. But here's the fascinating part. The Rhodesians didn't cow. God love 'em, they knew they were right and good. They knew it in their hearts. So, they stood their ground.

Thus, the great Bush War raged, and these intrepid gents fought the good fight and lived the good life while doing it. Perhaps they didn't know what they were up against. Perhaps they thought it was merely Mugabe and Nkomo. Indeed, if it were that simple, they'd have surely won.

In the space of a few seconds, Jack perceived all of this and more. The fall of Rhodesia – or rather, it's spiteful annihilation – is surely one of the cruelest travesties of recent history. And no one talks about it. Jack sorta knew but not really.

He would correct that. He had the means. He could probably learn a thing or two from these fine folks. Not to mention, it'd be nice to get some sun. And some fun. And some adventure.

Jack was suddenly energized like he hadn't been in a very long time.

"You right, mate?" Ozzie asked.

Jack blinked several times, then zeroed in on Ozzie. "Never better."

"You checked out there for a minute."

Jack's smile was wide and pure. "I think you've finally talked me into it."

"Have I now?" The change in Jack was sudden and dramatic. Like a rebirth. He went from weary and despairing to bright-eyed and optimistic. A profound metamorphosis. He was transformed. Infused with gleeful energy. "What was your uncle's name again? The Rhodesian fellow you've mentioned."

"Ah, Chester. What a life he lived." Ozzie beamed brightly. "As he used to say, Rhodesians Never Die."

"What happened to him?"

"He died."

Laughter.

"But he was old. It was his time. He lived a great life. Told me Rhodesia was the best country in the history of time, and I believed him."

The following day, Jack asked about money again. "We've enough for another week," Ozzie replied. "And I'll not be stealing from me Nan again."

"You're truly a man of principle."

"I already owe her fifteen grand."

"Maybe you should look for a job."

"Hey, enough o' your guff."

Jack grinned. "Perhaps it's time for the gambling thing."

"Yay."

"I didn't say we."

"I'm going with you."

"After the antics you pulled?" Jack shook his head sadly. "Probably best I go on my own."

Ozzie was crestfallen and Jack enjoyed watching him squirm. Bringing old Ozzie back had pros and cons. He certainly brought energy. And street smarts. And a raw passion for Britain. Scratch that, *England*. What did he say recently? *I'm not British mate. I'm an Englishman.* He'd said a lot of interesting things lately. And the negatives? Obviously, he wasn't great at following orders. And he had a chronic knack for stirring up trouble.

Ozzie was still staring straight at Jack. "It's you and me, old sport. We're a team. We can achieve immortality."

"We?"

"Definitely. You're Batman. I'm Robin. It's like the birth of a superhero."

"I do have an idea."

"Pray tell."

"Fall's coming. Perhaps a holiday to sunnier climes?"

"You've somewhere in mind?"

"I do."

"Out with it, then."

"Rhodesia, mate. Let's go see that great country your Uncle spoke of."

"But we won't visit Uncle Chester," Ozzie said with a grin.

Jack frowned and waved a scolding finger.

"This is gonna be a blast, mate."

Jack nodded happily. "After that, we'll go check out the Land of the Free."

Puzzled look.

"The Home of the Brave, mate. *America.*"

"What about our beloved England? Aren't we gonna save the Motherland?"

Jack smiled. "If we do things right, eventually we're gonna save them all."

A Note to the Reader

The infamous Cecil Rhodes once stated: "To be born an Englishman is to win first prize in God's lottery." Oh, how times have changed. Modern-day Britons have been defiled, humiliated, and reduced to second-class citizens. They are ruled by a hostile elite who seem intent on wiping them from the face of the Earth.

This trend is surely happening all through the West, but the poor English seem to be getting the worst of it. The enemy evidently hates them the most. Is it their colonial past? Or because they're among the whitest on the planet? As I've grown more cynical, I've come to suspect the latter.

Either way, the vast inward migration of hostile peoples into Britain has been reality for decades. The Brits never asked for it and never voted for it. In fact, it's always been against their collective will across all the social classes. One can only conclude it's been purposeful and malicious. An act of war.

Terribly upsetting, as the Brits might say. If they were allowed to, that is. Criticizing immigration is forbidden. Not surprisingly, most stay quiet. They ignore their slow and steady dispossession. It's easier to watch football, indulge in the drink, or attempt escape with the latest Netflix drama.

Ha, good luck with that. The subversiveness in pop culture has reached new heights. Reminders of aggressive white replacement are constant, as is the casual rewriting of history – *Britain has always been diverse.*

Go back twenty years and watch a Hugh Grant flick – England's portrayed as overwhelmingly white. Go back another twenty, and England herself was overwhelmingly white. Even London. Sadly, in movies and real life, those days are gone. The grotesque transformation of the Britain we knew and loved is surely one of the biggest stories in the history of time. Anyone with a smidgeon of common sense can see that.

Despite the tyranny, a few brave souls speak out. God bless them. God bless their moral courage and fortitude. They are the bravest of the brave. They risk job loss, ostracization, persecution, imprisonment, even death. They're modern-day heroes.

Myself, I don't have that kind of courage. I confine my dissidence to book-writing, and I've been at it over ten years, documenting the war on "First World" nations. My chosen form is fictionalized storytelling. Novels. However, of late the Western World has become so degraded, crafting plausible near-future *happy endings* has become difficult. With Britain, it was near-impossible.

'Twas a thorny dilemma for a writer intent on writing about the Mother Country. I didn't want to trot out a dreary black pill. Meanwhile, I'd been noticing nostalgic photos and videos of yesterday's Britain had become a popular genre on social media. Clearly, people were finding joy and comfort in these images.

Presto!

The idea for *Time Travel* arrived with a flourish. Using this device, I could take readers on grand adventures exploring the beauty and grace of not-so-long-ago Britain. All sorts of possibilities emerged. How was our present shaped? How can our future be shaped? Time Travel allowed me to write a book about England that was palatable, enjoyable, and even offered a modicum of hope.

The idea was so compelling, so fraught with possibility, I realized an entire series would be needed to properly tell the tale. Alas, the *FWAITAS Series* was born. It shall celebrate the beauty and charm of the West, and the singular magnificence of the Anglosphere.

There's so much to celebrate. We've been demonized so unfairly and for so long that we forget the near-otherworldly accomplishments of our ancestors. European men – particularly the British – invented the modern world. They built the finest nations on the planet from scratch, and they did it everywhere they went.

The high-trust communities they created transcended nature. The Western inhabitants of these derivative nations took the peace and prosperity for granted. They assumed it was the natural order. Of course, it was anything but. It was a unique and singular product of Western Man.

Where other tribes through history – the Mongols, the Romans, the Ottomans, the Zulus – might have annihilated indigenous populations, Englishmen showed an extraordinary capacity to transcend tribalism and seek a spirit of cooperation. No doubt, there were exceptions. They used force when threatened and they imposed laws to protect their people. But they generally sought to lift and enlighten others, to an almost pathological degree. They struggled to grasp that other races were not like them and never would be.

Over time, resentments formed, and those resentments were relentlessly stoked by the media and Hollywood. The *programming* began in earnest post-war and evolved into a non-stop anti-white pogrom. An endless series of vicious blood libels. In modern pop culture, only white men are allowed to be villains. Only whites are portrayed as uniquely evil.

And thus, life has imitated art. Now we have a world where only whites are undeserving of a homeland. The *powers that be* have acted in unison and with great precision to simultaneously attack – by means of demographic warfare – almost all formerly white countries. Certainly all with any hint of Anglo-roots. This open ethnic cleansing – historically dismissed as conspiracy theory – is no longer a secret. There's no more denial or subterfuge. The mask is off. Whites are being replaced in their homelands, and that's a good thing.

And so, this new series offers a lifeline. A much-needed dose of optimism for a people whose spirit has been badly damaged, in many cases, destroyed. Perhaps these books can help trigger a survival instinct? The Brits and their cousins around the world must re-remember the greatness from which they've come. And in doing so, they must recognize that greatness is still within them.

Critics might claim *Britain on the Brink* describes an idealized version of the past. A romanticized version. I reject the criticism. Certainly, parts of yesteryear's England were ugly and industrial and run-down. Even gloomy. Certainly, there was a measure of injustice and poverty. But the

English mind and soul was there. The land was English. The government was not authoritarian.

In fact, not so long ago, the same was true of America, Canada, Australia and yes, even Rhodesia. One may debate that final entry, but I'll cover that – *and then some!* – in my next book. The story of that tiny country, which shone so brightly for a brief period, portends the shocking depth of hatred and vitriol for Whites who stand up for themselves.

This will be explored, as will the path of other nations (including America). It's a lot to tackle really, but it's worth tackling. Destructive migration into Western lands is the biggest story of our age, and we're not supposed to notice or talk about it. The speed of demographic change has been mind-boggling. Are we witnessing the largest sustained genocide / ethnocide ever attempted? Sure feels like it sometimes.

A sad state of affairs, and we must all do what we can. Me, I'll continue quietly writing novels that take the side of indigenous Europeans. Yes, that means white people. I take the preposterous position that we have a right to not be destroyed.

If you enjoyed Book One, sit tight – there's more coming. You're in for a treat. Meanwhile, tell your friends, and be sure to leave a review. And if you feel like chatting, don't be shy. Contact me anytime at kmbreakey.com. I promise to respond.

About the Author

K.M. Breakey was born in Toronto and educated at Simon Fraser University in Vancouver, BC. He has previously published *Shout the Battle Cry of Freedom; Fearless Men, But Few; All Thy Sons;* and four other novels. To learn more, visit kmbreakey.com.

Also by K.M. Breakey

Shout the Battle Cry of Freedom

>From quarterback to Congressman, Thomas Baker's the All-American Boy. He loves hunting, fishing, and football. More than anything, he loves the United States of America – the greatest nation on earth.

But something's wrong with the American Dream. It's broken. Tom knows it. His friends do, too. When COVID hits, the insanity gathers steam. *Follow the science*, they say, and pay no attention to the violent crime, open borders, and descending Dystopia. Focus only on *the Current Thing* – be it COVID or climate or Ukraine. And the clapping seals obey.

From his perch in the DC swamp, it's obvious to Tom – America is under attack from within. He vows to fight back, but how? The surveillance state is everywhere. *The enemy is everywhere*, with unlimited funds, unlimited resources, and unlimited capacity for evil.

When Tom meets reclusive tech billionaire Noah Hughes, a spark of hope is kindled. Tom goes all in. He transforms into a populist juggernaut and declares war on the Regime. Together, they pursue an unlikely and dangerous path. With the General's help, they just might have a chance.

Fearless Men, But Few

Eamon Clarke is a proud Irishman. He's conquered the playing field, now he's a hero in the broadcast booth. He's larger than life. A national treasure. But things aren't all rosy. The land he loves has caught a vicious strain of *Progressivism.*

As Irish homeless sleep on the streets, Ireland is flooded with the world's waifs and strays, cost to taxpayers be damned. Tis a jarring disruption. Some call it an act of war.

They keep turning up, sometimes in the dead of night. They're given food and shelter and clothing. For them, opportunities abound in this wet and cold alien land. For them, everything's free.

Why is the government doing this? Is their intent to sow chaos? *To destroy Éire?* When Eamon's hometown is hit, he vows to fight – to risk everything. But it's not easy with his own life spiralling. When a dangerous nemesis emerges, Eamon's problems multiply.

Is it too late to save the ancient land? Eamon and a spirited band of patriots say *no!* And they're channeling Pearse and Collins to get the job done. Unfortunately, they've no idea what they're up against.

All Thy Sons

Life's unfolding on schedule for Tony Fierro. Raised in Vancouver by a loving Catholic family, he's blessed with good looks and self-confidence to burn. He gets the job. He woos the girl. He has the world by the tail.

But the world is acting strangely. Irrationally. Immorally. Tony questions the *progressive* mantras that pervade modern-day culture, but quietly. Better to ignore them, laugh at them, even as the absurdities multiply and turn dangerous.

His pal Ivan senses the evil lurking and warns of impending calamity. But Ivan's paranoid. An alarmist. He always was. Tony's got better things to do, like raise his boys, pay his mortgage, live his life.

When tragedy strikes, Tony's world crashes. He wakes from his slumber and sees a country at war with itself, a government complicit in the destruction, the pattern playing out across the Western World.

He can no longer stay silent, but will his message cross the line as a new Dystopian order rises? *All Thy Sons* explores a hellish future of chaos and racial violence. A future where remaining First World sanctuaries vanish with stunning rapidity.

What happens when there are no safe neighborhoods, or cities, or countries? Do we lapse into tribalism? Do we rise? Or does a *new* master rise?

Never, Never and Never Again

Audrey is a starry-eyed Brit, Pieter a tenth-generation Afrikaner. At the height of Apartheid, they fall in love. A life of splendour awaits, but the country is shifting underfoot. The winds of change fan revolution, and Michael Manzulu's rage boils. He is hungry, and will risk everything to destroy his oppressor.

When white rule gives way, trepidation is tempered by precarious optimism. Mandela will make the miracle happen. Or not. Twenty-three years on, South Africa has suffered unprecedented decline. The country unravels and fear is pervasive. Fear of persecution, land seizure, slaughter. Pieter and Audrey march on. They navigate the perpetual threat. They pray the wrath will not strike their home.

Recently, voices of protest cry out, none louder than the bombastic scholar, Kaspar Coetzer. World leaders cautiously take note, but will they take action? More importantly, can they?

Never, Never and Never Again is a story of vengeance, greed and corruption. A story the world ignores, but a story that must be told...before it's too late.

Johnny and Jamaal

Two athletes from different planets are on the verge of greatness. Johnny's a carefree Canadian making his mark in the NHL. Jamaal's set to follow LeBron and Kyrie out of the ghetto. When their worlds collide, the catastrophic clash ignites racial conflict not seen since Ferguson. The incident tests the fledgling love of Johnny's best friend Lucas and his African-American girlfriend Chantal, and sets them on a quest for truth and justice in the perverse racial landscape of 2016.

As chaos escalates across American cities, an MLK-like voice rises from the ashes. Wilbur Rufus Holmes may be salvation for Luke and Chantal, but can he stop society's relentless descent into racial discord?

Johnny and Jamaal is awash with sports, violence and political taboo, as America's seething dysfunction is laid bare.

Creator Class

Decades have elapsed since The Creators inflicted their vision on the planet. The population menace is tamed, resources are plentiful, and climate concerns abate. A sustainable world order has been achieved.

But the rigid restrictions of P-Class torment Shawn Lowe. Movements are tracked, conversations scrutinized, conformity enforced. It's wrong. The Laws of Earthism are wrong. When a treasonous outburst cements Shawn's fate, an unexpected communication from Creator Class sparks changes he could never have imagined.

A new life. A new family. Boundless opportunity. Destiny, it seems, has been rewritten. But an evil nemesis emerges, and a lust for vengeance points Shawn down a treacherous path.

The World Clicks

A powerful idea has descended on 30-year old Lane Craig, a corporate gunslinger who dreams of greatness. Simple beyond belief, powerful beyond measure, the idea won't go away. Lane knows that if managed properly, a new electronic organism will emerge and transform the Internet and his life forever.

He also knows he can't do it alone. Fortunately, suitable partners are nearby. Best pal Johnny is a glib slacker coasting in life's fast lane. Thomas is freakishly brilliant but has grown surly and awkward. What's he hiding? It's only the addition of hard-charging newcomer Gino that galvanizes momentum.

Will the idea triumph? Will it derail in a tumult of testosterone and alcohol? A brave face cannot mask Lane's self-doubt and paranoia. Nor can new love interest, Cat.

But as the saying goes, even paranoid people have enemies. Especially when it comes to Internet riches.

Printed in Dunstable, United Kingdom